Ticket to Intrigue

A Novel

Ticket to Intrigue

Alan Thomas Cowood

Ticket to Intrigue

National Library of Canada Cataloguing in Publication Data

Cowood, Alan T. (Alan Thomas), 1941-
  Ticket to intrigue
ISBN 1-55369-143-1

  I. Title.

PS8555.O92T5 2002   C813'.54   C2002-900051-3
PR9199.4.C69T5 2002

TRAFFORD

This book was published *on-demand* in cooperation with Trafford Publishing.
On-demand publishing is a unique process and service of making a book available for retail sale to the public taking advantage of on-demand manufacturing and Internet marketing. **On-demand publishing** includes promotions, retail sales, manufacturing, order fulfilment, accounting and collecting royalties on behalf of the author.

Suite 6E, 2333 Government St., Victoria, B.C. V8T 4P4, CANADA

Phone	250-383-6864	Toll-free	1-888-232-4444 (Canada & US)
Fax	250-383-6804	E-mail	sales@trafford.com
Web site	www.trafford.com	TRAFFORD PUBLISHING IS A DIVISION OF TRAFFORD HOLDINGS LTD.
Trafford Catalogue #01-0545		www.trafford.com/robots/01-0545.html

10   9   8   7   6   5   4   3

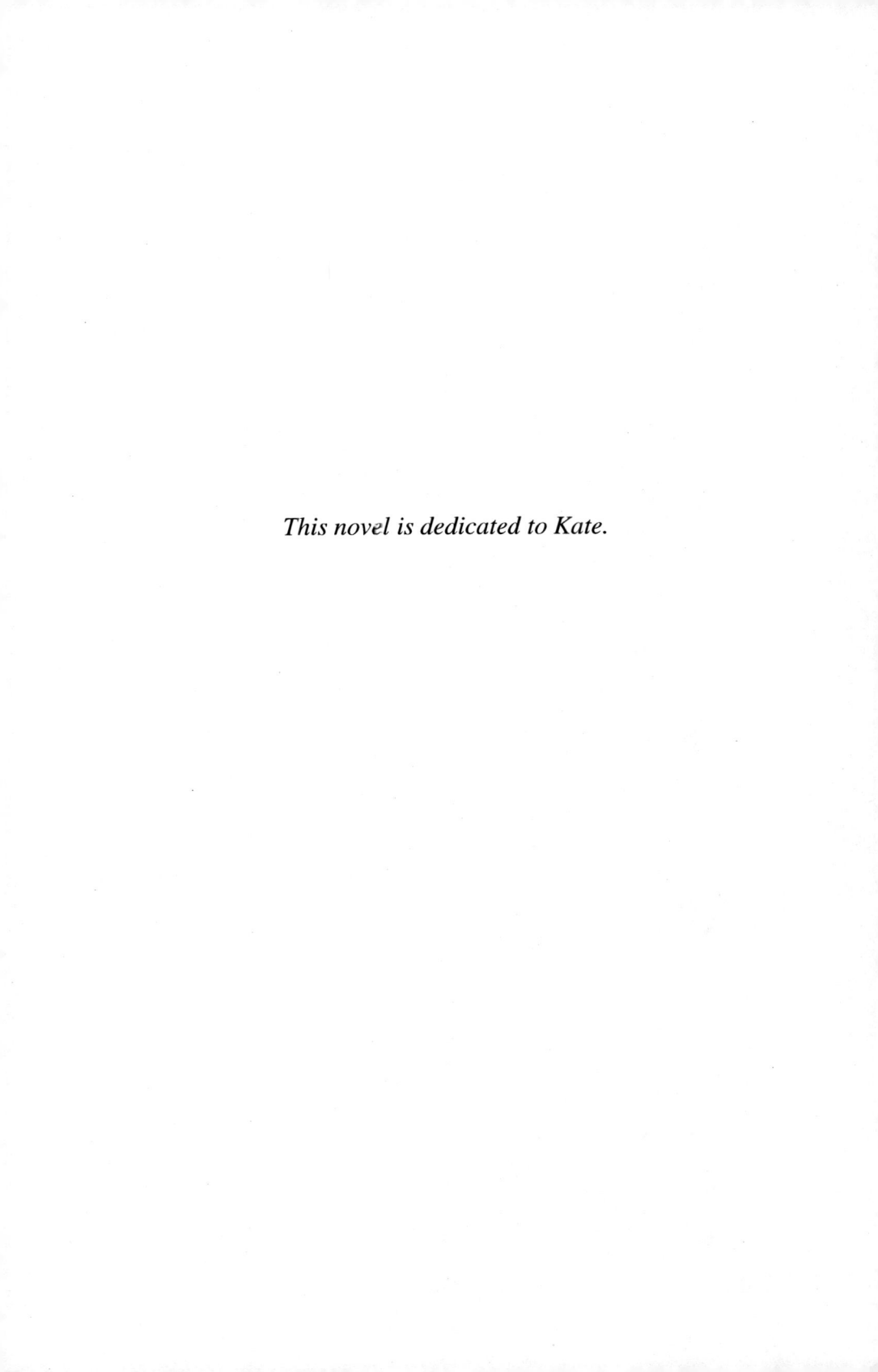

This novel is dedicated to Kate.

"The problem with opportunity knocking is that very often your knees are doing the same thing."

ATC

CHAPTER .1.

A man in his late fifties walked slowly through the park. He kept looking at the ground to make sure of his footing, as a late winter wind was in full sway and the leaves scattered on the pathway were wet and slippery from the previous nights rain. He did not want to slip and fall. He was dressed warmly with a plaid scarf around his neck and a heavy dark grey overcoat, which reached well below his knees. He was a solitary figure as he moved along the path. The wind was blowing strongly enough to make him bend into it slightly and the trousers showing below his coat were flapping back and forth.

He was deep in thought, remembering how he and his wife had walked through the park many times before, summer and winter alike. Sometimes holding hands, sometimes not, always discussing, gesticulating; and in particular, communicating. He smiled momentarily, recalling her opinion of the colour scheme of their neighbours house when it had been repainted and her disappointment at the resulting effect.

The smile left his face as he remembered the day, a year and a half ago, when she had died. He became angry as he thought of the hopelessness of the doctors to treat the cancer in her, which had become so widespread that treatment was out of the question. In the final few days of her life she was so heavily sedated with morphine that it was impossible to hold any kind

1

of conversation with her. That was the hardest thing he had had to bear since she had gone. There was no-one for him to communicate with; to explore with; to enjoy the rough and tumble of a good discussion on an interesting subject. That was the thing that had brought them together and had kept them interested in one another.

They had married late in life, too late to have a family and she had no siblings. He was two years older than she and though he had an elder brother, they had not kept in touch with one another. His brother lived half a world away in New Zealand and had been there for more than forty years. His last contact with his brother had been a letter from him sending condolences on the death of the mans' wife, and that was more than a year ago.

The man stopped for a moment and looked around him at the branches of the trees; bare of leaves now, they showed their shape. The twists and turns in their growth reminded him of the changes that he had experienced in his own life and the different paths he had travelled as he had grown from a child to the man he now was. He had always been something of a loner, not much of a team player. Even as a young man he had preferred his own company and had been rather too studious for his own good. He made acquaintances more than friends and was considered by those with whom he had worked, as something of a snob. Luckily for him he had not been bothered by this singularity as his life's work had been completely absorbing to him.

He had joined the civil service not long after his successful graduation from college and had been employed in the foreign office of the federal government as a translator. He had become fluent in German and Italian while at school, and subsequently at college where his flair for languages had been encouraged by his professors.

This career had taken him on a number of trips to Europe over the years where he was required to assist in translating the intricacies of contracts or treaties which were being entered into by various departments of government. For the

2

most part he had enjoyed this part of his life and in particular, the opportunity it presented for him to follow another of his interests, the study of archeology.

He started forward again on the path and was lost in thought for a few minutes, wondering if he should take the bull by the horns and make a trip that he had been considering for the last six months. This was to return to an archeological site in the south of France that he had visited while on the last of his work assignments, before retiring two years ago.

While at the site, he had met the leader of the dig, an Englishman, with whom he had enjoyed a lunch. They had spent the afternoon discussing the merits of excavating the area of the dig where they hoped to find evidence of a medieval religious settlement. They had exchanged addresses on leaving one another, and the man had received an open invitation to visit the site and participate in the uncovering of the history that would be revealed through the excavations and examinations conducted in the area. He had written back saying that he was unable to come last year but still hoped to have a chance in the next year and would write again to find out when the digging team would once again be at the site.

By this time the man had reached the end of the path and had to decide which way to turn. He took a coin from his pocket and tossed it into the air intending to call heads or tails, right or left. He missed the coin on its way down and bent to retrieve it from the ground which was covered by large dead leaves from a nearby maple tree.

In moving some of the leaves to find his coin he uncovered a mans hat. He picked it up and examined it; it was of good quality and although wet from the rain, it had obviously not been there very long. The man examined the inside of the hat looking for a name of the owner perhaps, but could only see the name of the store from whom the hat had been purchased. Feeling carefully around the inside lining of the hat, he felt a small piece of paper. Pulling it out he looked closely at it and discovered that it was a stub from a pawn ticket. Completely forgetting about his coin still lying there in the grass he turned

3

left and started to walk more briskly, heading for his home with the hat in his hand and the pawn ticket in his overcoat pocket.

On his way home he thought again about writing to the English archeologist and enquiring when the next opportunity to continue the excavations would be, and whether he would still be welcome to join the group. He made up his mind to write that evening and stepped out with a more purposeful stride than usual.

Arriving at his home he hung the hat he had found on a coat hanger and left it to dry on the shower curtain rod in the bathroom. The pawn brokers ticket he placed on top of the telephone to remind him to check in the telephone book to see if he could locate the address of the business. He also wrote down the name of the store that was on the inside of the hat, intending to make whatever enquiries he could about its owner.

He put the kettle on to make a cup of tea to warm himself, and went to his desk to write the letter to his archeological acquaintance. Looking up the address in his rolladex file he found what he was looking for, Peter Taylor. M.A. Phd. 113, Wellington Gardens, London S.W.4

He quickly wrote the letter and included the information that he was available at any time, and that he hoped the invitation was still open. After sealing the envelope he stamped the reverse side with his own name and address stamp, and was once again reminded that it still bore the name of his wife Carla, and his own name, Paul Brett. He had intended to buy a new one that would simply show his initials, as he always felt melancholy whenever he saw her name.

He was taken out of this mood by the whistle of the kettle and having made his tea, he sat down at the dining table with the telephone book and looked for the name of the retailer of the hat he had found.

Looking in the classified section he located the store and saw that it was in a nearby town, Westport, some twenty miles away from his own. He then checked to see if the Pawnbroker was listed and found that the business was also in the same town. He decided to drive there the following day and see what he could discover.

The following morning he set off with the hat and the pawn ticket on the passenger seat beside him. He always felt rather odd driving the car, as it had been Carla's, and he usually sat as the passenger because she loved to drive. He had not used her car much since her death, partly because of the memories it brought and because, he reminded himself, walking was much better for one than sitting and he enjoyed walking very much. He seldom listened to the radio when in the car but having mailed his letter to London before setting out, he was feeling very light hearted and decided to listen to some music. Searching around the dial he could find nothing but conversations. Then he noticed a cassette tape was still in the system so he pushed it in. *"Please put on your seat belt darling"* came a voice over the speakers.

Paul sat bolt upright; it was Carla's voice and he was not wearing his seat belt. He pulled off to the side of the road and stopped the car. For the next five minutes he listened to the tape. Carla had obviously made it shortly before her death. It was full of love and joy at the marriage that they had had and the good things that had happened to them when they had been together. The last part of the message made it very clear that she wanted him to get on with life and live it to the full by taking every opportunity that came along. The tape then played a piece of music which they had both loved. Paul sat there crying quietly to himself.

After a few minutes had passed he rewound the tape and listened again to the admonishment about his seat belt habit, and again to the words of encouragement that Carla had spoken about getting on with his life, making sure of living it to the full. He thought about the last year in particular and the plain truth that he had been far too remote and insular for his own good; spending too many hours thinking about the past, reminiscing and feeling sorry for himself. He began to think about the future, focusing on the concept of one day at a time.

5

Well, he had a focus on this day, "so, let's get on with it," he said to himself.

He started the car, put on his seat belt and pulled into the traffic. Within half an hour he had arrived at the outskirts of Westport. He knew the layout of the centre quite well and drove to the street address of the men's clothing store where the hat had been purchased.

Parking the car, he sat for a minute wondering to himself what he was going to say to the owner of the business. For some reason he decided to try the hat on his own head.

In the past, whenever he had been persuaded by Carla to buy a hat, or at least to try one on in a shop, the sales clerks had been quite unable to control themselves from laughing. He also felt silly no matter what style of headwear he tried on. As a result of this he had never owned a hat, Carla and he both agreeing that it was a hopeless situation.

It was a complete surprise, therefore, that when he looked into the rear view mirror to see himself, he appeared absolutely natural; the hat fitted perfectly and seemed to suit him. He was so pleased with this result that he got out of the car, still wearing the hat. He checked the street numbers and realized he had a block or so to walk. As he passed by the shop windows he could not stop himself from looking at his appearance, and on one occasion doffed his hat to a lady as she passed, eliciting a smile as he did so.

On arrival at the store he took off the hat and entered the establishment. This was no ordinary menswear store, but one which sold only hats and a quick glance at the prices of the items on display astonished him. The only staff member on hand was busy assisting another customer, so Paul walked over to a full length mirror and placed the hat on his head again to see if he still felt pleased with the result. He did. Hearing the door open and close behind him, he was about to turn and face the salesperson, when he heard a voice call. "Good morning Captain, what a pleasure to see you again."

As Paul turned around to see who was being spoken to, it was clear from the confused look on the face of the salesman that he had been addressing Paul.

"Oh, I'm very sorry sir," he said. "I seem to have made a mistake, I thought you were a client of ours. It must have been the hat you are wearing which is identical to one I sold a couple of months ago to a retired military gentleman. You and he are of similar build."

Paul took in this information, saying nothing for a moment. Then he approached the salesman, taking off the hat as he did so. He explained his reason for visiting the store and the circumstances surrounding his acquisition of the hat. He asked whether the store had an address of the customer on their files and was told that they probably did, as the customer had been a regular one and had purchased other items from time to time. Paul asked the salesman for the address, indicating that he wanted to return the hat to its owner that same day, adding that he hoped that the owner lived in Westport.

The salesman disappeared into the back of the store and came back with one of the store business cards on which was written "Captain Miles Dearborn, c/o No; 11, Wildwood Terr; Westport."

Paul then enquired as to whether or not the store had another hat of the same type and size, as he was seriously considering buying one for himself. The salesman disappeared again to the back of the store After a few minutes he came back. It seemed that this particular hat had come from a manufacturer in London, England, and had been a special order for the Captain. The store had simply been the intermediary for the delivery. If Paul wanted to, he could order a duplicate; however, he would have to pay for the hat beforehand and delivery would take approximately six weeks. Paul told the employee he would give the matter some consideration. He then left the shop.

As he walked back to his car he wondered to himself at the mistaken identity that had occurred. He had never before been likened to any other person that he knew of. He decided that it must have been the hat itself that had caused the confusion and was looking forward to meeting its owner; to see for himself the extent of any resemblance.

In his car he carried several street maps for the towns in the surrounding area. Opening up the one for Westport he located the Captains address. He had been intending to telephone the owner once he knew the name but there was no telephone number on the card given to him by the salesman. He picked up the pawn ticket and inserted it back into the lining of the hat, thinking that the owner wouldn't like anyone to know about his personal life.

He started the car and headed out to the area of the new address. It was on the south side of town and almost at the municipal limits. This area had at one time been one of the nicer residential parts of Westport, but had slipped out of fashion. Some of the large Victorian houses on Wildwood Terrace were now obviously converted into apartments. As Paul pulled up in front of No. 11, he could see a collection of names next to a row of buzzers on the wall beside the front door.

On a whim, he put the Captains hat back on his head and adjusted it to his satisfaction before getting out of the car, anticipating that the look on the owners face would be one of complete surprise and pleasure at the return of the missing item. He approached the front door and checked for the name "Dearborn". Sure enough it was there so he pushed the buzzer and heard it ring very faintly inside the house. After a few minutes he pushed it again; again he could hear it ringing. He bent down slightly to make sure he was pushing the right buzzer when he noticed that the curtain in the front room window was moving slightly. He looked up and saw a figure retreating into the background. He pushed the buzzer one more time and heard a door open and the footsteps of a slow moving person approach the front door.

Paul took a step back waiting for the door to open. "Who is it?" he heard in a high- pitched female voice. Paul stepped closer to the door and explained that he was looking for Miles

Dearborn, to return something to him. This information prompted the door to be opened revealing a woman wearing a shawl around her shoulders, over a green bath robe. Paul guessed that she was of a similar age to himself. In her hand she held a white cane.

"I thought you were Captain Dearborn," she said. "I don't see as well as I used to, but you looked like him from the window. My name is Mrs. Mactavish. I'm the owner of this house and I'm looking for him myself. He is seriously behind in his rent and he hasn't been here for weeks."

"Well," said Paul, "I found an item of clothing which I believe is his and I wanted to return it to him."

The landlady gave a shrug of her shoulders and a look of resignation came over her face.

"He is a bit of an odd chap, the Captain," she said. "Keeps very much to himself; never has had any visitors, and always carries lots of books with him whenever I see him."

"When was the last time you saw him?" Paul asked.
The lady thought for a minute, "February the fourteenth," she finally said, "I remember because I saw him with a bunch of flowers and wondered who they were for."
Today is March the eighteenth thought Paul.

"Has Captain Dearborn ever been away for this long before?" he asked.

"Oh yes", she said. "Last year he was away for two months in the late spring, but he paid in advance for his rent then, so I wasn't concerned."

At this point Paul could see no more use in staying where he was, so he took out his card and gave it to the landlady.

"If Captain Dearborn comes back, would you give him this and ask him to get in touch with me please; it has my address and telephone number on it. Sorry to have bothered you," he added, and doffing the hat, turned to retrace his steps to the car.

"Don't hold your breath for that to happen", she said, as he walked away. "He was down on his luck this time I think and I don't expect he will show up here again." Paul doffed the hat again, realising that it was becoming a new habit of his.

He sat in the car for a few minutes going through the events of the morning. In particular the fact that he had been mistaken for someone else twice and on each occasion he had been wearing the hat. He removed the pawn ticket from the inner lining again and decided that he would visit the pawnbrokers shop but this time he would leave the hat in the car. He reconfirmed the address and drove off.

When he reached the area where the pawnshop should be, he had to park in a parking lot a few blocks away from the street. This did not bother him as he wanted to walk a bit and think about what he was going to say when he got into the shop, as he had never been in one before.

There were three pawnbrokers' signs visible as he turned onto the correct street. He stopped outside the first one and looked in the window. There was no-one inside so he decided to go in and find out exactly what happened when one returned a pawn ticket. Behind the counter was a young man sitting on a stool, listening to the radio. As Paul approached, he turned off the music and asked how he could be of assistance. Paul asked the young man what took place when somebody brought in a pawn ticket to redeem an item.

"Well," said the chap, "you give me the ticket, I check to see how much is owing. You pay me the amount and I give you back whatever you pawned. Simple, isn't it ?"
Paul then asked the all important question as far as he was concerned.

"How do you know that the person with the ticket is the one who pawned the item in the first place?"

"We don't," said the youth, "and we don't care either. If you've got the ticket, that's all we care about. Sometimes a pawn ticket gets given to someone else as payment for a debt for instance, so we just care about the ticket. If you've got the ticket, and you pay what's owing, that's all there is to it. Have you got something to pawn?" he asked.

"No," said Paul, "but thanks for the explanation."

The young man turned away and turned up the radio again, indicating that the conversation was over as far as he was concerned. So Paul walked out of the shop.

He continued along until he came to the establishment whose address was on the ticket in his hand. Again he looked in the window. Unlike the first shop he had been in, this one had a display of musical instruments; trumpets, saxophones, accordions, etc. He pushed open the door and looked around. There was a musty air about the place and it was poorly lit from an old chandelier in the ceiling, in which only two of the five bulbs were working. He walked towards the counter where there was a steel grille all along the top with a small opening at one end; rather like an old bank tellers position. Looking at the other side of the grille Paul could see that the items on display here were mostly jewellery, and he assumed that the grille was there to protect the business from theft. There was a small bell by the open section of grillwork, so he pressed it and waited.

He heard a woman's voice say, "Coming," and from further back in the shop a lady appeared, carrying a small cat on her shoulder.

"Bringing in or taking out?" she enquired.

"I've come to redeem this," said Paul and handed over the pawn ticket.

Putting down the cat the lady took the ticket and checked the number.

"Hmm," she said to herself, "that's February". She then took down a ledger and found the relevant page. Sliding the ticket downwards she stopped at the corresponding number on the ticket. Pulling a calculator to her she entered a series of numbers.

"That will be $32.50 please."

While this had been going on, Paul had been thinking to himself about a couple of things. Obviously the lady did not recognise him in any way, but also, what was the item that had been pawned? Did he have any right to it, and what was he going to do with it anyway?

He decided that he would pay the money, retrieve the item and if necessary, return it to the owner by taking it to his address and leaving it with the landlady. Taking his wallet from his pocket he handed over the cash to the lady. "Wait here," she said, and disappeared into the back of the shop. In a few minutes she returned carrying an octagonal box.

"About the size of one of Carla's hat boxes," thought Paul.

"There you are" she said, handing it over to him.

"Thanks" he replied. "By the way, were you here when this was brought in?" The lady thought for a minute. "No," she said, "that was in February and I was away then; it must have been my husband that took it in."

"Well, thank you and good day," said Paul, and left the shop.

Walking back to his car, he felt rather relieved that he had not been mistakenly recognised for the third time that day and then remembered that the item he was carrying had been pawned in the presence of the husband at the shop. Somehow he felt that if he had been wearing the hat, and had met the husband, he would have been recognised.

This whole day had been full of surprises and all just to try and do someone a good turn he thought. Paul decided to drive back to his home before examining the contents of the box. "It's probably another of the Captains' hats," he thought to himself. Travelling down the road, he listened again to the tape that Carla had made for him and said to himself that it seemed that he *was* taking every opportunity that came along!

Later that evening after he had returned home and eaten his dinner, Paul sat down by the fire to examine the contents of the box and to look more carefully at the hat he had found. He put the box on his lap and undid the small brass clasp that held the top in place. Lifting off the lid, he saw a small black octagonal shape with a leather strap across it. He pulled this upwards and out came a concertina. He knew what it was, as he had seen one being played by street musicians outside the supermarket where he shopped . He put his hands inside the leather straps at both ends and pulled them apart, at the same time pressing at random on the buttons at either side. The musical notes he produced were not in any way a tune as he had no idea how to make any musical sense of the instrument. He put the concertina down and looked into the box to see if there was anything else there, but could see nothing. He also felt around the lining to see if there were any breaks or repairs of any sort, but there were not.

Setting aside this unexpected item, he returned to the hat. Basically it was a grey, fedora style, though with a wider brim than is usually found on this type. It also had a band around it which was very ornately patterned in green and gold colours. The band was held in place by two small gold pins. He removed these and lifted off the band. Turning it inside out he discovered that there was a completely different design on this side. Somehow he seemed to recollect that he had seen this design at some time in the past, but could not recall where or when. "Well," he said to himself, "that will give me something to mull over if I have trouble sleeping tonight."

He returned to the kitchen where the phone was to look up the telephone number of Mrs. Mactavish, the unhappy landlady, and make a note of it as he intended to call her in the morning. He found it with no difficulty and jotted it down on the notepad he kept close by.

The following morning Paul woke early. He had not slept well, unable to stop thinking about the previous days' events, and in particular the design he had discovered on the inside of the hat band. He knew he had seen it before, but could not place where. He made a quick cup of coffee, then put on his overcoat and left the house to go for a good long walk to forget about the details running around in his head.

Later that morning he returned home to put in a call to Mrs. Mactavish. The phone was answered very promptly and Paul recognised the voice at the other end. He identified himself and asked whether she knew if Captain Dearborn had ever played a musical instrument. There was a loud laugh at the other end of the phone.

"I should say not!" said the landlady, "and I should know as his room was directly above my own. All I ever heard from him was a lot of pacing up and down. He used to drive me crazy with his footsteps at all hours of the day and night. Why did you ask me that?"

"Oh, just on a chance", said Paul. "No special reason. I take it you haven't seen the Captain since I saw you last."

"No," she answered, "and I'm going to rent his room at the end of the week and throw his personal stuff, books and all into the garbage, and good riddance I say."

For some reason, and he couldn't say why, Paul asked if he might look at any books that she was going to throw away.

"Sure," she said, "but you had better be here by Friday noon, as the garbage men come on Friday afternoon."

Paul arranged that he would be there at nine-thirty in the morning and would help with the removal of the Captain's things. Putting the phone down he wondered to himself what he had done that for. This whole hat and pawn ticket thing was taking hold of his life and although it had been interesting, it wasn't that interesting, or was it?

Friday morning arrived bright and clear. As Paul made his way back to Westport, he mulled over what sort of books the Captain had been interested in, and how many of them there would be that might be of interest to him. It made him think about the sort of books that he liked to read. Mostly biographies and books on history he concluded, plus a fair amount about archeological discoveries. He was a subscriber to a quarterly review of archeological activities around the world, and always read each issue with great interest.

He parked his car outside the house at No 11. Looking at his watch he saw that it was about nine-forty. As he walked up to the front door, it opened wide and Mrs. Mactavish beckoned him in.

"I hope I'm not too late," said Paul.
"No, not at all," said the lady, and ushered him immediately up the stairs to a landing from which several doors led off to different rooms. The Captain's is the one at the front, directly over mine as I told you," she said, and proceeded to unlock the door.

Entering the room Paul stood and stared for a moment. The furnishings were minimal, a table with two chairs at the window, a single bed on the wall opposite with a wardrobe along side. Behind the door there was just enough room for a kitchenette arrangement. A counter and sink, plus a two burner hot plate. A feeling of melancholy came over Paul as he looked around at the sparseness of the place. There seemed to be no personal items, no trinkets, no photos that might have held memories of a life. The only sign of any occupancy was the table which was loaded with books and files.

At this moment, the sound of a telephone ringing prompted the landlady to say 'help yourself to the books and stuff on the table. I'll have to answer the phone as I have an advertisement in the local paper looking for a new tenant for this room. I'll be back in a minute or two."

Paul walked over to the table and began to examine the books. To his surprise they all seemed to be related in some way to archeology; indeed he had read some of them himself and even had a couple at his own home. Several of them were library books and a quick glance at the inside covers revealed that they were long overdue. There were two that he had not seen before and that he would be pleased to add to his own collection, so he set these aside on one of the chairs. Then he glanced through the files that were lying there. He felt as if he were prying into the personal life of someone else, and was uncomfortable doing this. One file in particular caught his eye; the tab on it read. "South of France," and in brackets "(Carcassonne)"; this one he set on top of the books on the chair.

By this time the landlady re-appeared.

"May I have these?" said Paul pointing to the chair on which he had placed the two books and the file.

"Certainly," she said. "In return you could do something for me. I'm going to empty all this stuff from the table into these boxes that I've brought up, and I know they are going to be heavy. If you would fill them up and take them out to the garbage, it would help a lot."

"I'd be glad to," said Paul and set about the task right away. While he was carrying the boxes out to the garbage the landlady brought up two large plastic bags and emptied the contents of the wardrobe into them.

"Not much here for a man of his years is there," she said. "Pitiful I'd call it. There's not one thing here that would be worth the effort, or cost, to try and sell to recover some of the lost rent."

To change the subject Paul asked her what she knew of the Captain, as he had obviously been a tenant for some considerable time, a year at any rate, from what she had told him.

"Well, I know that he was overseas during the war because he had ribbons on the uniform which he was wearing when he first came to rent a room, and later he told me that he had spent a lot of the war years in France. He used to get mail once in a while from France. I know that because I have to sort out the mail when it's delivered. It all comes in through the one mail slot in the front door. Apart from that, I don't know much else. As I told you, he never had any visitors that I saw, and seemed to keep to himself."

There appeared to be no more to be said, so Paul thanked the landlady for the opportunity to obtain the books, and file, which he had under his arm and started towards the front door.

"You weren't wearing your hat today," she said. "It was the hat you had on the other day that made me think you were the Captain, he had one exactly the same."

"Oh, is that so?" said Paul as he left and pulled the front door closed behind him.

Driving back to his own home he pondered over the type of individual that Captain Dearborn appeared to have been. Something of a loner, a bit bookish, and similar in physique to himself apparently, and of all things interested in archeology like himself. It was all very odd indeed!

Over the weekend he devoted his time to his garden. He was very keen on the roses he grew, and was often complimented by passers-by on their colour and fragrance. He and Carla had spent many happy hours together arranging the layout of the back and front yards. Despite the fact that she had been gone for more than a year and a half, he still found himself talking to her about the plants and flowers they had cared for together, asking her opinion, or offering advice while working away at the chores of pruning, planting and clean up. For Paul, this always seemed so natural and in some way he felt very close to her in the garden

On the Sunday afternoon he sat on his patio with a glass of his favourite wine, an Australian Chardonnay. He had brought out the two books along with the file he had picked up from the captain's room. He was particularly interested in the file marked South of France (Carcassonne.) On one of his trips to Europe, he had been sent to France to assist in some translation work for a government department attached to the aviation industry. The meetings had been held in Toulouse in the south of France, where the hub of the aviation industry in that country is located. Because the meetings were taking longer than expected he had had to stay over a weekend, and as a result had some free time. Paul had rented a car and driven the short distance to Carcassonne, as he wanted to visit this famous old walled town and explore as much as he could.

That whole weekend had been one of the highlights of his life as he had been able to immerse himself completely in the middle ages, Carcassonne being one of the very few remaining places in Europe where only pedestrian traffic is allowed and the buildings inside the walled town, are exactly as they were in the eleventh and twelfth centuries. For a minute or two he reminisced about that time; recalling the old buildings and the half timbered houses, the cobbled streets and narrow alleys that he had explored, and the feeling of another time that had captivated him so. As Paul examined the contents of the file it was clear that Captain Dearborn had also visited Carcassonne on more than one occasion. Including, from the dates on some of the notes he read, as long ago as the early 1940's, during the second world war. Other notes were much more recent, including some from the year before last. There were also two photographs in the file; one showing a young priest standing alongside an individual in uniform, on the back of which was the notation "Father Jacques," and the date March 7[th,] 1945. The other was a photo of the exterior of what looked like the front of a church, though the windows were boarded over. On the back of this photo were the words "Knights Templar".

Paul had read enough history to know that the Knights Templar were involved in the crusades of the eleventh and twelfth centuries, and that there was a connection between them and the town of Carcassonne where they had maintained a stronghold.

Reading through the Captain's notes, it was clear that he had been studying the history of the crusades and had been very interested in the part that the Knights Templar had played in these religious adventures.

Paul closed his eyes, and again cast his mind back to the time he had spent in Carcassonne to try and recall if he had ever seen the building that was in one of the photographs. He could see in his minds eye, the views as he had walked along the battlements which enclosed the town on the hill. However, he could not place the church or building in the photo.

He got up from his chair and went into the house. From his study he took a magnifying glass from one of the drawers in his desk. Returning to the patio he examined the photo of the building as closely as he could. A portion of the picture showed a large front door, presumably the main entry to the building. Over this doorway was a head carved in stone, and on either side of the carving was a decorated frieze work, also carved in stone. This caught Paul's eye, as it appeared to resemble the design that he had seen on the inside of the hat band he had found. "Well, isn't that a coincidence," he said to himself. He decided that he would take the two photos into town in the morning and have them considerably enlarged to get a better look at both the building and the two figures in the other picture.

The following morning he walked into town, taking with him the two photos, and wearing the hat he had found. He took the hat because he also intended to make a photo copy of the design on the inside of the hat band and have it enlarged at the same time.

The results from the enlargements showed that there was a distinct resemblance between the design in the stonework on the church building and the design on the inside of the hatband. It made Paul think that he must have seen the building when he was in Carcassonne some years before, and that he must have been struck by the fact that the church was boarded up and apparently not in use. The other photo, the one of the two individuals, revealed a young army officer about six feet tall with dark wavy hair. The priest, who seemed to be about the same age, was holding out a large envelope in his hands as if offering it to the young officer.

On his way back home, Paul made a slight detour to walk through the park where he had first found the hat. He stopped for a few minutes at the location where he had tossed up the coin. He bent down to make a brief examination of the ground, partly to see if there was any sign of the coin and partly to see if there was anything else to see. Since his last visit, the leaves had been picked up by the park employees but by chance, he saw his coin. What a stroke of luck he thought to himself; what are the odds of that I wonder? Putting the coin back in his pocket, he continued his walk home.

That evening he had a student coming to see him. He periodically took one or two promising ones who were studying the languages with which he was so familiar, and tutored them. He did this for his own sake as much as theirs, as he wanted to keep his own skills as sharply honed as possible and this proved an ideal way for him to do so. It also had the benefit of providing company for him with younger people and he very much enjoyed this part of his life. His student this evening was a girl from a Dutch family. She was in the last year of her university studies and was majoring in Italian with a view to becoming a translator like himself. Her command of the language was very good, so he needed to be on his toes.

The girl, Anka, arrived on time and the two settled down in his study to a discussion of current events, in Italian. Paul always insisted that the whole session be conducted in the language to be learned so that the student become familiar with all the simple things associated with a language that make up such a large and natural part of everyday speech.

It was his custom to take a break to enjoy a cup of coffee about halfway through the lesson. While the two of them were sitting together, Anka noticed the concertina and asked Paul if he was learning to play the instrument. Paul said that he had only obtained the concertina a few days before and that at the moment he had no idea how to play it. Anka asked if she might demonstrate some of the ways to learn. It transpired that her father had a similar instrument and that he could play it well. He had taught Anka how to play it when she was a teenager.

"Please go ahead," said Paul.

Anka picked up the instrument and commenced to play a familiar Viennese waltz. At the end of the piece, Paul clapped his hands together. "That was great" he said.

"I'll play one other tune," said Anka. "It's a sea shanty. Many of the tunes played on the concertina are songs about a sailors way of life." She commenced this one, which was using some different buttons than in the previous tune. She discovered right away that one of the buttons did not depress like the others, so had a difficult time with the music. Eventually she stopped.

"There must be something blocking the button inside," she told Paul.

"Well, I'll take a look at it later, but anyway, thanks for the concert; perhaps you could give me some beginners' lessons some time."

"Certainly," replied Anka, "anytime." Then she put down the concertina and the two of them resumed the language lesson.

Later that evening when Anka had gone, Paul picked up the concertina himself and pressed each of the buttons until he located the troublesome one. It was on the left hand side, bottom left he noted. He looked closely to see how to take the unit apart and found a series of small screws held each end onto the bellows.

Taking his smallest screwdriver from a kitchen drawer, the one which held the usual collection of bottle openers, bent forks, pens and pencils, string, etc., he carefully undid each of the screws on the end of the instrument. Very gently, he pulled and twisted until the two parts separated. Setting aside the end piece, he looked at the exposed buttons. He could see that each of them had a small spring-loaded mechanism which allowed them to go in and out. On the bottom left button, the spring was missing - it had been replaced by a small tightly folded piece of paper. Paul pulled this out and set it on the table. He then held the concertina upside down and shook it gently; sure enough he heard a faint rattle and out fell the missing spring. He replaced it in the appropriate position under the button and put everything back together again. While he was doing this, he was contemplating - what could the small folded piece of paper contain; someone had obviously put it there and presumably to hide it, but why?

As Paul took the paper and unfolded it, he could see that there were some words written on it. When it was fully opened up, he studied it for a moment and then was completely taken aback as he realised that there, drawn on the paper, was the design he had seen that very morning when he had had the hat band enlarged by the photocopy machine - the same design that he had also seen in the enlarged photo. Written underneath the design were the words "*calyx*" and "*blood.*"

In between the words and the design were a number of underlined spaces, as if someone were trying to complete a quotation or decipher a phrase by placing certain letters under parts of the design. Picking out a dictionary, he looked up the word Calyx. "The outer whorl of leaves or sepals at the base of a flower," he read. "Well, what does that mean?" he said. For a few minutes Paul sat back in his chair, closed his eyes and let his mind wander. He thought about Miles Dearborn, the Captain into whose life he had so strangely been drawn.

He surmised that there had been something that the Captain had been trying to discover, that had something to do with the Crusades, the Knights Templar, and Carcassonne.

Perhaps the captain had stumbled onto some archeological site during the war and had been attempting to solve some unexplained aspect of his discovery ever since. It seemed possible that the unusual design he had seen was some sort of code that the Captain was trying to unravel. But why was the piece of paper that now lay on his table so carefully hidden inside the concertina?

Who was the priest, Father Jacques? Obviously a religious figure, perhaps associated with the boarded up church in the photo; was he connected to this mystery in some way? What was in the large envelope that the priest had held in his hand? Paul's mind was spinning round and round.

That night as Paul lay in bed trying to sleep he thought back to the tape that Carla had left for him in her car. He recalled her request of him that he make sure to get all he could out of life, and to make the most of any opportunity that came his way. He turned over one more time, closed his eyes, and in his mind pictured the two of them walking together holding hands. Within a few minutes he fell asleep.

Over the next few days Paul visited his local library and read all the material he could find about the Knights Templar, and their connection with the town of Carcassonne. He discovered that the Knights Templar apparently existed in a rather secretive shadowy form to the present day - that they held themselves to be the true guardians of Christian faith. During the medieval period they had taken part in the wars of the crusades and when victorious in battle, had removed many important religious artifacts from the temples and churches that they had overwhelmed. These significant icons they had taken with them on their return to Europe, where they were subsequently carefully hidden. The whereabouts of these objects had been a source of great interest to scholars and archeologists for several hundred years.

One of the books that Paul had obtained from his visit to Captain Dearborn's room had a very comprehensive section on the history of Carcassonne, and its connection to the Knights Templar. Out of curiosity, Paul checked at the beginning of this book to see who the authors were. Listed among the several names was one, Frere Jacques Masson. Paul wondered if this could be the same Jacques in the Photograph he had found in the file. It seemed possible.

CHAPTER .2.

April 7th turned out to be one of the most important days in Paul's life. In his mail that day he received a letter from Peter Taylor the English archeologist, offering him a chance to join the group who were returning to the site of the ongoing excavation in France. They would be actively at work on the site starting on the 20th of the month. Peter went on to say that although Paul would have to pay his own way to the area, there would be accommodation and food provided, though the accommodation might be a bit spartan. Peter also advised that his team would be made up of several members from different countries and because of this, he hoped Paul would help out in the event that any translation was needed between individuals.

Paul immediately wrote back to say he would be delighted to attend and that he would, of course, be of any assistance he could with regard to translating. He walked to the post office that same day and sent his reply by special delivery.

For Paul the next week seemed to rush by. He had to make plane reservations, put a hold on his mail, and contact his students to advise them of his absence. He spoke to his immediate neighbour, with whom he intended to leave a key to his house in case of some emergency, etc, etc.

He decided to make a short stopover of two days in London, on his way to France. The reason behind this was his intention to visit the manufacturer of the hat he had found. He wanted to see if he could learn anything from the hat maker about the discoveries he had made since it had come into his possession.

To do this, it had been necessary to contact the shop in Westport to obtain the address of the maker in London. Paul sensed a distinct lack of enthusiasm from the salesman about giving him the information. At first he thought it was because of a potential lost sale to the store, but the more he thought about it, the more it seemed to be a real reluctance to pass on any details. While holding onto the phone, he had been able to overhear the sound of two voices arguing. Eventually the salesman came back on the line and gave him the address.

Two days before he was to set out on his trip he had a disturbing phone call from Mrs. Mactavish, Dearborn's Landlady. It seemed that she had been visited that morning by two men who at first claimed that they knew the Captain. She surmised this as they apparently were aware of his absence and said they were trying to find him. They asked if they could look in his room to see if he had left anything to assist in their search. She had told them that the room had been re-rented, and in any case, she had cleaned it out.

At this, the larger of the two men became belligerent and demanded to be let into the room immediately. She had been forced physically up the stairs, and made to unlock the door. Fortunately, the new tenant had not yet moved in, so the room was pretty much the way Paul had seen it when he had been there. The two men had searched everywhere - looking in every drawer, throwing the carpeting to one side to examine the floorboards; even pulling the wardrobe away from the wall to look behind it. Eventually the smaller of the two had demanded to know what had happened to the Captain's possessions. Mrs. Mactavish told him that she had thrown everything into the garbage.

"What was everything?" the man had asked. So she had told him all she could remember. He seemed to be most interested in the files she told him about.
"What was in the files?" he asked. She told him she hadn't looked inside them, just thrown them out.

"Damn and blast it!" the man said. He then raised his fist in front of her face and yelled: "don't you hold out on me!" At this point Mrs. Mactavish had burst into tears and collapsed against the table. The big man then pulled her cane out of her hand. Waving it in front of her he told her to keep her mouth shut about everything that she had seen; telling her not to contact the police. Then the two of them had then left the house. It took her a few minutes to get back down the stairs where she had nearly tripped over her cane which was lying across the last step.

Paul was, of course, absolutely amazed at this information, and asked her to go over the whole story once more, which she did, adding a few more details. Paul asked if she would be able to recognise the two men if she saw them again; she thought she might, but could not say for sure.

Then he asked if she had told them about his two visits to her house. "No," she replied; she had not told them anything at all. She had been about to just when the big chap had forced her up the stairs - when that happened she decided to say nothing.

Paul breathed an inward sigh of relief; the last thing he wanted was to get broken into and beaten up by a pair of thugs.

Mrs. Mactavish then told him that there was one thing she did remember. When the smaller man had raised his fist in front of her face she had been able to see a ring on his little finger. It had been so close that even with her poor vision, she could make out that the ring had a red cross on a white background.

Paul advised her to go to the police, and report the whole thing to them. However, it was clear from her comments that she was very much afraid to do so, and she felt that they were not likely to return, as they had not found anything and, in any case, there was nothing for them to find! After a pregnant pause, Mrs. Mactavish said goodbye, and Paul put down the phone.

All that day he could not stop thinking about what Mrs. Mactavish had told him. Clearly someone was after something that they thought Captain Dearborn had, and they were very desperate types. He began to feel that perhaps he had whatever it was that they wanted - that the note he had found hidden inside the concertina and the design on the inside of the hat band were all connected in some way to a mystery that Captain Dearborn had been trying to solve. And now he was in possession of these clues that were being so desperately sought.

"I sure wish I was getting on a plane today!" he said to himself.

Paul went to his bedroom and pulled out his suitcase and started packing for his trip. As he put things into the case, his mind was going over all the events that had occurred since finding the hat and the pawn ticket. Luckily, he had packed so many times over the years that he put the things he would need for the trip without really paying much attention to what he was doing - except when he put in some shirts. In the past, Carla had always folded these for him in a special way which he had never been able to duplicate. For a few minutes, he was lost in thoughts of her.

He came back to the present with a jolt. Closing the suitcase and locking it, he set it aside. Then he picked up a shoulder bag in which he intended to put the items he might need handy to him for the day of the flight. Passport, tickets, electric razor, toiletries bag, etc. He thought about what he might be doing a few days from today; when he would be absorbed by the activities at the archeological site and a long way from what had been transpiring around him here.

The location of the dig he was going to was about a three-hour car ride from Carcassonne. Paul intended to take with him the accumulated items that had been collected around the missing Captain Dearborn, including the hat, and the files. He intended to take some time away from the dig to try and uncover whatever he could about this enigma that had accidentally become part of his life.

There were many times in these last few hours before his departure that he thought about Carla's advice to him. "Well," he said to himself, "there is no doubt that I have taken her advice to heart!"

Luckily for Paul, his next door neighbour, the one with whom he had left the key to his house, had volunteered to drive him to the airport. He had also offered to pick Paul up on his return, as long as he had a day or two notice of the flight time. This gesture was much appreciated, and Paul promised to bring back a bottle of good French brandy for him on his return.

The trip from his home to Pearson International Airport in Toronto was made in good time and the flight to London was uneventful; the plane being only half full. It gave Paul the luxury of stretching out across three seats. As a result, he was able to sleep for more than four hours on the trip. Whenever he awoke, his mind went back to the things that had occurred in the past few weeks. In particular, the most recent call from Mrs. Mactavish and the physical abuse to which she had been subjected. He thought about how he might have reacted in similar circumstances and had to admit that physical violence was not anything that had been part of his world; he shuddered involuntarily.

He considered his plan to visit the hatmaker and wondered if the shop in Westport had been in some way associated with the visit of the two men to Captain Dearborn's room. He could not think of any obvious connection and decided he was only thinking in that way because that was the way in which he had located the Captain's residence. Notwithstanding this, he decided to be very careful about how he broached the subject of the purchase of a hat from this company in England, and to be on his guard while he was on their premises. He intended to take the hat with him when he visited the business but would keep it concealed in his shoulder bag as long as possible.

Eventually the plane touched down at Heathrow airport. Paul picked up his bag and made his way by tube to the centre of London. He then purchased a London street map at the station and located the address of the hatmaker. He took another underground train to Charing Cross and eventually emerged out on the street into the early evening rush of people headed home. With map in hand, he got his bearings. The hatmaking business was not far from where he stood, so he asked one of the station porters standing close by if there were any decent hotels in the immediate area.

"Yes there are," the porter replied. "For a fiver I'll take you to one that I know well. I often take travellers there, its only a five-minute walk. Give me your bag and I'll carry it for you. My name's Ted, by the way. First time in London is it?" he asked.

"No," said Paul, "I've been here a few times."

Then he made a quick decision. The porter was about the same age as himself, so taking some comfort in this, he handed over his bag and walked alongside.

The porter turned out to be as good as his word. The hotel was a short walk away and, though small, had a dining room with an adjacent bar. The room that Paul was shown was clean and adequately furnished. It also contained a shower and toilet; all very compact. The one thing missing was a telephone, though there was a public phone in the lobby area. Paul gratefully handed over the five pounds to his guide who had waited in the lobby to make sure that Paul was satisfied.

"Good night, guv'nor," he said as he tipped his cap.

Paul took a quick shower, which he always found so refreshing. Then he put on a complete new set of clothes, placed his airline ticket and passport in his inside jacket pocket and set out for a walk to become familiar with his surroundings. He also wanted to see how long it would take to walk to the hatmakers place of business.

There was still about an hour of daylight left before he would have any difficulty finding his way. He kept his street map open so as to enable him to pick out the street names as he came to them. After about twenty minutes, he turned into the correct street and started checking the numbers on the buildings. He had noticed for the past five minutes that he was getting into a more light industrial area, with a sprinkling of warehouses and he knew from his map that he was quite close to the river Thames.

He stopped outside the appropriate number on the street. Over the front door was a faded sign depicting a black top hat, underneath which was the name, "Burdett & Sons." The same name that was inside the hat he had found, and the same name that he had been given by the shop in Westport. Feeling pleased with himself at his navigation, he decided to walk back to his hotel by a different route, one which would take him alongside the river. At the same time he would see if this way was any quicker.

When he got back to his hotel he looked at his watch to check the difference; it was no more than five minutes and he had dawdled by the river watching the boat traffic, which was plentiful. So, there was not much in it, he decided.

At the hotel desk he requested a call in the morning at seven o'clock. That done, he retired for the night.

Paul was wide awake long before he heard a knock on his door advising that it was his wake up call. He had been unable to sleep for the last hour as he planned what he was going to do once he was inside the hatmakers. At one point, he had thought of telephoning to make an appointment but decided that he might well be put off by any employee he spoke to. He realised that this was a manufacturing facility and probably not open to the general public. Paul had made up his mind to take the hat with him, hidden inside his shoulder bag, and not to show it unless he had to. He had also taken the two gold pins off the hat band and placed the band inside his jacket pocket.

Because of the intrusion and treatment of Mrs. Mactavish, he decided to use a name other than his own while he was at the location and to tell a different story about why he was there.

In the dining room, Paul had what was called "a full English breakfast". This was considerably more food than he generally ate in the morning, however, he contented himself by saying that it was somewhere near his dinner time in Canada, and even if that wasn't true, he was hungry!

Leaving the hotel, he turned up his collar as the wind had started to blow. He retraced his steps from the previous evening and arrived at the street at a few minutes after nine o'clock.

He opened the door of Burdett & Sons and walked into a waiting area. There were a few overstuffed chairs and a table set up beside a counter. There was no-one around, but he could hear the whirr of a sewing machine and the sound of conversation. He opened and closed the front door with a bang and coughed loudly. This brought a response: "one moment please".

Paul sat down in one of the chairs and waited. As he sat and looked at his surroundings, he noticed that there was a small surveillance camera near the ceiling and assumed it was there to detect any unwanted intruder.

He looked up as he saw a figure approaching through a half glassed door behind the counter. The door opened and Paul was greeted by a man about the same age as himself, wearing an apron over his clothes.

"How may I be of service?" said the fellow.

"I'm interested in purchasing a hat from you," said Paul. "It has to be made specifically for my head and I have a very good idea of what I want."

"Well," said the man, "you've come to the right place; we specialise in making hats that are made to the precise requirements of a customer. My name is Burdett", he added. "I am actually the son of the original owner, my father, who passed away some years ago."

Paul could sense that he was expected to reveal his name at this point, however, he immediately began to describe the hat in his shoulder bag. After a minute or two, the owner reached under the counter and brought out two photograph albums. These were full of designs, drawings, and pictures of hats.

"Why don't you look through these," Burdett said. "I have to get back to my work but I'll come back in five minutes. I'm sure you will find something amongst these albums to help get us started."

Paul sat down at the table and started to turn the pages. About halfway through the second album he came upon the very hat, though the band around it was not exactly the same. He sat and waited for Mr Burdett.

When the owner returned Paul pointed out the hat to him.

"Well, well," said Burdett. "You have certainly picked a rare model; I don't think there are more than three or four of those in the world. I remember the last time we made one; it was for a chap in Canada. By the way," he asked, "you're from Canada aren't you? I thought I detected an accent."

"No," lied Paul. "I'm from the United states, Michigan, actually."

"I should give you some idea of the cost of this item," said Burdett. "It may be more than you are prepared to pay, but first let me get my assistant to come out and do some precise measuring of your head." With that, he disappeared. A few minutes later he returned with the assistant.

"This is Germain," said Burdett. "He has been with the firm for many years; he is one of the few true craftsmen left in this industry."

The assistant bowed to Paul and commenced to measure his head in a number of different ways, making notes as he went. At one point, as Germain was measuring from back to front, his hand was very close to Paul's eyes. On his little finger he wore a ring; the same ring that Mrs. Mactavish had described, a red cross on a white background!

Paul jerked his head in surprise, forcing Germain to measure again, allowing Paul a second opportunity to look at the ring, and confirm what he had seen.

"I'll have to look at our stock to see if we have any of the material we will need," said Burdett and left the room, taking the assistant Germain with him.

Once they had left, Paul had a chance to consider what he had seen. It seemed to him that perhaps there was a connection between the man who had frightened Mrs. Mactavish and this man Germain. Perhaps they were somehow in league with one another, perhaps members of the same group or organisation. In any case, Paul was now very alert.

Mr. Burdett came back into the room with a piece of paper in one hand and a pen in the other.

"I've worked out a price for you," he said, "but I need to know what sort of decoration, if any, you want for the hat band. We have many designs to choose from and some of them are outrageously expensive I'm afraid."

"As a matter of fact, I have a particular one in mind," said Paul, and pulled out from his jacket pocket, the headband he had placed there earlier. "It's my intention to use this."

Burdett was obviously taken by surprise at the sight of this, and for a moment or two seemed at a loss for words. Eventually, he asked if he might take a closer look at the hatband. Paul passed it over and watched as Burdett held it very close and examined it with a magnifying glass he had taken from a drawer under the counter.

To break the ensuing silence, Paul commented that he was sure that he could adjust the band to fit the hat that he was proposing to purchase. He then held out his hand for Burdett to return it to him. Reluctantly, the owner handed it back to Paul, who put it in his pocket. He then asked Burdett what the price would be and how long before the hat would be made.

The owner picked up his piece of paper. "The cost is fifty-eight pounds," he said, adding that the hat would be ready in one week.

Paul had already decided that he would give the impression that he would have to think it over, as it was more expensive than he had thought. He said to Burdett that he would think about it and call again in the morning, to say yes or no. With that, he picked up his shoulder bag and quickly retreated out of the front door.

He walked briskly down towards the river. When he reached the turn in the road he turned to the left and waited for a moment, then he looked back up the street. He was not surprised to see the assistant Germain come out of the building and head in his direction. As he left the business, he had a sixth sense that the hatmaker was not pleased with the outcome of their meeting, and wanted to learn from Paul how he had come into possession of the hatband, and exactly how much Paul knew about its significance.

Paul took to his heels and ran as fast as he could. He was very glad that he had taken this same direction the previous night and so was not held up to check if he was heading where he wanted to go. He did not look back until he was on the street where his hotel was situated. Turning this last corner, he had only a few paces to go before he was inside the lobby.

Once inside, he stood panting for a few seconds. Then he proceeded to the bar where he ordered a whisky. When the drink came, he took a seat close to a window that looked out onto the street. There he sat facing the way he had run. Less than a minute had passed when he saw the assistant turn and start to walk up the street toward his hotel. Paul watched closely as the assistant moved along looking from left to right, coming ever closer to where he sat. Paul left his place and moved into the washroom, there he sat down on the toilet. He waited as long as he dared and then returned to the bar.

He looked around and saw no one. Finishing his drink, he walked out into the lobby; picked up his room key and went straight to his room where he double locked the door.

Paul sat on the edge of his bed. He went through in his mind what had occurred at the hatmakers. He mentally kicked himself for having shown the hat band to the owner.

"That was not a good idea," he thought. On the other hand, he now felt sure that there was something very important to some people about what he had in his possession. Thank God he had not given his name or address to Burdett, or shown him the hat! What to do now was the question to be decided. Paul was sure that the ring on the little finger of the hatmakers assistant was the same as the one that Mrs. Mactavish had seen. He had to find out what the connection was, if any, between the people who wore these rings.

Somewhere in London there must be some information he could learn, but where to start his search? He decided to telephone Peter Taylor, he might know where to start looking. Of course Peter might well be in France by now, but it was worth a try.

Paul went down to the lobby to the public phone. There was no phone book so he went to the hotel desk and got instructions on how to call directory assistance. From the operator he got Peter's number and put in the call.

"Taylor here," came the familiar voice at the other end of the line.

"This is Paul Brett, your translator and all-around amateur archeologist on his way to France."

"Paul!" exclaimed Peter. "It's good to hear from you, where are you phoning from?"

Paul explained that he had decided to break his trip to France by stopping in London until the next day.

"Well, that's great," said Peter. Lets have lunch together and I'll fill you in on the plans for the next few weeks."

They agreed to meet at a pub called "The Judges' Arms," next to Chelsea bridge, on the north side of the river at one o'clock that afternoon.

Paul put down the phone. He hadn't felt like mentioning his quest to Peter while there were people walking by him in the lobby. He decided he was getting a bit paranoid!

Returning to his room he got out his map and found Chelsea Bridge. He was already on the north side of the Thames, so it would be a simple matter of walking alongside the river until he came to the right bridge; he guessed that he could walk there in less than an hour.

Paul made sure that he had his passport and airline ticket in his shoulder bag with him when he left his room. Dropping his key at the desk, he picked up one of the business cards of the hotel, thinking that it would be a good idea to give it to Peter in case he needed to contact him. Then he asked if there was a rear entrance to the hotel.

"Yes," said the clerk. "Just go to the end of the hall and turn left, the delivery entrance is right there. When you get outside, turn left again to reach the street."

Paul stood in the hallway for a minute or two to get the first few street names he would need in his head; then he set off. For the first few minutes he kept looking around to see if he was being followed, or if he recognised anyone - but the streets were full of people and traffic, and he became preoccupied about keeping his bearings.

His estimate of the time it would take to get to Chelsea Bridge was just about right, as he arrived just before one o'clock. The Pub was easy to find, so Paul went into the bar and ordered a beer. Luckily he was able to get a seat by the window, which had come vacant while he was ordering his drink. After about five minutes, Peter Taylor came into the bar and seeing Paul, came over quickly to shake hands.

"What would you like to eat?" Peter asked. "The menu is on the blackboard at the end of the bar. I've eaten here many times and the food is excellent." Paul chose a steak and kidney pie, and Peter went to the bar to order the meal and get a drink for himself.

"They'll bring the food to the table," said Peter.

The next half hour sped by as Peter launched into a complete update of the archeological site. Obviously, a lot of changes had occurred since Paul had been there and some very interesting things had been uncovered. The most exciting news was the discovery of an underground passage, which had been blocked up with debris when first found but was now completely cleared, and led to an entirely new area nearly two hundred yards away from the first dig. This new area was the one that the team were to work on during this trip. It was clearly connected to the first area but was thought to pre-date the first discoveries by more than one hundred and fifty years.

Paul enjoyed listening to the enthusiasm that Peter brought to the science of archeology. He was completely caught up in the realization that he would be there at the site in a couple of days.

By the time their meals had come and gone, they were talking about the loss of Paul's wife and the things that Paul had been doing since that time. It seemed to Paul that this was an appropriate time to change the subject, so he asked Peter if he knew anyone in London who was an authority on jewellery, and rings in particular. He described the ring he had seen, though not the circumstances surrounding seeing it.

"Well, said Peter, "although I am not an authority myself, I feel pretty sure that what you are describing is a ring that is worn by a group who call themselves the Order of St. George. I've studied the medieval period for most of my life and have seen drawings of such a ring. What you've seen sounds exactly like it. The people who wear this ring are bound up in a very shadowy society that stems from the days of the Crusades; and it is still in existence today. What little I know of the current society would make me stay well out of their way, they have a reputation for ruthless behaviour toward anyone who tries to penetrate their world. Where on earth did you see this ring?" he asked.

So, Paul told something of his visit to the hatmakers, leaving out the part about the hatband, but describing how he had come to see the ring while having his head measured. He went on to tell of the chase that had occurred when he had left the shop.

Peter, of course, did not understand why these things had happened but advised Paul to keep his eyes wide open until he was out of London altogether. He even advised Paul to change his hotel room, or even his hotel. Saying that, if nothing else, perhaps he was a target for a robbery.

On this rather somber note, they took their leave of one another; Peter to continue his organising of the dig before he left for France and Paul to make his way back to his hotel room.

Paul retraced his steps, going back the same way he had come. Walking along by the river, he was lost in thought. He stopped to look over the stone wall and stared down at the water running by. The remarks Peter had made concerning the likelihood that the ring he had seen had something to do with a society whose roots went back to the Crusades, seemed highly plausible to Paul. The number of connections he had found since first picking up that hat; the Captain, the town of Carcassonne, and the archeological aspect. The secrecy of the hiding place of the note in the concertina. The words that were on the note, and the feeling that the captain had been trying to decipher some code. All these things were connected somehow, but how? What about the experience at the hatmakers that morning? There was definitely more to this than he had ever imagined. Questions, questions - that was all he had at the moment.

He turned away from the river and putting his hands in his pockets, started off again.

In his left-hand pocket he felt the business card of the Hotel, the one that he had intended to give to Peter. "Damn!" he said to himself.

Thinking about the hotel, he went through the events of the morning again and the chase that had taken place. There was no doubt that the hatmakers employee was trying to catch him but with what in mind, he wondered. More unanswered questions.

Paul decided that he would stop at the next phone booth he saw, and call the hotel to see if anyone had been enquiring after him. The first phone booth he came to was occupied, so he continued on, the next one was also occupied, but he waited until it was vacated. Then he entered and dialled the number on the card.

"Handleys Hotel," said the voice. "This is the front desk, how may I help you?"

"This is Paul Brett," said Paul. "I'm staying in room 27; could you tell me if there are any messages for me?"

"No messages," said the voice, "but your brother-in-law was here asking for you."

"Oh?" said Paul.

"Yes," said the voice. "He showed me a picture of you, and asked if you were still at the hotel. I checked to see if your key was here, and as it was, I told him you were probably out somewhere but that we expected you back at any time. Then he said he would just have to phone later and try to catch up with you. After that he left."

"Thanks very much," said Paul. "I'm not too sure just when I'll return, probably later this evening."

Paul put down the phone, and noticed that his hand was shaking. He did not have a brother-in-law!

I should have asked the girl at the hotel what this person looked like, he thought. Though that might have seemed a bit odd, you would think I'd know what my brother-in-law looked like. Where the devil did someone get a photo of me anyway? Then he remembered the surveillance camera at the hatmakers. Of course! That's where it must have come from. Paul wondered if the girl had spoken his name to this so-called brother-in-law. Not likely, he thought, as she would have assumed that any relative would have known it. He wondered if this person had seen where his key was located when the girl went to check. "Rather more likely", he thought to himself, "I had better do some serious planning, thank God I called before I got back to the Hotel."

He continued to retrace his steps in the general direction of the hotel, turning over ideas as to what to do next. One thing was sure, he did not want to spend another night there. But all his luggage was in his room, how the heck was he to get his belongings out of the hotel without going there? He stopped walking for a minute and looked around him. A few steps away was one of the entrances to the underground for Charing cross station, this gave him an idea. He would try to locate the porter who had taken him to his hotel the day before. He hurried down into the labyrinth of passages and followed the signs to the main station. He eventually came up to ground level across from where he had been the day before. Paul approached one of the porters.

"Do you know where I can find Ted?" he asked.

"Ted who?" said the porter. So Paul described Ted as well as he could.

"Oh, that Ted," said the porter. He looked at his watch. "He'll be on a tea break right now I should think, but he'll be back in about ten minutes. He usually works the south side of the station," said the Porter, pointing to the exit that Paul had used the day before. "If you stand around over there you'll probably see him."

"Thanks very much" said Paul, and walked over to where he had stood on the previous day.

While he was waiting for Ted to appear, Paul thought about the idea that had come to him. It now seemed a bit flimsy, but as he could not think of a better one, he would have to give it a try.

At last he saw Ted emerge from the station looking around for a likely customer. Paul approached him and was recognised immediately.

"Looking for someone to carry your bags, Sir?" said Ted, smiling at him.

"In a way, yes," said Paul. "How well do you know the owners of the hotel you took me to yesterday?"

"Why, is something wrong?" said Ted, looking puzzled.

"Not exactly," said Paul, not knowing what to say next.

"Well, I should say I know them very well. My sister and her hubby own the place, have done for the last nine years." This bit of news was music to Paul's ears.

"I want to ask you to do something for me," said Paul.

"Not illegal is it? I'm not doing anything illegal, not for nobody!"

"No, it's not illegal," said Paul. "I'm concerned that someone is watching for me at the hotel, someone I don't want to meet. I can't explain it very easily, it's a long and complicated story. What I want you to do for me is to go to the hotel, pick up my room key, get my luggage and bring it back to me here. I'll give you enough money for the hotel bill, including tonight, and I'll pay you for your time."

Ted took off his cap and scratched his head.

"Dear me," he said. "That's the strangest thing I've ever been asked to do, and I've been asked some pretty odd things over the last twenty-five years."

Paul waited patiently while the porter seemed to be thinking over the proposition. Eventually he looked at Paul and said, "alright, I'll do it. But I'll call the hotel right now, and you ask to speak to Jean, that's my sister, and tell her what you want me to do, if she is agreeable, then ok."

Paul readily accepted the conditions and the two of them headed off to the nearest row of telephones. Paul got through to the hotel and asked to speak to Jean. When she came on the line, he quickly identified himself and explained what he wanted and why. The owner was naturally a bit surprised and asked to speak to Ted.

Of course Paul could only hear the words that Ted was saying, and there was a fair amount of "I don't know" and "sounds odd to me," with Ted nodding from time to time.

He handed the receiver back to Paul.

"You're sure you want Ted to do this?" Jean asked.

"Quite certain," said Paul. Then Jean asked what she should say to Paul's brother-in-law if he came back to the hotel. It seemed that she had been near the desk when the person had come in to the hotel enquiring after Paul.

"Tell him that I had to leave suddenly on a personal matter, and if he should ask for my name, please don't give it to him. Ask him why he doesn't know it himself seeing as he says he's related to me!"

"Yes, that's a good question", said Jean. "Alright, send Ted around to the hotel right away."

Paul put the phone down and pulled out his wallet. He handed Ted two hundred pounds, enough for last night and tonight's lodging.

"When you get to the hotel, see if you can find out what this person looks like and what exactly he said", asked Paul. "I'll just wait right here and look for you in about half an hour."

"Right you are guv'nor," said Ted, pocketing the money. "Half an hour it is then," and with that, he set off.

Paul walked back into the main station. He stopped at a small cafe, went in and ordered tea. Then he sat down at a vacant table to consider his next move.

He felt pleased with himself at his idea to use Ted to get his luggage back, what a stroke of luck that Ted's sister owned the hotel. It made the retrieval of his bags a whole lot easier to accomplish. He was sure that they were honest people, though they must think that he was a pretty weird individual. Once he got his luggage back, he decided he would go straight to the airport, take a room at one of the airport hotels and sit tight until it was time for his flight. He rechecked the airline ticket in his shoulder bag and confirmed that his flight to France left at nine-forty the next morning. Putting the ticket back, he took out the file of Captain Dearborn and re- read the notes that were in it. He took out the piece of paper with the words calyx and blood written on it and stared at the design above the letters. He felt that this piece of paper held the key to solving the mystery of the things that had been happening to him. He considered talking over this whole series of events with Peter Taylor, once he was settled in at the dig. Maybe he could shed some light on the puzzle.

Paul picked up the file, put it back in his bag, walked back out to the street entrance of the station, and waited for Ted. After ten more minutes, he saw Ted walking along the street towards him, with Paul's suitcase in his hand. A big feeling of relief came over Paul at this happy sight.

Ted put the suitcase down beside Paul. "What a mess! What a mess!" he said. "Your room was a ruddy shambles, clothes thrown all over the place, drawers tipped up on the bed, everything all upside down. Someone must have got in there and was seriously looking for something. If it was your brother-in-law, I should punch him on the nose."

To say that Paul was shocked at what he was told would be an understatement. He thanked his lucky stars that he had not gone back to the hotel. He took out his wallet to pay Ted for helping him retrieve his luggage. "Oh, no," said Ted, and handed over one hundred pounds. "Jean would not take any money for the room for tonight," he said. "Just for last night, and I took ten quid for myself for the trip. So that's that," he said firmly.

"Well, I'm very grateful indeed," said Paul. "Was Jean able to give you any idea what the person who was asking for me looked like?"

"No, not much," Ted answered, "except that he wasn't young, in his late fifties or early sixties, she thought."

"What are you going to do now?" asked Ted. "Do you want me to find another hotel for you?"

"No, I don't think so," said Paul. "I'll just get right out of town. I can't tell you how much the help of you and your sister has meant to me." With that the two men shook hands and Paul headed back into the main station to get a train ticket to Heathrow.

The trip out to the airport was uneventful and Paul was able to secure a room at an airport hotel with no difficulty. When he finally got into his room, he opened up the suitcase to see if anything was missing. Everything was rather jumbled up, but all the things he could remember packing appeared to be there. He sat down on the edge of the bed. "I reckon I've had about enough of this," he thought. "It seems to me that I could have had the same experience as Mrs. Mactavish, except that I probably *do* have something that these people want! However, they *don't* know where I am and they *don't* know where I'm going, and they *may not* know my name". This last one was a bit iffy, he decided. Whoever these people were - if they could find his hotel and then get into his room, the chances were they did know his name by now.

Paul got up and sorted out his belongings, repacking some things and hanging others up to get the wrinkles out. He picked up his shoulder bag and walked over to the departures lounge to check on his flight.

Everything was expected to be on time, he was told, but to be sure to check in an hour before take-off. With that done, Paul decided to walk the whole length of the airport and look at the various eating establishments, to help him decide what to have for dinner. He also stopped at a shop which sold newspapers from around the world and picked up the most recent Canadian one he could find.

Later that evening he returned to his hotel. He felt reasonably relaxed now, having eaten a good meal at one of the more expensive restaurants and finishing off the meal with a fine brandy. He had been spoken to by no one, other than his waiter. This individual was an Italian chap. Paul had enjoyed a discussion about the latest political scandal in Italy. They also spoke about the waiter's home town Padua, which Paul had visited some years ago. The whole conversation was spoken in Italian and Paul was complimented on his command of the language. He put a call in to the front desk to be wakened at seven o'clock. Then he had a very hot shower, which always relaxed him before going to bed. He opened up his toilet bag to take out toothpaste and brush, and noticed that the prescription label on his bottle of migraine pills was missing.

"Oh, no!" he said. "That label had my name on it, so whoever ransacked my room at the hotel today, *now certainly knows* who I am." The relaxed mood he had been enjoying disappeared and Paul knew he was in for another interrupted night, and not much sleep!

His morning call came right at seven o'clock and Paul woke up with a start, having only just fallen asleep at around four in the morning For most of the night he had tossed and turned - going over the incredible things that had happened to him. Paul regretted ever finding the hat and the pawn ticket. Instead of going on a wonderful, interesting, archeological expedition, something he had wanted to do so many times in the past, he now felt like a hunted man, trying to avoid capture by some powerful and frightening enemy.

If it wasn't for his own archeological curiosity about what he had found out so far, he would have abandoned the whole thing.

"In any case," he said to himself, "nobody knows where I am, or where I'm going. Once I get to the dig in France, it'll be like I disappeared off the face of the earth." Cheered by this thought, Paul packed his suitcase and left the hotel. He checked in at the departure gate much earlier than he needed to and got rid of his luggage. Then he went through airport security to the gate listed on his boarding pass, and waited for his flight to be called.

CHAPTER .3.

His plane left on schedule and arrived at Charles de Gaulle airport, where he had a two-hour layover before continuing on to Toulouse. He spent the waiting time listening very carefully to all the conversation around him, with a view to refreshing his comprehension of the French language. It wasn't his specialty, but he had a good vocabulary and used every opportunity to improve his accent. It was, he thought, rather like one of his tutorials back in his home, where he had insisted that all conversation be conducted in the language to be learned by his students.

He purchased a good road map of France in the airport and studied it carefully, with the idea of selecting the most convenient route from Toulouse to a town called Gaillac, the sight of the dig.

The last time he had been in this town, he had been coming from the north but this time he would be going in a northerly direction from Toulouse. He cast his mind back to that first meeting with Peter. They had met one another purely by chance. Paul had learned of the site from a conversation with his host while staying overnight at a small hotel in Gaillac. He had driven out to the location the following morning hoping to be able to take a look at the activity. He had introduced himself to Peter and, although Peter was a bit stand-offish at first, he quickly realized that Paul was a serious amateur student of archeology, and the two had struck up an immediate liking for one another's company.

Peter had taken him under his wing and shown him much of what had been uncovered; how the work would proceed, and why. Many of the individuals working on the site were much younger than Peter and spoke either French or Italian as their native tongue. Paul got the distinct impression that as he and Peter were of a similar age and both spoke English, his arrival had been a welcome breath of fresh air.

Paul's flight from Paris to Toulouse was with Air France. The passenger sitting next to him was a young lady on her way to her home just outside their destination. She told Paul that she had been in Paris to sit exams for an entry into university.

"How did you make out?" Paul asked.

"I think I did well enough," said the girl, "but the questions were much harder than I had expected". On the other hand, she felt she knew her subjects, and considered that she had been able to demonstrate her knowledge sufficiently well for that to be recognised.

The conversation between them was a mixed bag of things. She had realized, despite his command of the language, that he was not French. Paul had told her something about life in Canada and some of his reasons for being on the same plane. When they landed at Toulouse airport, they walked together to the baggage carousel. While they waited for their bags to appear, the young lady's father arrived to pick her up. Paul was introduced to him.

"My name is Jean Carbonne," he said, as they shook hands.

"I knew a Carbonne some years ago," said Paul. "He was with the ministry of aviation here when I was on assignment with the Canadian government."

"That was probably my father," said Jean, "he retired about seven years ago."

"Well perhaps when you speak to him next, you'll remember to mention my name," said Paul. "He and I had many discussions regarding a joint venture between the French, Italian and Canadian aviation industries at that time."

"I'd be delighted to," said Jean. "My father wanted me to go into aviation too, but I became a television news producer instead. I'm afraid he did not approve of my choice at the time, but he has come to accept it over the years."

By this time their bags had arrived, so they said goodbye and parted company.

Paul had organised a car rental when he had booked his trip, so he went to the rental booth and completed this arrangement. Picking up the keys, he walked out to the parking lot and found his vehicle in the company compound. He put his suitcase in the trunk, took out his road map and set it on the passenger seat, started the car and drove out of the airport.

His spirits were lifted by the knowledge that he was master of his own destiny for the moment. He had a couple of days to reach his destination, no one knew who he was, or where he was going. His mind went back to the last time he had been in Toulouse. Some of the streets were familiar to him and he had a good idea of how to proceed. He thought about Yves Carbonne, the father of the man he had so recently met. Yves was a structural engineer and had one of the best brains that Paul had come across. "I wonder what he is doing with himself these days," Paul mused. "Come to that, I wonder what I'm doing with myself!"

By the time he had left the outskirts of Toulouse it was early evening, so Paul decided to pull up at the first decent looking hotel he saw and get a room for the night.

He was now travelling north and the traffic was light. After about twenty minutes he came to a small village. He parked his car in front of a restaurant that had a sign in the window offering accomodation.

Walking into the entry hall of the establishment, he was greeted by a woman carrying a big tureen of soup on a tray.

"Yes sir?" she said enquiringly.

"I'm looking for a room for the night", said Paul.

"Yes," she said. "No problem." If he would wait until she had served the soup, she would show him to a room. A few

47

minutes later she returned, carrying a handful of keys. She asked Paul to follow her while she lead the way.

He was shown into a large bedroom at the rear of the house. Looking out of the window, he could see a large garden full of fruit trees in early blossom and a number of flower beds around the base of each tree.

"Perfect," he said to his hostess. "I'll take it. Now, to make my day complete, do you have any more of that delicious smelling soup that you were carrying?"

"Certainly," said his hostess.

Paul arranged to move his car to the back of the restaurant, get his luggage and be in the dining area in half an hour.

That night he slept well for the first time in a week, he felt completely at ease and relaxed. In the morning he had the usual hot croissant and strong coffee - so common in France. Along with the croissant he received a poached egg, cooked just exactly as he liked it. He was able to eat his breakfast on the patio at the rear of the restaurant and was the only customer. His hostess was delighted when Paul told her he would like to stay for another night before continuing his journey to Gaillac. He wanted to go for a long walk in the countryside and simply enjoy the day, which was warm and sunny.

"Would you like me to make up a lunch for you to take along?" she enquired. Paul could think of nothing he would like more, and said so.

Half an hour later, with his lunch packed in his shoulder bag, Paul set off to explore the area with a sense of freedom and adventure. He found himself talking to Carla as he walked along, telling her how much he wished that she was with him, and describing the flowers and shrubs to her as he came across them. The roads he travelled on were almost devoid of traffic except for the occasional farm vehicle, and the sense of quiet filled him with joy. He made his walk in a large circle from a tourist map of the local area that he had picked up in the restaurant hallway. It showed various routes that one could take, depending on the distance one wanted to travel, and indicated points of interest along the way.

Paul had his lunch by a small lake. At the end of his meal, he polished off a bottle of beer that his hostess had thoughtfully provided. He got up and started walking again, and eventually returned to the restaurant in the late afternoon.

On his return, he thanked the owner of the restaurant for the lunch she had provided. She then asked Paul to make a selection for his dinner from the choices available. They all sounded delicious, so he left it up to her to decide, saying that he would be pleased with her decision, whatever it was.

Paul returned to his room and sat down with the file he had taken from Captain Dearborn, and re-read all the notes that were in it. Once again, he sat with the piece of paper with the design on it and the words *Calyx* and *Blood*, and tried to see how the Captain had arrived at these. He turned the paper around and around, he took parts of the design from different locations and tried to marry them together, but nothing he tried made any sense.

Paul's mind went back to the Captain himself. What could have happened to him, how did his hat come to be laying on the ground in the park? He was sure that the Captain did not just lose his hat, perhaps there had been a chase or a struggle and he had lost it in the melee. What was he doing in Paul's home town? Paul shook his head, he had more questions than answers, it was all very frustrating.

He left his room and went into the garden at the rear of the restaurant. Wandering about among the trees and the flowers, he wondered if his neighbour was watering his own garden, as he had arranged.

"I must remember to get that bottle of brandy for him," he thought.

He had an enjoyable meal that evening and went to bed at an early hour. He slept well again, and woke up feeling refreshed and ready for the day. He was on the road by eight o'clock the following morning, having paid his bills and thanking the owner for her kind attention to him.

Paul had looked at his map while having his breakfast and knew he would be in the town of Gaillac at around noon, if he just took his time.

The day was warm and sunny and the traffic was light again. As a result of this, he was able to enjoy the scenery as he passed by the villages and farms of this very rural part of France. The countryside was dotted with small rivers and rolling hills. If it hadn't been for the television aerials on the roofs of some of the houses he could be back in the eighteenth century he thought to himself.

Paul arrived in Gaillac a little after noon and made his way to the post office. He had an address for his accomodation from Peter Taylor, and was sure the postal service would know where it was. It took a few minutes for him to write down the directions he was given, and for the postal employee to draw him a map of the streets he should take. Back in the car, Paul held the map in one hand and the steering wheel in the other. He followed the instructions with no difficulty and arrived at a large house on the edge of town. The house was old and set back from the road, about one hundred yards. There was a semi-circular driveway leading up to the house, alongside which were very tall poplar trees, obviously planted some years ago.

He parked his car and walked up to the front door, rang the bell and waited. In a few moments the door was opened by a young man. Paul asked if this was the place where the team of archeologists were staying, and if Peter Taylor was in. The young man confirmed that it was and introduced himself as Michel. He invited Paul to follow him. They walked down a wide hallway and then turned in to a dining area set up with several tables. Here a group of ten or twelve men and women of various ages were eating lunch. Michel called out to everyone and introduced Paul to the group. That having been done, Paul was invited to join one of the tables. There he re-introduced himself and sat down. He was asked what his speciality was. He explained that he was there as a guest of Peter Taylor; that he had no specific contribution to make, other than an enduring passion and interest in the subject of archeology. He added that his career had been the study of languages, and that he hoped to make himself useful by aiding in any translation that might be needed. One of the two ladies at the table, a woman in her mid-forties he guessed, introduced herself as Maria Bernardo. He discovered while talking to her that she was from Florence. She had a similar interest in languages, spoke perfect English, and was Chair of the Department of Linguistics at the university in her home town.

When the meal was over she invited Paul to join her. She was going to the dig site that afternoon where there was to be a general meeting of the group. Peter, who was at the site, would distribute the work into small sections and allocate the bodies available into several smaller units. Each of these groups would be reporting to him.

Maria had her own car. She and Paul chatted easily together on the way to the site. He noticed that she had the habit of describing things with her hands as much as with her voice when she was emphasising a point. It made the short drive a bit more of an adventure than it might have been. She told him that she had arrived the previous day and was already familiar with the roads leading to the dig.

At two o'clock the group were gathered in a large trailer that was parked at the site. Paul had been able to speak briefly to Peter and had been asked to explain any linguistic misunderstandings to members of the dig who might not have understood what they had been told. There were five different European countries represented by the group and though they were all certainly competent archaeologists, they did not all speak, or understand, the English language. Paul could see that he was going to be busy and that Maria would be a big help as well. She was fluent in Greek and had a working knowledge of some Slavic languages too.

The rest of the afternoon was spent orienting the working parties to the site; making sure that each of the newly arranged smaller divisions of people were as compatible as possible. Apparently, there were still five more individuals yet to show up, though they were expected later that day or the next. Each of the new groups had at least one specialist, plus a scribe, who doubled as a sketch artist. When any new discovery was made, the specialist in that field would be brought in to supervise the team.

Peter had made the best use of the individuals, and this system of his had proved quite satisfactory in the past. It helped to build a team and also allowed a camaraderie to develop in each of the smaller groups. He gave Paul the job of roving translator. He was to move between the teams as he was needed, and at the same time, look for any dissension amongst the workers. If he detected anything of this nature, he was to report it to Peter and not get involved personally. Maria had been assigned to one of the teams to act as the scribe/artist. This was mainly because of her fluency in English and skill in other languages.

As daylight faded, the whole group returned to the house in Gaillac where an evening meal had been prepared. A cook and kitchen staff had been hired for the duration of the dig, which made life much more pleasant, allowing the archeologists time for socialising in the evening.

Paul and Maria had travelled back to the house together. Paul went to his room on the second floor. He had only briefly examined his quarters on arrival, as there had been just time enough to drop off his suitcase before heading to the site. The room was small, sufficient only for a single bed, a dresser and a wardrobe. From the window in his room, he could look out of the front of the house and see a herd of cows in the field across the road. "All very bucolic and serene ", he thought.

He removed his toilet kit from his shoulder bag, intending to use the bathroom to clean up before heading down to dinner. As he left the room, he noticed that there was a key in the lock of the door. He removed this and tried it from the outside. It was a bit stiff but it did lock his door. He was very glad for the privacy that would result from this.

At the end of the landing was an old fashioned bathroom. The sounds of activity emanating from this room made it clear it was occupied. Paul decided to wait on the landing, guessing that if he left he might well miss his opportunity to use the facilities. Two minutes later, another person arrived carrying her toilet bag. Fortunately the bathroom door opened at this moment and Paul stepped inside, turning the lock behind him. It was obvious that the toilet arrangements were woefully inadequate for the number of people staying in the house. Paul could foresee plenty of problems ahead in this department. He dressed carefully, making a special effort to look his best and wondering if any of the rest of the group would be doing likewise.

When he entered the dining area, he looked around and saw that most of the others were still wearing the same clothes that they had worn at the dig site. One of the exceptions was Maria. She had changed into a black skirt and a cream coloured blouse, Paul thought she looked very fetching. She was deep in conversation with one of the other archeologists, however, when she saw Paul enter the room, she came over to join him and the two of them sat next to one another at one of the tables.

During the evening meal, the participants in the dig naturally gravitated towards one another by the language that they spoke. However, after the meal was over they moved around the room to talk to each other about the work to be commenced in the morning. Paul was constantly asked to translate something for one person or another. He could see why Peter had been so keen for him to join the team. As the evening wore on, two of the group brought out a violin and a guitar. They entertained everyone for an hour or so with a wide selection of music which included some tunes that the group could sing together. Paul was reminded of his student playing the concertina back at his home.... and realized that he had not thought about the problems of the Order of St. George for a whole day. "What a relief," he said to himself.

For the next three or four days, he and Maria drove together to and from the dig. He learned that she had been married when she was in her late teens but the relationship had not gone well. Her husband was jealous of her academic interests and had eventually left her. There had been no children from the marriage, and Maria had become more and more involved in her work. The position she held at the university had never been held by a woman, and she was obviously very proud of her accomplishments.

Paul talked about his working life and the places he had visited. He told Maria of the death of his wife and the impact that it had made on his life since she had died. The two of them seemed to be able to converse quite easily, which made it very pleasant for Paul, and the days seemed to fly by. At the site of the dig, they were both involved in different areas, so did not see much of each other during the day.

A number of new items had been unearthed, a pewter dish, a piece of leather clothing, and a selection of coins. These coins were of great interest, as some of them were dated, which helped to confirm the period of the site. The group that Maria was working with had been gradually uncovering a section of wall and had reached a point where there appeared to be a doorway. She was very excited about this and showed her sketches to Paul one evening. Paul was suitably impressed by her drawing talent, which was undeniable.

Her capacity for translation into English, of the work being done, was also first class. It was made even more impressive, in Paul's opinion, by the fact that one of the members of her group was from Greece and spoke only his native tongue. He was one of the late arrivals and something of a know-it-all, which was rather aggravating. To make matters worse, his attitude toward Maria was very condescending and as she was the scribe for the group, she had to put up with more than her fair share of his remarks. She and Paul discussed this problem on their way to and from the site, and Paul promised to talk to Peter about the issue. At the house, he had a word with Peter about Maria's problem, and from that time on, the chap from Greece was the soul of discretion and politeness with her, though not with the rest of his associates.

At the end of the first week, there was agreement to take the Sunday off and relax. Some of the group were going to make a trip into the surrounding countryside and explore the area. Others had personal matters to attend to.

Maria was anxious to do some sketching of the new part of the site that her group had been uncovering. She asked Paul if he would accompany her. As he had no plans, he readily agreed, suggesting that they stop in the town to pick up some lunch items to eat while they were at the site.

In the morning they drove to the market square in Gaillac, where there were stalls set up, offering everything one could want in the way of lunch. This included some wonderfully fresh bread and a great selection of cooked meats. They shopped together, with Maria making most of the food decisions. She was in her element, negotiating the price of items and examining in detail the way some foods were cooked. All this in a mixture of French and Italian with much arm waving, just as though she were at home in Florence. Paul was quite happy with this arrangement and spent some time admiring the flowers that were for sale. He purchased a bottle of red wine for them to enjoy with their meal and happily tagged along behind Maria carrying the various bags she accumulated.

Once they arrived at the site, Maria got busy with her pad and pencils. Paul watched her for a few minutes, then left to do some exploring for himself. He had been so busy with the interpreting he had been doing, that he had not had time to look around at all the areas where work was being done.

The site seemed very different with no-one else around. There was definitely an aura of melancholy and loneliness about it. To shake himself out of this feeling, Paul decided to do a bit of digging at the site in the area where the coins had been found. Using the usual tools of the trade, a small shovel and a stiff brush, he carefully removed small amounts of earth. He had been working away at this for a short time when he felt his shovel touch something hard. Digging very slowly he uncovered the haft of a sword. He pulled it gently toward him and it came free. There were only a couple of inches or so of the blade attached to the haft, and it appeared to have been broken off. Paul shouted for Maria to come and see what he had found. He was excited beyond words.

"Look! Look," he yelled.

Maria came running over. When she saw the sword handle, she was as pleased as he was. "I'll get my sketch pad," she said, "and make a drawing of it right away." While she was gone, Paul brushed the dirt off the haft, holding it by the piece of blade that was still there. He could see that it was quite ornately made. "It must have been owned by someone of rank," he said to himself. By this time Maria had returned. She took the object and placed it on a nearby rock, then sat down to draw it.

Meanwhile Paul continued to dig at the spot to see if he could locate any more of the sword. He dug carefully for half an hour but nothing came to light. By this time, Maria had completed the drawing of one side of the sword handle and had turned it over to draw the other. She carried a small paint brush with her pencils to brush away any dirt that might get on her drawings. She was using this to clean off the imbedded earth on the other side of the handle. As she worked away at this, she saw a decoration in the centre.

"Come and see," she said to Paul. He came to join her just as the last of the dirt was brushed away. It showed a red cross on a white background !

Paul felt as though he had been kicked in the stomach. He sat down and took the haft from Maria, and looked closely at the decoration. Despite the fact that his hand was starting to shake badly, he could see that there was no doubt about the similarity between this design and the ring he had seen at the hatmakers in London.

"Whatever is the matter with you?" asked Maria. "You're white as a sheet, are you alright?" Paul looked up at her and sighed. "I was absolutely alright until a few moments ago, now I'm not too sure."

"Please tell me, if you can, what has upset you so."

"Well, it's a long and complicated story", he replied, "and I'm not sure that I should tell you anything as it may place you in some danger."

"I'm not a child," said Maria, "and I'm not easily frightened. Why don't we stop working and have our lunch. I'll set everything out that we've brought to eat, and you go and find some way to open the bottle of wine. While you're doing that, think about whether or not you want to tell me what is worrying you."

With that, Maria left to go to the car and bring the food to a table that was outside the trailer. It was used during the week for coffee breaks and for a flat surface to write notes on.

Paul took the bottle of wine behind the trailer where he knew there were a few tools in a box. He took out an old screwdriver and a hammer. After a few attempts. he managed to push the cork down into the wine bottle without spilling too much. He walked around to the front of the trailer and sat down at the table, opposite Maria.

While he had been opening the bottle, he had been thinking about whether or not to tell her anything at all. In the end, he finally decided that it might help if he got the whole business talked through with another person.

CHAPTER .4.

Over their meal together, he told her the whole story. She listened intently to what he had to say, interrupting him from time to time when she couldn't follow the details. When at last he had finished the two of them sat in silence. Finally, Maria asked if she could see both the hat and the paper with the word puzzle written on it. "I might be able to find a way to decipher those missing letters," she said. "Don't forget that my special area of interest is the translation of ancient documents and I have had some success at it." Paul re-emphasized his concern for her safety. "What do you think will happen to you if you are able to make sense of the puzzle? Remember what happened to Mrs. Mactavish, and to me in London. If these people find me and can link you to me, you will be in serious danger."

Maria agreed that this was so, but she still wanted to examine the hat and the paper. They agreed to return to the house taking with them the sword haft that Paul had discovered.

They both knew that this was rather bad form in archeological circles, but did not want to leave their discovery at the site unattended. When they got to the house they would hand it over immediately to Peter, to let him decide what should be done with it. Paul knew that he would be the centre of attention for the first little while when they arrived. Each time some object had been found, there had been lots of discussion and opinion as to the age and significance of the discovery. In this instance, one of the German archeologists who was an authority on weapons would be in his element for days.

When Paul and Maria arrived at the house, Paul went off to find Peter to show him their discovery. Maria decided to make the most of the fact that because many of the group were away, she could take advantage of the empty bathroom to have a leisurely soak.

Peter was thrilled to learn of Paul's discovery. "We'll make an archeologist of you yet,' he declared! "Let's keep it under wraps until our weapon's expert returns, then we'll bring it out after tonight's dinner." Paul was quite content with this idea. He handed over the sword to Peter, who looked closely at it. A moment later, he stared up at Paul. "Isn't this the very same design you were talking to me about when we had lunch at the pub in London?" he asked.

"Yes," said Paul. "I'm sorry to say I think it is." Then he went on to tell Peter about his hotel room being ransacked, his escape plan to get his luggage back, and the experience at his hotel at Heathrow airport.

"What a damn good job you are here at the dig with us," said Peter. "Whatever these people want, they will still be looking for you, I'm sure of that." He stopped talking for a minute, obviously going over what Paul had told him. "You know, if they've got your name from your prescription pills, they may be able to trace your flight to Toulouse."

"Yes," agreed Paul, "that's something that has occurred to me. They may even have found which rental car agency I used at the airport, but they don't know where I am now. My God!" he added, "they must have a lot of influence in some high places to be able to get passenger lists from airlines. I thought such things were strictly controlled."

"I wonder what you should do now?" said Peter. "Just carry on as usual I suppose, but keep an eye out for anything suspicious, and let me know if you see something or you need some help."

"Thanks," said Paul "I will."

Once back in his room, Paul locked the door behind him and took down his shoulder bag. It had been a week now since he had taken out the hat or the file with the notes in it. He had been so pre-occupied with the thrill of being at the dig that he had not given much thought at all to the other reason for his being in France. His pleasure at the companionship that he was experiencing with Maria had made him do some serious thinking about how ordinary and uninteresting his life had become at home. He compared her to Carla. She was different in appearance. A little shorter and her hair was very dark, where Carla's had been fair, but they both had green eyes and long lashes. Maria was also blessed with that wonderful quality of being naturally happy and she had the same love for good conversation. He realized how much he looked forward to seeing her each morning.

Leaving the items on the table he left his room, locking the door behind him. He went to Maria's room and knocked on her door. "Come in," she called. Paul opened the door just enough to stick his head around, and asked her to come with him to his own room to look at the hat and the notes, along with the enlargements he had made of the design.

"I'll be right there," she said, so Paul waited on the landing. The two of them returned to his room.

"Put the hat on," said Maria, "I want to see if I think it suits you as much as you think it does." Paul obliged.

"Well, I agree that it does look good on you," she said. "Now let's get down to business. Please show me the papers with the drawings on them, and take the hat band off so that I can see everything at the same time." Paul spread all the papers out on the table. Taking the pins out of the hatband, he placed this on the table as well. Maria poured over the material - looking closely at each piece, she felt like a detective trying to solve a selection of clues. After examining the hat band, she said: "this pattern on the inside was sewn quite recently. I can tell by the relative freshness of the stitching. It is certainly not as old as the design on the outer side, which could be as much as a year old. As to the design or pattern on the building in Carcassonne, I agree with you that it is very like the pattern on the inside of the hatband. I think the drawing with the letters underneath is also a copy of the same pattern. It's hard to be precise because there is obviously some weathering that has occurred over the years on the stonework of the building. Did you say that you have seen this place when you were in Carcassonne?"

"I just can't remember." said Paul. "There are so many old structures in that town. The thing that sticks in my mind is that it seems to be boarded up and unused. Perhaps it has become unsafe and dangerous for people to use."

"Well," said Maria. "I can't see any obvious relationship with the design and the words Calyx and Blood. What is a calyx anyway? I thought my English was pretty good but this word escapes me, is it something to do with flowers?"

"Very good," said Paul. "That's what my dictionary at home said, something about the petals at the base of a flower."
At this point in their conversation, the sound of the bell calling the group to dinner could be heard.

"Please keep all this to yourself," said Paul. "The less anyone knows, the better I'll feel." Maria agreed. Replacing the items in his bag, the two left the room, locking the door behind them and went down to dinner.

Paul was thinking now about the partial sword he had found. He was looking forward to its being shown to the group at the end of the meal, and the pleasure that he would feel at bringing a contribution to their discoveries.

At the end of the dinner Peter called them all together, and asked Karl the weapons expert to come and sit beside him. Then he placed the broken sword on the table and removed the cloth in which he had wrapped it. "What can you tell us about this find that Paul made today?" he asked.

Karl stared down at the object for a moment or two. "What an incredible discovery," he said. "I never expected to find anything like this, and in such recognisable condition."

By now the rest of the group were gathered around the table and there was no escape for Paul. He had to tell them exactly where he had unearthed the sword handle, the depth of ground he had uncovered, and a dozen other questions. For the next hour he and Maria, with the others, discussed the importance of the find and what it meant about the site that they were uncovering.

There was, perhaps, a different aspect to the dig. Peter had always thought that this site had only been a religious community, but now with this find it could have also been fortified - or maybe it was attacked and defended. The possibilities were endless.

Meanwhile Karl had been able to examine the broken sword more closely. He pronounced that it was definitely from the twelfth century, and that in his opinion it had been made in France for a person of high rank and that it was very likely owned by a crusader. Paul asked why Karl thought it had a connection with the crusades. According to Karl, the red cross on a white background had been the chosen insignia for many of the crusading knights. It was very often seen on the tunics of these men, particularly when going into battle. At that time, there were strongly held beliefs that wearing these colours offered some magical protection to the wearer. Having the insignia on the handle of the sword was a further extension of the same idea, giving the holder protection from his enemy. Karl went on to say that the chances of being able to identify the owner of such a sword as they had found was highly unlikely, as during the eleventh and twelfth centuries many such weapons had been made.

Paul and Maria looked across the table at one another for just a moment. The finding of the broken sword was certainly energizing the group, and everyone was excited at the prospect of further discoveries at the site.

For the next week, Paul continued to do his job as a roving translator during the day. In the evenings he spent time with Maria as often as he could. They were able to go for lengthy walks now, as the evenings were getting lighter and the weather stayed pleasant. On these walks, the two of them thoroughly re-visited every aspect of Paul's connection with Captain Dearborn. Maria had made no progress with the puzzle and had suggested more than once, that to really have the best chance of solving it, she would have to visit

Carcassonne and see the stonework for herself. Though Paul had told her that he intended to go there himself while he was such a short drive away, he was very adamant that she should not accompany him. He insisted that it was too dangerous for her, especially as she now knew so much.

All the arguments she came up with to support her desires, he objected to in one way or another. His objections only made her more determined to go with him. At one point in one of their walks, they were both waving and gesticulating at each other with their arms, and Paul was reminded of the same thing happening when he had been walking with his wife, Carla. In fact, he thought, there are some definite similarities between Maria and Carla. Even though they had known each other such a very short time, he was certainly very drawn to this intelligent woman.

At the archeological site, work was proceeding rapidly in the area of the wall where the doorway had been discovered. Inside the doorway there was a lot of loose dirt and rocks. As these were removed, it became clear that they had entered another passageway leading back toward the original dig site. It seemed to suggest that the two passages had formed accesses to the first part of the excavations. This meant that there was a great deal more to be uncovered to reach this lower level, and also perhaps that the site was considerably older than had at first been thought. Peter was delighted with this new discovery as it would allow him, if correct, to continue obtaining funding for several more years into the future.

By the end of the second week, Paul had decided to drive to Carcassonne on the Saturday and stay overnight, returning on the Sunday. When Maria heard this, she immediately asked to be allowed to accompany him. Paul could no longer deny her. She had continued to spend hours poring over the drawing and the lettering, and was convinced that only a visit to the building would help her efforts to decipher them.

Peter had known that Paul would be taking time away from the dig, but reminded Paul that he could be walking into the lions den, so to speak, by going to the town. When he heard that Maria was going with Paul, he was both pleased and concerned. On the one hand, he was losing his two best translators. On the other, he felt that Paul would be safer with a female companion, as it would appear as though they were simply a couple of tourists on a visit to a famous town.

The two of them left Gaillac early on the Saturday morning. Maria suggested that they take her car to avoid anyone finding Paul's rented vehicle in Carcassonne.

"This lady is really thinking," said Paul to himself. "I should have thought about that, especially if Peter is right, that the people searching for me may well know who I am."

They drove steadily for an hour or so, then stopped to have a light breakfast and some coffee. As the day wore on, the traffic became more heavy and their progress was often reduced to a crawl - especially as they were using smaller roads from time to time, and had to pass through villages where market day was in full swing.

Just after mid-day, they came over the rise of a hill and could see the walls of the town and the battlements outlined against the sky - it was an impressive sight. Maria was filled with amazement at the view. She had read about Carcassonne and seen pictures in travel books, but nothing could match the sight of it in real life.

"My goodness!" she exclaimed, "I'm going to pull off the road and just take in this scene for a few minutes. You know something of the history of this place don't you?" she asked Paul. "Please tell me what you know".

Paul told her that Carcassonne was named after a woman. In the time of the reign of Charlemagne, the town had been under siege by his troops. The siege was into its third year and the residents were desperately short of food and water, and close to surrendering. A woman named Carcass had the idea to feed one of the few remaining pigs in the town with the best food available. When the pig was well fattened, she threw it over the battlements to the invading troops below the walls, giving the impression that the inhabitants still had plenty to eat. Charlemange's troops were so discouraged at the thought of this that they gave up and lifted the siege. As the troops were leaving, the bells rang out all over the town to celebrate their departure. The town was named Carcassonne, after Madam "Carcass", and the French word for the ringing or sounding of bells, "sonne". Hence the name, Carcassonne. The actual settlement had been there long before the time of Charlemagne and was a gathering place for some of the first crusaders in the eleventh century.

Maria was going to make a remark about the superior intelligence of women, then thought better of it. She simply started the car and rejoined the traffic.

During the drive there, Paul and Maria had worked out a plan of what they would do once inside the walls. They knew that they would have to park the car in one of the many parking lots below the old town, as no vehicular traffic was allowed inside. There were many places to do this but the lots were already full, indicating that there would be plenty of tourists walking around. Eventually, on the third try they found a place to leave the car. They took with them the items they thought they might need - Maria's sketch pad and pencils, Paul's shoulder bag containing the hat, and the drawings. They set off toward one of the gates leading into the old town proper.

They had decided to walk all the way around the battlements so that they could look down into the streets to see if they could identify from above, the building or church, whichever it was. Once they had found the structure, they would pinpoint it on the tourist map that they had purchased when entering through the gate of the old town. For an hour they walked along with all the tourists, most of whom were admiring the views from both sides, looking in on the town and also looking out at the countryside spread out before them. Paul and Maria concentrated on the inside of the town, marking their way by the map that Paul held in his hand.

On two occasions, they thought they had seen the building and had descended the steps which were periodically located at points along the wall, to take a closer look. Each time, the building they had seen was not the right one. After their second descent, they stopped to have lunch at one of the many restaurants.

Every place was extremely busy, so they were obliged to join a table that was meant for four people, where another couple were already seated. They made brief introductions to each other before concentrating on the menus placed before them by their waiter. The waiter was clearly overwhelmed by the number of tables he was trying to cope with and the several languages that customers were using, or trying to use, to order their meals. This situation prompted Paul and Maria to speak French together, in the hope of endearing themselves to him. The couple sitting with them were obviously tourists and spoke only English. When the waiter finally arrived at the table to take their orders, they had difficulty being understood, so Maria volunteered to solve the language problem for them. She received a sincere look of relief from the two of them, and the waiter. As a result of this act of kindness, some sporadic conversation ensued amongst the four of them. It appeared that their lunch companions were a couple from Scotland and were on a coach tour of historic sites of France. Part of the tour included a two day visit to Carcassonne and this was their second day. They had explored everywhere, "walking miles and miles," said the wife.

Paul decided to take out the photo of the building to see if they had seen it in their wanderings. "You never know," he said to Maria as he passed the photo over to the husband. The couple from Scotland looked at the picture for a few moments. "I have seen this place," said the man. "You remember dear", he said to his wife, "that's the place where we saw that fellow climbing over the railing around the building. We wondered what he was doing there, as the place was all overgrown and derelict looking."

"That might well be it," said Paul, "can you place it on the tourist map that I have?" "Let's have look," said the man. He turned the map around a few times. "Yes, it's somewhere

here," he finally said, making a circle on the map with a pen. "It's a bit off the beaten track, we only saw it because we got lost for a while yesterday." Paul took the map back and looked at it. The circle made by the Scotsman was much further along than he and Maria had walked so far.

"Could you describe the person you saw climbing over the railings, by any chance?" asked Paul. "Well, it's funny you should ask that", replied the Scotsman, "because he looked quite a bit like you, though a bit older I should say. But about your build."

"Did he say anything to you?" asked Maria.

"No," said the Scotsman. "I got the feeling that he regretted having been seen at all, and he ran off very quickly."

"We were about to ask him for some directions," said the wife, "but he took off before I could get the French words sorted out."

At this moment, the waiter appeared with their various meals and conversation died while they all got down to enjoying the food. Paul couldn't help recalling the two occasions when he had been mistaken for someone else and that person had been Captain Dearborn. "I wonder if somehow the Captain is here in Carcassonne," he thought. "It's certainly possible!"

At the end of their meal, Paul and Maria said goodbye to their lunchtime companions and thanked them for the help they had given. Paul stood for a few minutes outside the restaurant studying the map to find the most direct route to the circle drawn by the Scotsman. Like many medieval towns, the streets and alleys wound around all over the place and there was no direct way for them to proceed. The overhanging second storeys of some of the old buildings made it difficult for any sunlight to penetrate down to ground level.

"We'll have to go a few streets at a time," said Paul. "Otherwise we'll just get lost, like those two did." For the next while they walked along checking the map as they went. The streets were full of tourists in this section of the town, as most of the gift shops and restaurants were located here. After about twenty minutes, they noticed the crowds were becoming less and less, until turning one corner they found themselves alone.

"We must be really close to the building now," said Paul. "It's probably down one of these alleyways on the right, maybe we will be able to see it in the distance." No sooner had he said this than they stopped at a corner and, looking to the right, Maria said: "There it is, I'm sure of it!" The alley was about two hundred yards long. As Paul walked towards the building, he had a sense of deja vu and knew he had been here before. His mind went back to the time when he had visited the town during that weekend away from Toulouse, a few years ago.

This part of town attracted far less tourists than the rest, and they saw no-one as they came out of the end of the alley and stood across a small square from the building. As they walked toward it, Paul was thinking about the photo of Captain Dearborn and the priest. He wondered to himself if the priest had at one time been resident at this church, for that was what the building looked like the closer they came to it.

"I must try to find out what happened to that priest", he thought. "Perhaps I can locate someone from the Catholic Diocese here who can tell me."

Paul and Maria now stood at the main entrance. In front of them was a picture of complete neglect, overgrown weeds, rusted railings, old weathered boards covering the windows. The front door was locked with a large rusty lock and surrounded by cobwebs. Yet despite all these signs of abandonment, there was a solid look to the place. The stones with which it had been built were not badly decayed or lying at odd angles.

"Whoever built this church did an excellent job," said Paul. "They must have been master masons. This place is very old indeed, perhaps as old as the site we are excavating in Gaillac."

"I wonder why it is not used as a church?" questioned Maria. "Maybe there are just too many other ones in the town. In any case, I can see the design work in the stone around the top of the doorway. I am going to compare it to the photos and the drawings, and see if I can see any discrepancies between them. Why don't you climb over the railings and take a good look inside the entry of the main doorway?" she suggested. "I think I can see something above the centre of the door inside the entry but it is too much in the shadow to make out."

Paul put down his shoulder bag and clambered up over the railing. Grunting with the effort, he eventually dropped down on the other side. "Hell", he said, "I guess I'm not as agile as I thought." He walked into the entryway and stood in front of the door. It was massively built and made no movement as he pressed against it. He looked at the hinges, they had not moved for a long time. Stepping back, he looked up over the door. At the centre of the arch was a carved skull, around which was a Latin inscription. Roughly translated, it appeared to say *THIS IS A TERRIBLE PLACE.*" "What a strange thing to have over the front door of a church," he thought. "It doesn't make any sense." Stepping back into the daylight, he told Maria what he had seen.

"Are you sure that's what it said?" she asked

"Yes I'm pretty sure," said Paul. "Though I don't understand it. I'm going to walk down each side of the building to see if I can find anything else worth discovering. I'll be back in a few minutes."

Maria went back to her study of the stonework. She drew what she saw very carefully, without reference to the photo or drawings, so that she would not be influenced by them. She kept thinking about the inscription that Paul had described to her, like him she couldn't understand why such a thing would be there.

While she was drawing, her concentration was broken by the sound of a footstep. She looked around but could see no-one. "That's odd", she thought. "I could swear I heard something." She turned quickly around again and caught just the glimpse of a shadow disappear into the alley from which they had come.

At that moment Paul re-appeared. "Well there's nothing much to see, I've walked all around the church and it's the same everywhere. Just plain old disuse and only a few more boarded up windows."

Maria was so keen to show Paul her work that she forgot to mention the footstep or the shadow as she handed him her drawings. "What do you think?" she asked.
Paul looked from her drawing to the stonework and back again several times. "I think you've done a great job. Perfect in fact! Now let's make our way back to the car, find a hotel for the night and then examine everything at our leisure over a glass of wine."

"I'm for that," said Maria. "It's starting to get colder and it looks like we may be in for some rain later."

Paul clambered back over the fence - it was a little easier this time. He picked up his bag and the two of them made their way back toward the gate leading out of the town, down to the parking lot. On the way, they talked over what they had seen. Paul was especially surprised by the inscription over the skull. Whatever could it mean? He recalled that in the photo he had found, the words Knights Templar had been written on the reverse side. He knew that the Knights Templar had built churches in different parts of Europe, perhaps this was one of them. On the other hand, Maria was very pleased with the fact that they had found the church and that she had been able to get a good look at the stonework. She felt that her drawing was accurate enough, and that any differences between her work and the drawings would be fairly easy to spot.

They drove out of the lower town, and into the countryside for a few miles. On either side of the road were vineyards and small chateaux. They came to one that advertised accomodation and meals. Maria turned onto the gravelled road that led to the house and pulled up in front. "Lets go in and see what the accomodation is like," she said
"And what's on the menu," added Paul.

70

The front door was opened by an elderly man as they approached. "I saw you drive up," he said. "Do you want to purchase some wine?"

Maria said: "No, we were looking for two rooms for the night and an evening meal, and also some wine to enjoy with the meal."

"Please come in." said the man. "I'm the owner of the vineyard and I'll show you our accomodation." He led them right through the house to a courtyard in the rear, where there was a small detached cottage. "Here you are," he said and opened the door. Inside the cottage there was a sitting room and kitchen plus two bedrooms with a bathroom in between. "This place is normally occupied by the manager of the vineyard," the owner explained. "At the moment, he is away visiting his mother in Germany. He goes every year at this time for a month, so we rent it out to travellers."

Paul looked at Maria, she was smiling, so Paul said that it would be fine.

"You can bring your car around to park it in front of the cottage," said the owner. "It makes it easier to unload any luggage."

Maria handed her car keys to Paul. "Why don t you do that. I'll go and find out what's for dinner." She and the owner walked back into the house. There Maria asked him for two bottles of wine and discovered what they would be eating that evening. When she left to go back to the cottage, the owners wife called out, "dinner will be served at eight o clock, here in the house."

By this time, Paul had taken everything out of the car, and placed Maria's things in one bedroom and his in the other. The drawings he had placed on the table in the living room. There was an acorn fireplace in the corner of the room and Paul busied himself lighting it from a supply of kindling lying nearby. Meanwhile, Maria told him what they would be having for dinner and opened a bottle of the wine. At last, the two of them sat across from each other and studied the results of Maria's efforts.

Her attention to detail was easy to see. There were some differences between her drawings and those of Captain Dearborn. Also, comparing the old photo and the enlargements, one could see that some detail had been lost due to shadow.

At the use of the word shadow, Maria told Paul what she had heard and seen when she was working that afternoon, while Paul was away exploring the rest of the church. He was thoroughly alarmed by this news. He immediately speculated that the people who were after him had found out that he was in Carcassonne. Now he had the extra worry that they might well connect Maria to him, if they had been seen together. He insisted that Maria tell him if anything like this happened again, and told her to yell at the top of her lungs for him if he wasn't in sight.

Maria was concerned herself, but did not want to let Paul see this, so she simply said that she would do as he asked, and went back to her drawings.

"You know," she said, "I think that the answer to this puzzle is to try and use some different alphabets from other languages. Maybe Captain Dearborn was just guessing or didn't know enough ancient languages to enable him to understand. I'm going to test this theory when we get back to Gaillac. I have a number of different dictionaries and material on some of the forgotten languages that are no longer in use." Paul thought this was a good idea. "Let's clear away all the paper and look at it when we get back to our base. Tomorrow I want to visit the Roman Catholic diocese or the main man of the church here and see if I can find out anything of the priest, Father Jacques. There must be someone here who knows of him or knew him." Maria agreed that it was worth searching while they were in the area. Having said that, she suggested they have another glass of wine, put their feet up and watch the fire until it was time to go and eat.

They had their dinner with the owner and his wife and eldest daughter, all sat around the same table together. The meal was excellent, the main dish being a cassoullet. Maria wanted to know what the recipe was and as many of the cooking details as she could learn. Paul watched with pleasure as the two ladies had an animated discussion on the merits of using certain spices in some dishes. Both of them were obviously excellent cooks. The owner of the vineyard was generous with his servings of wine - offering a different one for the main course, and a special dessert wine at the end of the meal, which had been the creation of his absentee manager. This was delicious and they toasted the good health of all present.

Paul and Maria made their excuses for the evening and returned to the cottage. He stoked up the fire and the two of them sat together quietly for an hour or so, until Maria announced her intention of going to bed. They stood up together, Maria held Paul's hands in hers and planted a light kiss on his cheek. "Thank you for letting me come with you this weekend," she said.

Paul was completely taken off guard by this gesture, and fumbling for words for a moment, simply said "good night."

In the morning they both woke early. Paul heard Maria in the bathroom singing softly to herself. He turned over and listened until he was sure she had vacated the room. A smile came over his face at the pleasure she had brought into his life. They had the inevitable croissants and coffee with the owners wife, the owner having left to work in the vineyard. Paul asked if she knew where the largest Catholic church was in Carcassonne. She was a practising Catholic and was able to give them good directions. She herself would be going to mass that evening, but not to the same church. She explained that there was one just two miles further along the road that they had been on yesterday which she regularly attended.

Paul paid the bill for the accomodation and with that done, he and Maria departed to return to the town.

They were able to park a little closer this time, as the tourist crowds had not yet arrived in force, and they were in a different part of the town. The wife of the vineyard owner had given them excellent instructions and as a result of this, they could see the spire of the church they were going to visit quite plainly. On entering the main door, they realized that there was a service going on, so finding a place to sit down, the two of them waited. Maria, who was a Catholic, took part in the balance of the service and helped Paul find his way in the prayer book. She suggested that they could both use a bit of help from on high, and pray accordingly.

As the service was ending the two of them hurried out to the front steps, and waited while the priest greeted the congregation and said a few words to some of them. After the last one had left, the priest came over to Maria and Paul.

"I am glad to see you both." he said. "Are you visitors to our famous town?"

"Yes we are," said Paul, "and we are enjoying ourselves very much, I was wondering", he continued, "can you tell me the name of the Bishop in this diocese and where I can find him? I would like to talk to him."

"I'm very sorry," said the priest. "The bishop is in Toulouse at a conference and won't be returning until the end of next week. Is there something I can help you with?"

"Well," said Paul "I am trying to find some information about a priest whom I believe was here in the early nineteen-forties. I think he was called Father Jacques."

"I'm afraid I don't know any such person, I've only recently arrived at this parish. However, there is someone who might know of him. She is an elderly lady now, but she was the housekeeper for the Bishop for many years, her name is Madam Dupree. She might recall this Father Jacques. She lives with the Sisters of Charity, who run a home for old people here. The house is just around at the back of the church. If you turn right at the corner here, and right again, you'll find the house with no problem."

Paul thanked the young priest, and he and Maria set off. As they walked along, Maria turned to Paul and said: "these housekeepers often knew more about what was going on in the diocese than the Bishop himself. We might learn a thing or two here."

At the house they explained the reason for their visit. One of the sisters took them into a small sitting room and asked them to wait while a member of the staff would bring Madam Dupree to meet them. The Sister told them not to expect too much from her as she was very frail, and rather deaf. Nevertheless, she had a very good memory if prompted in the right way.

Maria spoke to Paul while they waited. "Let me handle this, I can probably get more information from this lady than you can." Paul agreed. Handing her both photos, he said: "she might be able to tell you something about the disused church as well. It's worth asking anyway, while we're here."

After a few minutes, Madam Dupree was brought into the room and was helped to a chair. She stared blankly at Paul and Maria. Maria pulled her own chair close to the old lady and spoke to her in a very clear, loud voice. She spoke of the life that Madam Dupree had probably lived, and it wasn't long before it was obvious that she was getting through to her. Maria showed the photo of the priest and Captain Dearborn to her. The old lady held it right up close to her eyes and nodded in recognition. She had known Father Jacques. According to Madam Dupree, he was a very devout person and well loved in the town. Maria asked if she knew his whereabouts now. She shook her head and said no. Then she started talking about the period during the war. From what she said it seemed that Father Jacques had been working with the allies, and was part of the underground that helped to get allied servicemen out of the country. At that time, no-one knew that he was doing this dangerous work but after the war was over, his contribution had been recognised by the French government and he became a hero. "Yes," said Madam Dupree, "a great hero!"

At this point, Paul asked Maria to show her the photo of the church. Maria took the first photo from Madam Dupree, and put the second one in her hand. She held it close for a moment and then threw it on the floor. "Bad, bad," she shouted, and at once appeared to be very frightened and agitated. Maria tried to calm her but it was no use, she was clearly very distraught.

One of the Sisters came running into the room to see what was happening. Taking one look at Madam Dupree, she turned to Maria and Paul. "I think you had better leave right now," she said. "When she is upset like this, it takes a long time for her to settle down. Please leave."

There was no point in staying and making things worse, so they picked up the photo from the floor and made their way back out into the street.

"I wonder what caused all that!" said Paul. "She certainly knows something about the abandoned church, and whatever it is, it isn't good."

At that moment, one of the Sisters came out of the house and spoke to them.

"I can tell you where to look for Father Jacques. He runs the St. Vincent De Paul shelter down in the lower town, but he is no longer a priest. We still call him Father when we speak of him, though he was dismissed from the priesthood a long time ago for spreading heretical views. He is no longer accepted by the Catholic diocese here, and is considered a bit of a renegade. Despite this, he is well loved at the shelter and does a lot of good work there. If you have a pen handy, I can give you the address, though I should warn you, it's not in the nicest part of the town."

Maria took a pen out of her purse and wrote down the address, along with a few instructions as to how to get there.

"Thank you so much," said Paul. "We'll go there directly and hope to find him. I wonder if you can tell me why Madam Dupree was so upset at this photo that we showed her?" Paul handed her the picture of the abandoned church, the sister looked at it then she pursed her lips and frowned. "I think you had better ask Father Jacques about this place," she said handing it back. "Very well," said Paul, feeling a bit bewildered, "and thank you again for your help."

Paul and Maria walked back to her car. "There is obviously something about that building that sets people off," she said. "I wonder if it's just Catholics that don't like it."

"Well, hopefully Father Jacques can answer our questions," Paul replied. "Let's go and find this St. Vincent de Paul shelter."

Driving to the shelter, Paul was thinking over what he had been told about Father Jacques. He knew that there had been an underground system for getting airmen out of France and back to England. He also knew that those involved in this very hazardous business took a lot of risks with regard to their own lives. Father Jacques must have been a very cool character indeed. He wondered if the underground was part of Captain Dearborn's reason for being in Carcassonne, and if he and Father Jacques had been working together. From the date on the photograph, it seemed a possibility. He pulled the photo out of his bag and looked at it once again, and at the date – nineteen-forty-five.

Maria parked her car across the street from the building which housed the St. Vincent de Paul shelter. The Sister had been right about the area, it was run-down and shabby looking, in complete contrast to the tourist part of the old walled town.

"Maybe you should stay in the car," said Paul. "There could be some pretty unsavoury characters inside this place."

"I'm coming with you," insisted Maria. "I think I'll feel safer with you than waiting out here."

The two of them walked into the building. Once inside, they found an office on the left of the hallway with a glass partition which was open. Paul knocked on the glass and looked inside. A young woman was seated at a desk, talking on the telephone. Gesturing to Paul to wait, she continued to talk for a few minutes more. Then putting the phone down, she asked if she could help.

"We're hoping to meet Father Jacques," said Paul. "I understand he works here.'

"Yes, that's right, but he is out at the moment. I expect him back in about half an hour or so. Would you like to wait, or is there something I can do for you?"

"No, that's fine," said Paul glancing at his watch. "We'll come back later, around two o-clock"

"Can I give him your name?" asked the woman.
"No," said Paul, "it wouldn't mean anything to him, we'll just come back."

He and Maria crossed the street again and got back in the car. "Let's just sit here and watch for him," said Maria. "I don't think I want to walk around here! Let's plan what we'll have for dinner, and where we will stop on the way back to Gaillac. We still have a lot of driving to do today."

There was very little traffic on the street and only a few pedestrians passed by as they sat together. They were having an animated discussion about desserts, when Paul looked up to see a figure approaching. "That's him," he said. "I'm sure of it. I'm going to go and meet him before he gets into the building, you wait here please."

Paul got out of the car and crossed the road. The closer the person came toward him, the more sure Paul was that this indeed, was Father Jacques. "Good afternoon," said Paul. The man looked up and smiled back at him. Paul held out his hand. "Are you Father Jacques?" he asked.

"I used to be," said the man, "but that was a long time ago, now I'm just plain Jacques."

"I believe you and I have a mutual acquaintance," said Paul.

"Oh, and who might that be?" the ex-priest asked.

"During the war I believe you had a friend called Miles Dearborn, a Captain.". At the name of the Captain, Father Jacques stared back at him. "You say that he is a mutual acquaintance? How do you know of Captain Dearborn?"

"If we could talk together somewhere," said Paul," there are some things I would like to tell you, and some questions I have that you may be able to answer."

"Before I spend any time talking to you, I have some work to complete right now," said Father Jacques. "If you want to wait until I've finished, you can come into this shelter where I spend my time and I'll speak with you in my office."

"I have a lady friend with me," said Paul. "Do you mind if she comes with me?"

"That's alright with me," said Father Jacques. With that, he walked on into the building

Paul ran across to the car and took out his shoulder bag. "Let's go," he said to Maria. "it *is* Father Jacques.'

Inside the tiny office to which they were directed, they waited until Father Jacques made a number of telephone calls. When he had finished, he looked up at Paul and Maria expectantly. "Well?" he said. Paul took a deep breath. "Here goes," he thought. "Stay calm and listen, don't talk too much."

Paul took out the photo from his bag. "Is this you?" he asked, handing it across the desk. Father Jacques gazed at it intently. "Yes, that's me," he replied.

"I believe the officer standing next to you is Miles Dearborn," said Paul.

"That is also true," replied Father Jacques. "Please tell me how you come to be in possession of this picture and tell me who you are, before I say anything more."

Paul identified himself, and Maria. He then gave a quick sketch of how the photo had come into his possession. Father Jacques looked back and forth between Paul and Maria. When Paul had stopped talking, Father Jacques said: "there is clearly a lot more that you know than you have said so far. So, I suggest you listen to me very carefully for a few minutes.

First of all, you are both in considerable danger. There are a group of people who will stop at nothing to find you and discover what you know. If they knew where you were, you might already be dead. As for me, I do not fear death. I have been threatened many times in my life. To most people, I am just a poor priest who has lost his faith, but they do not know my whole life. I'm very interested to hear every detail of your story," he said, "but this is not a good time or place. Let's arrange to get together later in the evening perhaps. Where are you staying in Carcassonne?"

Paul explained that they had to get back to Gaillac that evening, as they had responsibilities to their host.

"Well then," said Father Jacques, "I suggest that I come to see you both next weekend in Gaillac, well away from here. If you give me your telephone number there, I'll call you on Friday evening to tell you what time I'll arrive. There is a regular train service from Carcassonne, and that is how I shall come. It will be safer for all of us if we are not seen together here in this town."

With that, Father Jacques stood up to indicate that their meeting was over. "Please excuse me," he said, "I still have work to do."

Paul and Maria were escorted to the front door, which was firmly closed after them.

"What do you make of that?" said Paul.

"My intuition tells me that there is something going on here," she replied. "I think Father Jacques is being very cautious and I also think he is not telling us anything more than he wants us to know. I think that for every question he asks, we should ask one in return. We must try not to reveal any more than we absolutely have to, until we are satisfied with what he says."

"I think that's a good way to proceed," said Paul. "I don't think we should ignore his warning about those people who are pursuing us either. After my experience in London and the ransacking of my hotel room, I believe what he told us. These individuals mean business, so please, be extra careful. Now, let's get on the road again, we've a long way to go today. On the way, let's look for a restaurant that will give us the desserts we were talking about earlier. I'm hungry too!"

As they left Carcassonne behind them, the rain that had been threatening all day started in earnest and Maria was obliged to concentrate on her driving. Occasionally, she had to ask for directions from Paul, who was studying the map. Conversation was sporadic and there were long pauses while both of them digested all that they had learned over the two days.

Eventually, Maria pulled into a restaurant parking lot. By this time the rain was really coming down and they had to run quickly to avoid getting soaked.

"I don't care what's on the menu," said Maria. "This is where we eat!"

The restaurant was full, so Paul and Maria sat at the small bar sipping wine until a table became vacant. There was nothing on the menu that particularly appealed to either of them.

"Let's just eat something basic," said Paul, "and then get on our way again. I promise that when we are back at the dig, I will take you out for dinner and we will have all the dishes we were talking about in the car earlier." Maria locked up from her menu and smiled at him.

They arrived back in Gaillac around nine o'clock that evening. Peter was in the dining room with some replacement archeologists who had arrived over the weekend. He was slotting them into the gaps in some of the teams, caused by the departure of others who had not been able to stay for the entire duration of the dig.

"Welcome back," said Peter, and introduced them to the new arrivals. "Fortunately for me, most of this group have come from Cambridge University, so the language problems will be somewhat alleviated. We're going to have a general meeting at the site in the morning to plan our next weeks' work, so we should all be there no later than eight thirty. You two look as if you could use a hot bath and a good nights rest, so we'll see you later."

Paul and Maria left the dining area and headed up the stairs to their rooms. As they parted on the landing Paul turned to her. "Thanks for your help and your company," he said.

"My pleasure," said Maria. "See you in the morning."

CHAPTER. 5.

The following morning, the whole team gathered again in the trailer and Peter outlined his plan. Since the discovery of the second passage in the previous week, and the fact that it had lead them back to the original area of excavation, they would concentrate their combined efforts on opening up this area. This would allow them all to work in close proximity to one another. He hoped that in this way, after two or three days, at least one or two new leads would be worthy of even greater concentrated effort. This proposal was accepted, and the smaller groups divided up the site.

Maria and Paul were once again separated, he to continue his role as roving translator, and Maria to rejoin the group she had been working with for the previous two weeks. Fortunately, the fellow from Greece had returned to his own home, so she and the others in their group were saved from his sardonic remarks. Peter had replaced this spot on her team with a new member of the group who had arrived on the weekend; a young lady who had come from the University in Kiev. Apart from her own native tongue, she spoke only German. She told Maria that her father, who was German, had been in Kiev during the war. Here, he had met and fallen in love with her mother, who had nursed him when he had been wounded in the fighting around the city. After the war was over, he had gone back to find her and had smuggled her out of Russia into Germany, where they had married, and where she was born. She and Maria became friends right away, and a great deal of conversation could be heard between them as they worked at the site.

For the next two days, large quantities of earth and boulders were removed from the site, using wheelbarrows. Whenever Paul was not busy translating, he took many loads away from the dig in this manner. He told Maria that he regarded this as a healthy exercise and felt pleased to be doing something physical for a change.

On the morning of the third day, there was great excitement as one of the teams had uncovered a set of steps leading down to the second passage that had been found earlier. From this discovery, there had been some new developments. A grave had been uncovered containing a partial skeleton and beyond the grave, some foundation walls had been exposed. This lead to speculation from some of the archeologists that perhaps they had broken through into the crypt of the original building. That evening, after their meal, the teams became thoroughly involved in discussion as to what the latest discoveries could mean.

Paul and Maria knew from experience that this would go on for several hours, so they took the opportunity to slip away from the house and go for a good long walk. For the last two evenings, Maria had been reading the books she had brought with her that provided detailed descriptions of various ancient alphabets, and extinct or obscure languages. She told Paul that she was beginning to think the design in the stonework was a clever compilation of more than one language and alphabet. She assumed that this had been done in an effort to make it almost impossible to translate, unless one was familiar with a wide range of ancient writings. She went on to tell Paul that she thought one of the languages was Cyrillic, as there were a number of places in the design that closely resembled the lettering of this alphabet. However, there were other parts of the design that did not match up with anything Cyrillic. Paul was very excited about Maria's research and asked her to let him take a look at what she had tried to do. Maybe they were going to finally make some progress.

As they were returning to the house, he asked her to keep Thursday night open as he intended to fulfil his promise to take her out for the best dinner he could find in Gaillac. Paul was up very early on Thursday morning in order to take a leisurely bath and have a careful shave; he wanted to look his best for his evening dinner date with Maria. He went down to the dining room and ran into Peter, who was sitting there with a cup of coffee, making up schedules for the various groups. There was no-one else around at this early hour.

"Sit down and tell me what happened in Carcassonne," he said. Paul told him of their finding the building and what they had learned about the background of Father Jacques, along with their brief meeting with him.

"He sounds like quite a character," said Peter. "Doing that kind of resistance work during the war was very dangerous, and not always popular with the residents of this part of France."

"I think he knows a great deal about Captain Dearborn, and the disused church," said Paul. Then he went on to tell Peter of the meeting they planned to have on the weekend. By this time, other members of the group were coming into the dining area for breakfast, so Peter changed the subject and started talking about the work at the dig site. "I think we have discovered a crypt under the site," he said. This would confirm my belief that we are uncovering a very old religious site. I wonder what we will find in the next few days."

That evening Paul and Maria left the house at seven o'clock. They took Paul's car and, as he drove down into the town, he could not stop himself from looking over at Maria, sitting beside him. She was wearing a light green summer dress that was a perfect match for her eyes, and had arranged her hair in a way that revealed her long neck. "She is really very beautiful," he said to himself; "what a lucky fellow I am to have such a companion for dinner."

The restaurant he had chosen was on the other side of the town. It was situated overlooking the river which wound its way through Gaillac. Paul had arranged with the proprietor to reserve a table next to a large bay window. This gave a perfect view of the garden at the rear of the establishment

84

which sloped down to the waters edge. Their dinner included several of the items that they had been discussing while sitting and waiting for Father Jacques in her car, on the previous Sunday. A soup that Maria had suggested; a wine that Paul had insisted she try; and a main course of rack of lamb, which was done to perfection. The dessert was one they had mutually agreed on; crepe suzette. During the meal, they talked about the previous weekend in Carcassonne and the new discoveries at the site in Gaillac. More than once, Paul thought to himself, "this is the best time I have had for a long time. I wish it would just go on forever."

There was still enough daylight left when they had finished their meal, for them to take a walk through the garden and admire the flowers. From the garden, they wandered down to the river bank where the owners of the restaurant had thoughtfully provided a number of patio chairs. Paul and Maria sat together for a while and watched the river flow by. As it passed along the bank, it made a soft swishing sound. Eventually, the daylight started to fade, so they returned to his car, to drive back to the house.

Maria turned to Paul before he started the engine. "That was a truly lovely evening", she said. "I don't know when I have been so content."

"I was thinking the same thing," said Paul. "It seems a lifetime to me since I was in my own home in Canada. The things that have happened since then are quite amazing." They drove back in almost complete silence; Paul savouring the evening and the way he felt. As they pulled into the driveway, Maria said, "I'll bring you what I have done on the puzzle. I'd like to know your reaction and whether or not you think I'm crazy, or if you think I'm on the right track. Give me a few minutes to change and I'll come along to your room."

"Sounds like a terrific idea to me," said Paul.

He sat in his room waiting for Maria. At one point he got up and looked in the mirror. "Where is all this leading?" he said to his reflection. "In some ways I feel invigorated, and in some others I feel afraid. Am I on the road to a completely new way of life? Or just in over my head?" His confused thinking was interrupted by a knock on his door. "Come in," he called. Maria came into the room carrying several books and a file folder. She and Paul sat down at the table where she laid out her own drawings of the frieze work design, and opened one of her books to a page that displayed the Cyrillic alphabet. Pointing to one of the letters, she said: "do you think this one is a match for this part of the design, and that there is a strong resemblance between this other letter and this next part of the design?" Paul examined them both. "Yes," he said, "I agree that both of them look very similar, especially the first one." With that, Maria took out a sheet of graph paper from the file and showed Paul where these letters would be if they were placed appropriately below the design. They appeared at more than one point. Then Maria replaced this paper with another one. On this, she had added the words *Blood* and *Calyx*, and had taken the letter "*L*" and placed it in a position underneath another portion of the design. "I'm not too sure about the letter *L*," she said, "but I think it bears a strong resemblance to the one in the alphabet. At this point, I am stuck. Nothing else in the design looks anything like the rest of the Cyrillic letters."

"Well," said Paul. "I think you've done a great job. I still don't know what we are looking at, but I think the idea that more than one language has been used to create this enigma, is certainly worth pursuing. I also agree that those Cyrillic letters are amazingly similar to the shapes in the design on the stonework. Whoever created such an intricate piece of masonry must have taken great pains."

"I'll leave these drawings with you," said Maria. "I need to step away from them for a while, and think about something else. I'm off to my own room now. See you in the morning, and thank you again for a lovely dinner."

After Maria had gone, Paul sat staring at the letters that she had added to the puzzle. He tried to recall what he knew of the origins of the Cyrillic alphabet. There had been a "St. Cyril" he remembered, but where this Saint belonged in terms of an historic time period, he did not know. Nor did he know where he had lived or his sphere of influence. In the morning, he would ask the other archeologists if any of them knew anything about St Cyril. It seemed likely that there would be at least one or two with some knowledge.

When Paul arrived in the dining area next morning, he saw Maria and her friend from Kiev sitting together, having a very animated discussion. He walked over to their table with his coffee and croissant in hand. Maria looked up. "Sit down," she said, "and listen to this. My friend here, Annaleiza, knows quite a bit about St. Cyril, the creator of the Cyrillic alphabet. Her mother who, as you know came from Kiev, told her about St. Cyril when she was growing up. He spent most of his life in southern Russia preaching Christianity there. She has offered to look at the design, and tell us what she can."

"I thought we might find someone with this kind of knowledge amongst this group!" said Paul. Turning to Annaleiza, he asked if she would join them after dinner that night to look at the photos and papers together. "Of course, I'd be pleased to help if I can," she said. Paul reminded Maria that they were to receive a telephone call that evening from Father Jacques, and that they had better make sure they were back at the house in good time. "You can bet I haven't forgotten," she replied. With that, they set off for the dig.

Throughout that Friday, Paul was unable to concentrate on the work at the dig. He was pre-occupied with thoughts of Father Jacques, and how he would tackle the business of learning more about Miles Dearborn. He tended to agree with Maria that Father Jacques was likely to be very circumspect and perhaps evasive about any information he divulged. It was a real "cat and mouse" game he was going to have to play.

In the latter part of the afternoon, he and Maria returned to the house before the rest of the group, hoping that they had not missed the call from the ex-priest. On enquiry, they found that there had been no telephone calls for Paul.

In fact, the call they had been awaiting occurred in the middle of dinner. Paul went out into the hallway to answer it.

Father Jacques' voice was quite recognisable on the line. "I shall be arriving at one twenty-eight in the afternoon," he said.

He went on to say that in the event that he thought for any reason that he was being followed, he would carry a rucksack in his hand. If he thought he was not being followed, he would have the rucksack on his back. In the event that he was being followed, Paul was not to meet him, but to go to the site of the dig. Father Jacques would try to meet him there once he had eluded any pursuer. Paul was to wait until four o'clock. If he had not arrived by then, Father Jacques would call again later that night.

When the dinner was over and the rest of the group were discussing the days' activities, Paul, Maria, and Annaleiza met in his room so that Annaleisa could examine the design and confirm whether or not the letters from the Cyrillic alphabet did appear to her to be part of this design. It took only a few minutes for her to agree that the resemblance was definitely there. She also thought the letter "*L*" that Maria had added was a very good match to part of the design. Like Maria, she could not see another area where there was any kind of a match. She was naturally very curious about what she had been looking at but Maria explained that it was a private matter, and had nothing to do with the archeological work that they were all involved in. Annaleiza would just have to be happy with this explanation. They both thanked her for her help and indicated that she should now leave them alone so that they could continue to concentrate on the problem themselves.

Once she was gone, Maria was intent on learning the details of the call from Father Jacques. Paul told her what had been said, emphasising the details of the plan to avoid being seen together, if he was being followed. Maria suggested that she meet the train instead of Paul, using her car. She reasoned that if Father Jacques was being followed, the pursuer would probably be looking for Paul. Also, the pursuer would not likely connect Maria with the ex-priest. On the other hand, Father Jacques had seen Maria's car and would probably make the connection. Paul reluctantly agreed that she was right. If she did not pick up the ex-priest, she was to return to the house until just before three o'clock, and then come to the dig site. He took Maria's hands in his own, re-emphasizing his concern for her safety. "Don't do anything that might connect you to Father Jacques unless you're sure it's safe, be patient and watch carefully. If you sense anything wrong at all, just drive away, ok?"

She looked up into his face. "Don't worry," she said with a smile, "I won't take any chances."

On Saturday afternoon, Maria sat in her car outside the station in Gaillac. She had at least ten minutes to spare before the train arrived. She had left Paul at the house, where he had been talking to Peter before he collected the drawings and photos to take up to the site. She knew that Paul had asked Peter for the keys to the trailer so that they could meet in privacy, and avoid any prying eyes or ears.

The train arrived on time and Maria sat intently watching the passengers exit onto the street.   She saw Father Jacques talking with a mother and two small children. He was carrying his rucksack in his hand! When she saw this, she continued to look carefully at the rest of the passengers, and at the same time, keep an eye on where the ex-priest was going. Father Jacques walked across the street and went into a cafe. Maria turned back to look at the station exit. All the other passengers had gone, except one - a middle-aged man carrying a raincoat over his right arm. He stood still for a minute, looking across at the cafe; then turned and walked to the end of the station building and sat down on a convenient bench. Maria started her car and drove slowly past him to try and get a good look at his face; then she continued on over the railway bridge and out of sight. From her brief look at the mans face, she noted he had dark hair, a small moustache and was wearing a brown sports jacket. "At least I can tell Paul what to look out for", she thought to herself.

While this was going on, Paul had driven up to the site. As it was Saturday, there was only one small group of workers on hand.   They had volunteered to continue wheelbarrowing away the accumulated earth and rocks, so that on the following Monday the archeologists could continue their exploration. Paul offered a quick "hello"; then unlocked the trailer and went inside. At one end of the unit, there was a window that looked out onto the road leading to the site. He decided to spend an hour trying to fit either Latin or Greek letters to the design, in the hope that Maria was on the right track about more than one alphabet being used in the puzzle. By this time it was around two o'clock. Then he sat by the window and watched for anyone coming along the road.   It had been spitting with rain for most of the morning and from the dark grey clouds, it looked as though there was more to come. While Paul worked away at the desk, he could hear the rain beginning to bounce off the tin roof of the trailer and he was feeling sympathetic to the group outside. As the weather worsened, he heard one of them call an end to the day. Looking out of the window, he saw them depart in their van and watched it disappear down the road.

"If Father Jacques does get here today," he thought, "he's going to be soaked to the skin. I hope Maria was able to pick him up."

Paul sat at the window watching the rain stream down the hill, causing puddles to start to form in the parking area. "What rotten luck to have this weather today of all days," he thought!

There was a kerosene stove in the trailer, so Paul decided to light it, to take the chill off the room. He also filled a kettle from one of the portable containers of water that were kept in the trailer and placed it on top of the stove. "I could use a hot drink," he thought, "and I may not be the only one." Paul looked at his watch for the umpteenth time; two forty-five it said. He glanced up and saw a figure on a bicycle coming up the road towards the site.   It can only be one person he thought. As the individual drew closer, Paul recognised him. Without a doubt, it was Father Jacques.   As the ex-priest dismounted from the bicycle and walked up to the site, Paul waved at him and beckoned him inside.

The two of them shook hands, Father Jacques took off his raincoat and threw it over a nearby chair.

"Phew!" he said, "it's a long time since I pedalled this far on a bicycle; I'm not as young as I was!"

"Come over and sit by the stove," said Paul. "I've got some water nearly boiling and I can make some good strong tea for you." Father Jacques sat close to the stove and held his hands out to warm himself. "It's a good job you didn't come to the station," he said. "I was followed by someone; I'm sure of it. I managed to give him the slip though. When I got off the train, I went into a cafe across the street and left by a back door. Luckily there were two bicycles just outside the door, so I borrowed one for the afternoon."

"What did the fellow look like who was following you?" asked Paul.

"Middle-aged I would say," said Father Jacques, "small moustache and a light brown jacket. I don't know who he is," he added.

"Why would anyone be following you?" asked Paul.

"I can't say for sure," Father Jacques replied; "unless somebody knows that you were enquiring about me and that you came to see me. It's odd to me that I had the same feelings that I used to get during the war; a sort of sixth sense that I was being followed. That sort of premonition saved my skin more than once in those days."

"Well," said Paul: "why don't we start this talk by going back to the time of the war. I've got some questions, and I know you've got some too. It makes sense to try and do this in some chronological order. But first of all, let me pour you a cup of tea; then you tell me how you came to know Captain Dearborn."

Father Jacques agreed to this as a basis for discussion, but insisted that each of them be able to ask a question in turn. "I'll start the ball rolling," he added.

Father Jacques explained that during the last war, there were a lot of men parachuted into France to aid the resistance and help them make life unpleasant for the occupation forces. In 1941 Miles Dearborn was parachuted into France with two other men. They were supposed to act as an independent team and were to carry out sabotage work on the railway system. One of the reasons why Dearborn had been chosen for this job was that he had been brought up in Montreal and was fluent in the French language. They worked successfully for six weeks; then one of them broke a leg falling from a railway bridge. They got the wounded man to a doctor with the help of a member of the resistance and at this point they were separated. Dearborn was placed in a farmhouse a couple of miles from the others. After only a few days, the third member of the group had gone to visit the wounded comrade and the two of them were picked up by the French police.

It turned out that the doctor was a sympathiser with the German occupation forces. At that point, Dearborn started to try and make his way south to the Spanish border on his own. He was given some help at different times by the French underground and had been handed over to Father Jacques for safety when he reached Carcassonne.

"At that time, I had no experience at hiding allied personnel," continued Father Jacques, "and did not know what to do with the Captain. I couldn't keep him in my small apartment for very long; too many visitors coming and going, so the day following Dearborn's arrival, I went out to look for a suitable place. I had gone to check out an empty house I knew of, and discovered that it had been taken over by a group of nuns who were using it as an orphanage. While I was in that area of the town, I found myself in the square where the old abandoned church is located. That would make an ideal hiding place, I said to myself. So, that night I took Dearborn there and we broke in through one of the boarded up windows at the rear. I was curious to see what was inside the building, so the Captain and I had made a cursory inspection. Of course it was almost pitch dark, so we had to move around very carefully trying not to make any noise. The main church seemed to be completely empty, but there were several doors leading off, which we could not open. I left the Captain there with the few candles we had brought, promising to return the next night with some food and water."

The following night when Father Jacques arrived, he brought a supply of food and some containers of water. Dearborn told him he had managed to open two of the doors which were simply stiff from having been closed for so long. When he had opened the first, he had nearly killed himself as there was a large hole in the floor, which he had just missed falling into. He had been unable to see the bottom of the hole, but had decided to use it for a toilet. Inside the other door he had found himself in a small room, in which there were some planks and two very old wooden benches.

During the day, he had discovered that there was a bit of light coming in through two small slits in the masonry in this room, about twenty feet up from the floor. There were several of these slits at regular intervals in the walls of the main building, so Dearborn had been able to move about in a sort of gloomy half-light. Father Jacques had told the Captain that there was a concerted effort by the police to round up any people known to be assisting the resistance. Because of this, he would have to stay put for a while, but he would come with supplies as often as he could. Then he told Dearborn that he would try to contact London by radio to let them know that he was safe.

At this point in his story, Father Jacques stopped to drain his cup of tea. Paul refilled it without asking, and Father Jacques continued.

Over the next ten days Father Jacques was only able to visit Captain Dearborn intermittently. However, one night he arrived with some news. He had managed to contact London and had been told that the Captain was to stay where he was and become part of the underground. He was to assist in providing a safe stopping place for any allied personnel on the run. Dearborn was disappointed at this instruction, as he had been hoping to get back into the war but he recognised that he had to obey orders, so accepted his lot.

"That's enough from me for the moment," said Father Jacques. "Now you tell me in detail, the background of why you are here."

Paul described what had occurred when he had found the hat and his attempt to return it. He explained how he redeemed the pawn ticket, found a hidden note and what this had lead to. He also described his visit to Dearborn's room, the material he had taken from there, and the surprising fact that he had been mistaken for Dearborn more than once. He went on to explain his interest in archeology and his invitation to the dig here in Gaillac and his curiosity that the Captain had also had an interest in archeology.

At this point, Paul decided he had said enough so he asked Father Jacques if he was one of the contributors to the book that he had found in Dearborn's room.

"Yes," said Father Jacques; "that was me. One of my passions has always been religious history. When I left the priesthood I studied in Paris for several years and obtained a degree. I taught history at a college in Toulouse and while I was there I pursued my interest in medieval studies. I wrote several papers on the subject and was lucky enough to have some of my work included in various publications. I sent a copy of one of the books to Miles Dearborn some years ago and I assume that is the same one that you now have." Here the ex-priest stopped talking; "your turn, I believe".

Paul then told him that he had been to Carcassonne some years before, and that the invitation to assist in the dig in Gaillac had prompted him to try and discover what Dearborn had been looking for while he was so close to the town. He told Father Jacques about his trip from Canada, and the visit to the hatmaker in London, plus the ransacking of his hotel room. He had to go back a couple of times to explain the two incidences regarding the rings with the red cross on a white background. The ex-priest wanted Paul to go over these events in as much detail as possible, so Paul obliged. While he was repeating his description of the hatmakers' assistant, they heard a vehicle approaching.

Paul got up to look out of the window. He recognised Maria's car and went to the trailer door to open it. She came running in, as the rain was continuing to fall in torrents.

While she took off her wet coat, Paul re-introduced her to Father Jacques and told her what the ex-priest had been telling him about Captain Dearborn.

When he had at last brought her up to date, she said: "now, I've got some information for you! I went back to the house after the trip to the train station to wait until the time you had said to come up here. About an hour after I got back, there was a visitor to the house. I was on my way to the bathroom and overheard the conversation down in the hallway. I recognised Peter's voice, and heard the other man asking about the broken sword, the one with the red cross in the handle, that we found at this site. The man said he was a colleague of our German weapons expert and had come to Gaillac in the hope of being allowed to see it."

"At that point," Maria continued, "I leaned over the banister railing to get a good look at him. He is the same man who got off the train earlier; he had a moustache and was wearing a brown jacket! Even more than this," she said; "he was carrying a raincoat over one arm and I could see his hand. He had a ring on his little finger. I'm sure it was the same ring with a red cross on a white background! Peter invited the man into his office, so I finished what I was doing and then got in my car and waited for him to come out. He was there for about half an hour; then when he came out, he stood for a few minutes and seemed to be hesitating."

"By this time, it was really raining hard. He turned toward the centre of town and I followed him in my car, staying well back. He eventually got to the railway station and went inside. I parked the car and walked over the road to look down onto the platform. I could see him there, so I waited a few minutes, standing in this awful rain. When I looked down again and he was still there, I got back in the car and came straight up here."

"From the description you've just given us," said Father Jacques, "I'm sure that's the same person I thought was following me. There can be no doubt about that now."

"Well at least he is out of here for the time being," said Paul. "Let's get back to the unravelling of this whole business. Tell me what you know about the disused church that Dearborn was hiding in."

"That is a very strange story," said Father Jacques. "I'll tell you what I know. Some is fact; some is legend and it is difficult to know which is which. We do know that it was built during the first crusades, around 1120. We know that the builders were the Knights Templar. We also know that it was used as a place of worship in the late 1100's, and that it was an important stop for crusaders on their way to the Holy Lands.

As you may know, there was a hiatus of around seventy to eighty years between the first and the second series of crusades. The second ones were at the instigation of a new Pope. These new crusaders were from all over Europe and included a large contingent from England. It was impossible in those days to co-ordinate the movement of all these groups from different countries. They were all leaving at different times, and there was a great deal of confusion as to who would lead these Knights and the troops that accompanied them. The Knights Templar came into prominence when they attempted to achieve some order among this polyglot of religious zealots. This church was an important place at that time, and some meetings were held here to determine who should play a leadership role. Legend has it that there was murder committed in the church by factions trying to hold sway over other contenders. Near the end of the second crusade, a group of English Knights were returning home after sacking the city of Jerusalem. They came to this church as a temporary resting place. Several of them were wounded and they were not able to continue the journey. No-one can say exactly how long they stayed, but we can assume it was as long as several years.

When they left, the building was unused for a time, however, at some point it was taken over again by the Knights Templar somewhere in the fourteenth century, and was occupied by them. They were no longer involved in any crusades of course, but they had great influence in the economic affairs of Europe at that time, particularly with the various guilds that controlled the trade regulations in existence."

"Over the years, The Catholic Church has had many quarrels with the Knights Templar and its various branches. These have been basically power struggles over influence and wealth, some of it going back to the crusades when the loot that was plundered from the holy sites in and around Jerusalem, was taken by the crusaders and never given to the Pope of the day. Anyway, that is some of the background of the building where Dearborn was hiding out."

"Now," said Father Jacques; "I believe that you may have learned something from the books and file you took from Captain Dearborn's room; would you show me what you have of his?" Paul took the file and handed over some of the original pieces. He did not pass over the hidden note or the work that he had done with the enlargements, nor the translation efforts of Maria.

Father Jacques looked again at the two photos. "I had forgotten all about these," he said. "One of the nuns who were operating the orphanage I told you about, took these just before the end of the war. I remember that Captain Dearborn wanted a photo of the frieze-work around the entry, to study it after the war was over. He had gone back to London by the time the film was developed, but I had the address of his mother in Montreal and sent them on to him there."

"How long was Dearborn hiding in the church?" asked Maria.

"More than two years, I think," said Father Jacques. "He wanted to leave many times, but the intelligence people in London kept refusing him because of the success he was having getting downed airmen back to continue the fight. He was leading a very hair-raising existence and had some close calls, but he was never caught."

"Do you know why he wanted to study the stone frieze-work?" asked Paul.

"Well, that requires a bit of background," said Father Jacques. "As you know, he was a keen student of archeology, like yourself. We spent a lot of time together when he was holed up in the church, and much of that time was spent talking about the people who built it and the place it had in history. He didn't know a great deal about the crusades or the Knights Templar, so I brought him some reading material which he found very interesting. You can imagine that being shut up inside for many days at a time, he had made a thorough examination of the whole structure. He certainly knows more than anyone else what is in there. For instance, he discovered an entry to a crypt under the main floor from tapping on the stones and listening for an echo. He also discovered that the hole he was using for a toilet, had at one time been a well."

"He became convinced that some of the loot stolen from the religious sites in the middle east was hidden in the building somewhere. He spent hours searching for a hiding place, but never found anything. Now, on the subject of finding things, please tell me, what is this broken sword that Maria talked about? Did you find it at this site?"

Paul gave him the details of the discovery of the sword, plus a description of the red cross built into the handle. Maria had brought one of her sketches with her and handed it to Father Jacques.

He looked at it carefully. "It's amazing that you found it in such a recognisable condition," he said. "My guess is it was made in France during the time of the crusades."

"That's pretty well what our weapons expert here at the dig told us," said Paul. "But I want to return to the question of Captain Dearborn. Did he ever leave the building during the day time?"

"Yes," said Father Jacques. "In the early part of 1944 it was becoming obvious that the Germans were going to lose the war. Dearborn had less and less work to do moving allied troops back along the underground to Spain. He was anxious to get out of the hiding place so I arranged with the nuns who were still operating the orphanage, for him to go there occasionally and do some repairs to the building, which was in a very sorry state. He turned out to be pretty good at masonry work, and rebuilt some walls and repaired a chimney which was collapsing."

"The nuns were told not to ask any questions about him, and they did as they were asked. One evening when I came to visit him, he was quite excited. He had been looking at the exterior of the church and told me that he thought the front entry way had been added on some time after the church had originally been built. He also believed that the decorated stone frieze-work around the entry was added later. I didn't argue with him, as I wasn't as interested as he was. However, I know that whenever he could get out during the day, he would spend time staring at that part of the entrance. A few weeks later, he got orders to leave and return to England, which he successfully accomplished, using the same escape route that he had helped to create.

I lost contact with him entirely, until one day in the spring of 1945 he showed up at my apartment! We had quite a party I can tell you, it lasted well into the wee small hours. It was on the following day that those two pictures were taken, just before he took off to rejoin his unit. The envelope you see me handing to him in one of the photos, had some drawings in it that he had done of the stonework around the entry to the church. He had given them to me for safekeeping until the war was over, and that seemed a good time to return them. The drawings here are the ones that he did when he was in Carcassonne during the latter part of the war."

"Do you have any idea why he was so interested in that stonework?" asked Paul. Father Jacques picked up the photo of the front of the building again.

"Well," he said, "the Captain thought that the additions were made when that group of English crusaders were living there; the ones I told you about earlier. Dearborn seemed to think that the intricate frieze-work in the stones might hold the clues to the hidden religious artifacts that he thought were somewhere in the building. Personally, I think he was just having a flight of fancy after being bottled up in that place for so long. He was living on the edge for those two years; sometimes seeing no-one for days on end. It would be enough to drive anyone slightly crazy, don't you think?"

"Now, let's talk about this business of the men who wear the same ring with a red cross on a white background!"

"Your friend Peter was probably right when he told you of the society who go by the name of the Order of St. George," said the ex-priest. "These people claim direct descendancy from the English crusaders of that same medieval period. One of their main objectives is to protect the secrecy of the hiding place of some of the most sought after religious artifacts - those that were taken from temples and churches when they were destroyed or taken over by the crusaders. It's also possible that they no longer know where some of these items are hidden and are trying to locate these objects themselves. Whatever the case, they are not to be taken lightly. The fact that I was followed today leads me to think that somehow they know of your visit to me at the shelter, and that they hoped that I would lead them to you. Unfortunately, I think they have achieved that goal. Now, my guess is that they will watch you closely and follow you until they are ready to move in. I also think, from what you've told me, that Captain Dearborn knew that they were closing in on him and got away just in time. Though how they found him in Canada after all these years, is something I can't begin to explain! Only one person knows the answer to that conundrum."

At this point, Paul was on the brink of showing the work that Maria had done; then he changed his mind and said nothing.

"What will you both do now?" Father Jacques asked.

"My hunch tells me that I should vanish into thin air," said Paul, "and that's what I'm going to do. Maria and I will make a plan that only we will know; but first I want to thank you for coming to see us today and for telling us all that you have. I hope you feel that you learned something from what we have told you. In the very beginning, all I was trying to do was a good turn, returning a hat to somebody. Now, I'm going to do some serious thinking about my future."

With that said, Paul put the photos and papers back in the file.

"We'll get you back to the station by car, and drop off the bicycle outside the cafe. I hope the owner isn't there to greet us!" he added. The rain was continuing to fall as they put on their coats and prepared to leave.

To see if it made any impression on Father Jacques, Paul took out the Captain's hat from his bag and placed it on his head. "Just the thing for a miserable evening like this," he said as he adjusted it.

"Yes," said Father Jacques, looking up. "I wish I'd brought one with me."

Paul decided that the ex-priest had never seen the hat before, and also that it did not make any impression on him. "Well, so much for that," he thought.

Paul and Maria traded vehicles after putting the bicycle in the trunk. It didn't fit, but was jammed in tightly enough not to fall out. Paul then drove Maria's car to the station and dropped off Father Jacques. "I'll be in touch with you sometime in the next week," he said as they shook hands.

"Be very careful from here on," said Father Jacques. "I'll look forward to hearing from you at anytime, and thanks for returning the bicycle for me."

Paul drove around to the back of the cafe and propped the bike up against the wall; luckily there was no-one about. He got back into the car and drove away quickly.

Returning to the house, Paul asked Peter if they could have a private meeting, so the two of them went to his office. "I believe you had a visitor today," said Paul, "someone who was interested in the broken sword that I found."

"Yes," said Peter, "a strange sort of chap really - he claimed he was an associate of our German archeologist, the one who is our weapons expert. I am sure he knew something about medieval swords from our discussion, but I don't think he was a close friend of our expert, as he kept getting the name wrong. He seemed much more interested in the people we have here at the dig; where they had come from, and how long they had been here. I told him that I thought his questions were rather inquisitive, and a bit out of line. I actually wondered if he was checking out the house, with a view to trying to steal the sword - it wouldn't be the first time that something like that was tried! Anyway I eventually showed him the door, and sent him out into the rain. Why are you asking me about him?"

"Did you notice if he was wearing a ring similar to the one I told you about, the red cross on a white background?"

"No, I can't say that I did," Peter replied.

"Well," said Paul, "let me tell you about what transpired this afternoon". So he filled Peter in on the events.

"What are you going to do now?" asked Peter.

Paul hesitated for a moment. "I'm leaving tonight. I won't tell you where I'm going, so please don't ask. It's my intention to disappear for a while and see if I can shake off these troublemakers. I hope that you'll understand, and I'm sorry about not being able to help with the dig right now."

"Have you told Maria that you're leaving?" asked Peter.

"No not yet," Paul replied, "that's where I'm going now."

The two friends stood facing one another for a moment. Peter held out his hand. "Take great care," he said, "please call on me if you need help." With that Paul went to his room and started to pack his things.

A few minutes later there was a knock on his door.

"Paul, it's me, Maria, Can I come in? "

"Yes, the door's open," he replied.

"You're leaving," said Maria, seeing the suitcase partially packed on the bed.

"Yes. I'm going to vanish into thin air. I'm leaving in an hour."

"Can I come with you?" asked Maria.

"No," said Paul firmly, "it's too dangerous. I don't want anything bad to happen to you. I'm going to lay low and see if I can complete the puzzle on my own. I've been thinking about all the things that Father Jacques talked about today. Maybe there is something hidden in that abandoned church in Carcassonne. Somehow I feel an obligation to Captain Dearborn to complete the task he started. I'll call you on Wednesday night from wherever I am and let you know what's happening."

"It seems to me that you've made up your mind." said Maria, with a look of resignation. "Though I hate being left out, I do want to see you again and help if I can. I'll loan you my two books on ancient languages - you may find them helpful in continuing to unravel the meaning of the design."

"Thanks very much," said Paul. "I'm sure they will be a great help." With that, Maria left the room and returned in a few minutes with the books.

"I was going to try using the Greek alphabet next," she said. Paul took the books and put them in his shoulder bag, along with all the papers the two of them had worked on. He turned to face Maria.

"You have been a fantastic help, and a great companion," he said. "I promise to keep in touch." Then he kissed her on both cheeks. "I promise," he repeated.

CHAPTER .6.

Paul loaded his car, checking that he had taken everything with him. He noticed that he would have to fill up the car with gasoline before he went too far, as the gauge was hovering around empty. He backed out into the driveway and turned towards the road. Looking back, he saw Maria standing in the doorway waving to him. He waved back and tooted his horn. For a moment he regretted not having her with him, then set his mind on driving carefully as the rain, which was continuing to fall, was making the roads slippery.

As he drove along, he decided to stay at the same small hotel that he had stopped at on the way to Gaillac a few short weeks ago. He felt sure that no one would find him there. He was feeling good about his decision to get away and vanish, though he was worried about Maria. If he could, he wanted to stay at the hotel for a couple of days and plan his next move. He knew he was going to go back to Carcassonne at some point, but did not want to do so until he had figured out the puzzle of the letters. He intended to concentrate all his language skills on solving this problem first.

Paul arrived at the village where he had previously spent a couple of nights, and pulled up in front of the hotel. Luckily, he had left the rain behind on the journey, so was able to gather his luggage from the trunk without getting wet. There was only one light on in the front of the building and no sign of life in the restaurant window. He found the door bell and heard it ringing inside the house. At last a light came on in the hall and the door opened slightly. Paul asked if there was a room available, mentioning that he had stayed at the hotel recently and that he had been very happy there. Just then, the woman he had met the last time, arrived at the door. Fortunately, she recognised Paul and invited him to come in.

"Yes," she said there was a room available, the same room he had enjoyed earlier, if he wanted.

"That would be fine," said Paul. He was ushered up the stairs and into the accomodation he had known before. The woman told him that he could come down for breakfast any time after eight o'clock and then wished him goodnight. Before she left, Paul asked if he could move his car around to the back of the building, and was told that he could. Having done this, Paul turned in for the night. He was feeling elated on the one hand and rather lonely on the other.

He did not sleep well, there were too many things flying around in his head. At around two o'clock in the morning, he heard the wind pick up and start to blow really hard. "I wonder if that is going to bring more rain, or a clearing away of the bad weather", he said to himself.

He eventually got up at six-thirty. Looking out of his bedroom window, he could see the sun just coming up over the distant hills.

"Well, that looks a lot more pleasant," he said, "perhaps I will be able to get some walking done while I'm here."

After finishing his toilet, Paul sat down at the table with his shoulder bag and emptied out the contents. He picked up one of Maria's books and started to leaf through the pages. Throughout this book, there were a number of illustrations of various alphabets and examples of the writings of some ancient languages. He took Maria's latest translation effort and started to try and match up any letters he could from the chapter on ancient Greek lettering. Only two or three looked anything like a match to the design but he made a mental note of them and continued to look at others.

He moved further along in the book and came to a chapter on the Aramaic alphabet. This was described as the language that Jesus Christ would have spoken when he was alive. Because of this religious connection, Paul thought that there may be some resemblance to the design lying in front of him;

so, he turned to a page which outlined this alphabet very clearly, with good illustrations. Right away, he could see a very good likeness between two of the letters in the book and the design on the paper in front of him. Translated into English equivalents, they gave the letters "*N*" and "*I*".

He placed these letters in the appropriate positions on the paper. He now had, if the transcriptions were correct and in the right place, more than half of the missing letters. Even though he had spent less than half an hour on this particular part of the puzzle, he had a feeling that he was on to something, and that his placement of the letters was correct. He immediately thought of Maria and wondered if she would be supportive of his thoughts. Not likely, he decided. She was too much of an academic to place so much faith in such a serendipitous outcome. Nevertheless, he felt really good about what he saw on the paper in front of him, and very buoyed by his efforts.

Paul left his room in great good humour and went down to the dining room to have his breakfast. He asked his hostess what the weather forecast was for the day, and received the good news that the bad weather from the north was going to bypass them, leaving some warm and sunny days.

"In that case," said Paul, "could you please give me a similar lunch to the one I had the last time I was here, as I want to go for a good walk." The owners wife said that that would be no problem, and suggested that he take a different route from the one he had gone on before. She told him of an abandoned chateau roughly five miles away that she thought he might like to visit, and pointed out the route he should take from one of the tourist maps she had in the hallway.

"That's perfect," said Paul. It was his intention to walk at a brisk pace on this day, and to go over in his mind his additional words from the mornings studying, to see if he could come up with a phrase, or saying, that made any sense to him. He would try to add different letters from time to time, using a process of elimination of the alphabet from A to Z.

After his meal, he dressed in sensible walking clothes, including wearing his boots. These were the ones that he had been wearing at the dig in Gaillac, and they were now thoroughly worn in and extremely comfortable. With his lunch packed in his shoulder bag, he set off to enjoy himself. At first, he walked along, neither looking to the left or right, so engrossed in his efforts to work his way through the letters of the alphabet, hoping for another brainwave, but nothing he tried made any sense whatsoever. By the time he reached the letter "P", he was totally fed up with this idea of his and abandoned himself to the pleasure of the countryside and the lovely scenery.

When he reached the abandoned Chateau, there were several other visitors wandering around the outside walls. He walked down past a garden area, which was also abandoned, and through a small orchard, until he came to the bank of a stream. Here he sat down to enjoy the lunch that the hotel had provided. Looking at the water running slowly by, he was reminded of the dinner he had enjoyed with Maria when they had strolled together at the rear of the restaurant in Gaillac. The memories of that evening brought a smile of pleasure to his face and he sat contentedly, re-visiting the whole event, right from the moment they had set out in his car when he had noticed her beautiful neck for the first time.

The sound of children's voices brought him out of his reverie, as two youngsters came along the bank of the stream playing with a small raft that they had built out of some pieces of wood tied together with string. He watched them until they disappeared around a bend in the footpath which ran alongside the water.

Paul now put his mind to work on what he was going to do to avoid being found by these people who were pursuing him, and how he would return to Carcassonne without their knowledge. He felt that he would have a better chance of losing his pursuers if he returned the rental car to the airport at Toulouse. Once he had done that, they would not be able to trace his whereabouts so easily. Thinking about the airport reminded him of his arrival a few weeks ago, when he had met the son of Yves Carbonne, Jean, the father of his travelling companion from Paris.

"I think I'll give Yves a call tonight from the hotel", he decided, "perhaps he can suggest somewhere to lie low for a few days." Cheered by this thought, Paul gathered up the remains of his picnic and walked back through the orchard to the grounds of the Chateau. It had certainly been a grand house in its time, with large windows and several turrets on the roof. The view from the south side was a beautiful vista out over the rolling hills. Paul examined the stonework on the exterior and decided that it was not as well built as the abandoned church in Carcassonne. In a few places, there were stones missing, having fallen out over the passage of time.

Around the area of the grand entryway to the house, there was a porte-cochere. At the front of this, there was a coat of arms carved in the stonework, with a motto below. It had been damaged and Paul was unable to make out much of the detail. Some of the stones were also missing underneath this decoration, so, the motto of the family who had at one time owned the chateau was obscured.

While he was examining this part of the house, a couple came walking by. "Hello," said Paul, and was greeted with a smile from the woman.

"Do you happen to know the name of the family who owned this Chateau?" he asked.

"Yes, I do," she replied, "the name was Brisebois. I know this because that family was at one time related to mine, a cousin of some sort."

"How interesting, said Paul, "do you know why the place is abandoned?"

"Well, it's a long story," she said. "But in a nutshell, the family were nobles at court in the late seventeenth century, which is when the house was built. They fell out of favour with the government some time in the latter part of the eighteen hundreds, and the property was seized for unpaid taxes. Since then, the family and the authorities have had many legal battles as to its ownership. In the meantime, it has been left to the elements. These things move very slowly in this country," she added.

"What a terrible waste," said Paul. "Thank you for the history lesson anyway." The couple moved on leaving Paul to wonder at the ways of the world.

On the way back to his hotel, he was considering what he might say to Yves Carbonne about what he was doing in France. Yves would certainly ask him! He decided he would simply explain that he was here doing some amateur archeological work, and then let the conversation go where it may.

That evening he put a call through to the telephone operator in Toulouse and was lucky enough to get Yves' number. When he made the call, the phone was quickly answered. Paul identified himself to Yves.

"Yes, yes," said Yves. "I knew you were in France, my son Jean mentioned that he had met you at the airport. I'm so glad you called. Where are you calling from?"

Paul explained that he was on his way to Toulouse airport to return his rental car, but that he intended to stay in Toulouse for a few days. "I wonder if you could suggest a good place to stay?" he asked Yves.

"Why don't you stay here at my home?" Yves suggested. "There's lots of room, and I would enjoy the company, I don't get around much these days as one of my legs doesn't work as well as it used to."

"That would be great," said Paul, "I really appreciate the offer."

The two of them arranged to meet at the airport the following day at one o'clock, in the main entrance.

"I hope we will be able to recognise each other," said Yves, "it's been a few years. Look for a white haired man with a walking cane, that will be me."

After dinner that same evening, Paul put a call through to the house in Gaillac, hoping that he would be able to talk to

Maria. Peter answered the telephone and after their brief conversation, went to get Maria from the dining room.

"Hello Paul," he heard Maria's voice. "Where are you now?"

Paul told her where he was and what his plans were.

"Oh, I'm so relieved to know that you are alright," she said. "I was worried about you." Then she went on to say that she had received a call from the dean at her University in Florence. He had requested that she return there as quickly as possible, so she was driving back to her home in the morning. "Please give me the telephone number of your friend in Toulouse," she asked. So Paul gave her the number. "How long are you going to stay with him?"

"Two or three days," he replied. "Then I am going back to Carcassonne. I should tell you what I have added to the puzzle," he went on. "I was looking through one of the books that you loaned me, and found some lettering in the Aramaic alphabet that is a very good match for another part of the missing words. I know you won't think it was very scientifically done, but I have a feeling that I am right."

Maria asked him which letters he had now added, and where he had placed them so that she could include them in her own copy. He could hear her making notes on the other end of the line.

"I can't wait to see what they look like," she said.

She then went on to give Paul her home number in Florence. "Please call me before you go back to Carcassonne," she asked, "and if I am able to get away from work for a week, please let me join you there."

Paul agreed to call her before he left Toulouse. He asked her if there had been any more strangers at the house, or at the site.

"No," she told him. "No one". They had only been able to go to the site once since he had left, as the weather had continued very wet, leaving the site unworkable.

They then said goodbye to each other, with Paul telling her to drive very carefully, back to her home.

110

He spent the balance of the evening trying his best to add more letters to the word puzzle, in the hope of completing at least one or two words which might give some overall sense of it. He found himself going round in circles and eventually gave up. "It will have to wait until my brain is unscrambled," he said to himself, " maybe tomorrow will be better."

The morning dawned bright and warm, Paul was up early. He ventured down to the dining room. Finding nobody about, he picked up the previous days newspaper and caught up on the rest of the world news - all the while waiting for the familiar smell of fresh coffee brewing. At last, he heard someone stirring in the kitchen area and finally the voice of his hostess wishing him "good morning", and bringing with her a steaming cup of strong coffee. She asked if he was leaving today, and he told her he would be on his way after his breakfast. Once again, he thanked her for taking such good care of him and for providing the delicious lunch he had enjoyed the previous day.

After he had eaten his meal, he went to his room and gathered his luggage. In the foyer of the hotel he paid his bill, once again thanking his hostess for her kindness. Then he packed his luggage in the car and set off toward Toulouse.

He started to think about Yves Carbonne as he drove along. It was certainly very decent of him to offer a place to stay. He realized that he hadn't asked after Mrs Carbonne, and felt badly that he had completely forgotten her name.

Paul had lots of time to make the journey so he drove slowly, pulling over whenever he saw that he was holding up the traffic. In this way, he arrived at the airport around noon.

Parking his car in the same lot where he had picked it up, he made a note of the mileage on the back of his road map. He wanted to make sure that his bill for the rental had the correct mileage cost. Picking up his luggage, he checked the car for any mislaid items, then entered the main terminal building and proceeded to the booth of the rental agency. He quickly completed the return of the vehicle, paying his bill with cash, thinking that it would make it more difficult for anyone to trace him than if he used a credit card.

Paul took his bags to a nearby locker rental and deposited them inside, then he walked over to a cafe and sat down with a drink to wait for the arrival of Yves. From where he sat, he could keep an eye on the main entrance and felt sure he would be able to recognise him when he appeared.

At a few minutes before one o'clock, he saw Yves coming through the automatic doors. There was no doubt that it was him. Though he was several years older and now had white hair, his height gave him away. Yves was one of the tallest men that he had ever met. As Paul approached, Yves recognised him and smiled. "You look just about the same as the last time we were together," he said.

"Well, thank you," said Paul, "a bit thicker around the middle I'm afraid. Please wait a minute while I get my bags from the locker, and then we can be on our way." Paul retrieved his luggage and the two of them walked out to the parking lot. As they walked to the car, Paul could see that Yves was moving very slowly and relying heavily on his cane.

"I need a new hip," said Yves, "and I hope to get one next month. I've been on the waiting list for ages. Perhaps you would do the driving as it is a bit painful for me to operate the pedals."

"Certainly," said Paul.

Yves' car was an old black Citroen. "It's getting on a bit, like me," he said, "but it's still the most comfortable car I've ever had."

They left the airport, and with Yves giving directions, they were soon on their way.

"I'm sorry to have to ask this," said Paul, "but are you still married?"

"I was," said Yves, "but my wife died three years ago, she had a massive stroke and never recovered. How about you?" he asked.

Paul told Yves of Carlas' death and something of the effect it had had on his life. After a few moments of reflection, Yves

112

enquired as to what Paul was doing in the south of France. So, during the drive to Yves' home, Paul filled him in on the archeological site at Gaillac and how he happened to be there. By this time, they had arrived at Yves' home. "Just leave the car in the driveway." said Yves. "Let's get your things into the house and then we can sit out on the patio and have a glass of wine. I'm so glad that you decided to give me a call, it will be a real treat for me to have some companionship for a change. I have a housekeeper who comes every other day to keep things tidy and to make me some meals. She is a great cook, but a bit boring when it comes to good conversation."

"Take your things upstairs to the second door on the right, on the landing. I had the housekeeper make up the bed in that room this morning, when I knew you would be coming. I'd show you myself, but I try to avoid going up and down stairs as much as possible with this bad leg. You'll find the bathroom next door to your room. I'll be out at the back of the house with a bottle of chilled wine, come down when your ready."

Later, when they were both sitting outside enjoying the warm afternoon sun, Yves asked what Paul's plans were, and why he was staying in Toulouse. Paul explained that he was trying to avoid being found for a few days while he worked on a piece of archeological puzzle. Despite his best efforts, it was impossible not to keep explaining to Yves why certain things had occurred. Over the course of the next couple of hours, he had told enough of his tale that Yves had a broad understanding of the way Paul's life had been, since finding the hat and the pawn ticket.

"My God!" he exclaimed, "what an amazing story. It's no wonder you want to disappear for a while. I should think that you will be safe in this house though, no-one knows of our friendship, and in any case, it was a long time ago."

Paul agreed that it was unlikely any connection could be made between them, and that for the moment, he was as safe as he could be.

Yves mentioned to Paul that it was his habit to take a nap in the afternoon, and that he hoped he would be forgiven for not being the best of hosts if he slept for a while. For Paul, this presented no problem as he wanted to spend as much time as possible working away at completing the frustrating word puzzle. He thanked Yves again for his hospitality and left to go back to his room. He took out of his shoulder bag all the material again and laid it out on the bed. He also pulled out the hat, as it was getting rather bent out of shape and put it on again in front of the mirrored dressing table.

As he stared at his reflected image, his mind went back to the hatmakers' establishment in London, he certainly regretted having gone there, as he felt sure that it was there that his problems had really started.

This Order of St George was probably headquartered in London, and his unexpected arrival had stirred up a hornets nest. Looking at the hat on his head, he said. "Well, you might look good on me, but you've surely caused me a few grey hairs!"

Sitting down on the side of the bed, Paul picked up one of the books which Maria had loaned him and turned again to the section on the Greek alphabet. Once more, he studied the two letters that he had considered using before, back at the hotel. There was a pretty good match alright but not exact. He leafed through the next few pages and found another set of illustrations of the same alphabet that predated the first examples. There were a number of letters that had not changed, but there were some that had been modified slightly. There he saw the exact reproduction of several parts of the design in the stonework!

"Eureka," he yelled, "now we will see something!"

Placing these new letters on the most recent piece of paper that he had worked on, he finally had a phrase which made some sense;

"*BEHIND THE MIND LIES THE CALYX OF BLOOD*".

"What the heck does that mean?" he thought. "Calyxes are flowers or petals or something. What bloody flowers?" he said to himself frustratedly.

Paul tried moving the words around but nothing made any better sense than the way he had first written them. "In any case," he said to himself, "that's the way I first found them, so, Captain Dearborn must have placed them in that order for a reason. I wish I could talk to him," he thought. "I wish I could tell Maria too, but she'll be on the road somewhere, and won't be in Florence until tomorrow night at the earliest. Well, I can still tell Yves about my discovery, as soon as he wakes up. What a relief to finally have something to go on. What a stroke of luck that Maria let me have that book. What a stroke of luck that he had met Maria at all," he said smiling to himself. It was a touch of genius that she had considered the answer to the puzzle would be found in a number of different ancient languages. If she had been there with him, he would have given her a great big hug and a kiss!

"Now," he said, "back to those bloody flowers, where do they fit in?" He cast his mind back to the abandoned church in Carcassonne, he could not recall any floral decoration in the stonework, anywhere on the exterior. Maybe there is something on the inside he thought, but how to get inside without raising any suspicion. The only people who had been inside the building that he knew of, were Captain Dearborn and Father Jacques. As he didn't know where Dearborn was, or even if he was alive, that left Father Jacques.

However, before he made contact with the ex-priest, he wanted very much to talk to Maria. First, to tell her of his discovery, and then to listen to any ideas she might have about floral decorations. Maybe she had seen something when she was making the drawings outside the church.

It was at this moment that he realized he had been pacing up and down the room for the last five minutes, busily talking to himself.

"I'd better just calm down", he said, "go for a walk, get some fresh air."

He put on his jacket and left his room. In the hall downstairs, he heard Yves call his name. Paul opened the door to the living room and poked his head around the corner. Yves was sitting up on the sofa.

"Nice hat," he said. "Are you going out?" It was only then, that Paul realized he was still wearing the Captain's hat. He took it off immediately.

"Yes," said Paul. "I need a bit of a walk to clear my head. I've made some excellent discoveries about the puzzle in the last two hours, and I need to think them through."

"Well, why don't you go for your walk," said Yves. "When the housekeeper was here this morning, I asked her to make us a casserole for our dinner this evening, so, I'll put it in the oven for us and we can eat it whenever you get back. When we have finished our meal, you can tell me what you've discovered, if you like."

With that said, Paul put the hat on a table in the front hall and left the house.

He didn't know the area around Yves' home, but as it was near the top of a hill, he could see down into the centre of Toulouse, so, he set off in that direction. As he walked along, he kept turning over the phrase that had resulted from the latest translation. "Behind the mind", he repeated to himself. "What mind? Who's mind?" This was going to be the part that he would need to understand before any more progress could be made.

By the time Paul arrived at the main shopping centre in the city, he realized that he had been walking for more than an hour. He went into a bakery to buy one of the delicious looking desserts that were on display in the window. He wanted to bring something as a contribution to the meal that they would be having that night. He stopped in at a wine shop on his way back to the house and bought two bottles of wine, one red and one white. "At least I'm doing a bit to return Yves' hospitality," he thought.

Arriving at the house he had to ring the doorbell, and Yves came to let him in. "Here's a key," he said, as Paul entered. "Keep it until you leave, it will make life easier for both of us."

116

"Thanks," said Paul. "I've brought some dessert and wine to have with our dinner, but first I'd like to take a shower, if I may. That's a long walk uphill from downtown and I got rather warm."

Later that evening, the two men sat across from each other at the table. During the meal, Paul had told Yves about the phrase that he had deciphered. The two of them had discussed its meaning but had come to no satisfactory conclusion. Eventually, Yves asked to look at the enlargements that Paul had done of the stonework at the front of the church, and at the drawings that Maria had done. Paul got them from his room and laid them out on the table in front of him.

"How old did you say this building is?" asked Yves. Paul gave him the dates that Father Jacques had told him.

"For a building of that age it is in a remarkably good state of repair," said Yves. "It must have been built by the finest Masons of that period. As you know, I was a structural engineer in my working life and, although I ended up in the aviation industry, I spent the first few years of my career in the construction field. I had a hand in a number of the larger buildings that are in the city centre here. I have great respect for the builders of the middle ages. How they overcame height problems, and weight and stress-related difficulties with the instruments they had, is a marvel."

Paul mentioned the state of the abandoned chateau that he had visited on the previous day.

"Oh yes," said Yves. "I know the one you are talking about, I've been to see it myself. It comes up in the newspapers here from time to time whenever the original family tries to get it back from the government, it's a pity it is in such a bad state. If it had been built by the people who built the church in your photo, there wouldn't be any stone falling out of the walls. They knew how to cut stone to the precise angle in order to maintain structural integrity."

Yves seemed to be in a mood to reminisce about his life, so, Paul leaned back in his chair and let him talk. He felt that Yves, like himself until recently, had been on his own rather a

117

lot in the past few years and was enjoying having an audience to communicate with for a change. Eventually he said, "well enough about me, I hope I didn't go on too much. Now, if you'll excuse me, I'm off to bed.... see you in the morning."

The following day, as they sat in the kitchen over a cup of coffee, the telephone rang and when Yves came back into the room, he told Paul that his son Jean had invited them both to lunch, and that they were to meet at a restaurant near his office. Yves explained to him that today was his birthday, and that the lunch was a celebration of the event.

"Well, congratulations and many happy returns of the day," said Paul.

"What a nice change it would make," he thought, to do something other than chase puzzles around in his head."

At the restaurant, Paul met Jean's wife and renewed his acquaintance with Yves' granddaughter Simone, the young woman he had travelled with from Paris. Their lunch turned out to be a double celebration, as Simone had just learned that she had passed her exams and would be going to Paris in the fall. Paul and Yves told them some of the funny stories that had occurred years ago, when they were both involved in the aircraft industry. When the lunch was over and they were getting ready to depart, Jean took Paul aside and thanked him for coming.

"My father doesn't get out much anymore," he said. "This is the most animated I have seen him for a long time. It's been good for him to have you at the house."

"Well, it's been a treat for me too," said Paul, "but I can't stay for long on this occasion, I have some work to finish up."

Driving back to the house, Paul broached the subject of his return to Carcassonne.

"I'll be leaving in a day or two." he said. "As soon as I've spoken to Maria. I'm going to call Father Jacques and arrange to meet him again."

Yves said that he was disappointed that Paul would not be staying longer, but that he understood why.

118

In the evening, when they were sitting in the livingroom watching the news, the telephone rang again. Yves picked up the receiver and after a few moments handed it to Paul. "It's for you," he said.

It must be Maria, Paul thought, she's the only person who knows I am here. He heard Maria say: "Hello Paul. I just had to call you. I think I've had an inspired thought. You know the word Calyx in the puzzle? Well, I've been thinking about it as I've been driving along. I think Dearborn was using the Greek alphabet to try to solve the design, and he made a mistake. Maybe at that point he didn't realise that there were several languages being used to hide the meaning. Anyway, if you use the letter "Y" from the Greek alphabet, you get the word Calyx, meaning petals or flowers. However, if you substitute the "Y" for an "I" from Latin, you still get Calix, but it doesn't mean the same thing."

"Well," said Paul, "slow down a minute. I've been doing some work myself and I think I have solved the phrase." He went on to describe what he had found in her book at the second set of Greek alphabet illustrations. Then he told Maria the order of the words that had finally appeared.

"BEHIND THE MIND LIES THE CALYX OF BLOOD."

"That is absolutely fantastic," said Maria. "Now, what do you think Calix means in Latin?"

"I don't know," said Paul. What does it mean?"

"It means a cup, or in this instance, a Chalice," said Maria. "It seems to me that Captain Dearborn was on the right track. That there is something hidden in the abandoned church after all. It could be an ancient cup that was used in religious services, perhaps symbolising the blood of Christ. Now, wouldn't that be something!"

"Quite unbelievable," said Paul. "If you are right, that it is a significant religious artifact that was stolen during the crusades, heaven only knows what an uproar that could cause today."

There was silence on the phone for a few moments while both Paul and Maria tried to digest what they had learned.

119

Eventually Paul asked, "where are you calling from, are you at home?"

"No," said Maria. "I'm at my office. I came straight here to take care of the problem that brought me back to Florence. It's nothing but a storm in a teacup, too many academic egos getting in the way of each other. I can solve it quickly enough, but not until tomorrow. After that, I'm free to finish my vacation. I don't suppose you'd like me to join you, by any chance?" she said hopefully.

"You bet I would," said Paul. "When can you get here?"
"I'll have to check the flights in the morning and see if I can catch a plane after I've dealt with the problem here. It will probably be sometime in the late evening before I can get out of town".

"Just call and tell me when you are arriving, and I'll meet you at the airport," said Paul. "What a marvellous conversation we've had, your powers of deduction are terrific. I can't wait to talk to you about everything when we meet. See you soon," he said putting down the phone.

"I gather your friend Maria is coming to Toulouse," said Yves.

"Yes, tomorrow I hope. But that's not all!" He explained what Maria had said about changing the "*Y*" for an "*I*" in the word Calyx, in the puzzle, and the meaning of the word in Latin.

Yves was silent for a minute. "You know," he said. "If there is some ancient religious item hidden in that church and you are able to find it, you won't just be the object of a chase from the Order of St George. There will certainly be a number of religions that will try to claim ownership of it. You'd better be ready for that possibility."

"You are right," said Paul. "I've been thinking about that myself. However, we are getting the cart before the horse. We don't know the meaning of the phrase yet, or even where to look. "*BEHIND THE MIND*" could mean anything, it could be something like, 'until you truly believe in God, you cannot be accepted into the Church'. I am not a particularly religious person," he added. "I'm more interested in the here and now, than the hereafter. I'm also enough of an archeological enthusiast to want to discover something from our past if I can. I don't want any fame or notoriety at all. Nor do I want to be the quarry of the Order of St. George. But I have come this far, and I want to see this through to its conclusion, whatever that is."

The resolute manner in which he made that last remark gave fullest. Well, he was surely doing that! Paul a bit of a surprise. He was reminded again of Carla's words to him, to take every opportunity to live life to the fullest. Well, he was surely doing that!

CHAPTER .7.

Paul decided to call Father Jacques that evening, to let him know that he and Maria would be returning to Carcassonne. He got through to the St. Vincent de Paul shelter but could not get hold of Father Jacques. He was told that the ex-priest was not expected until the morning. Not wanting to leave a message, Paul simply said that he would call again.

Yves asked Paul if he was going to tell the ex-priest about the phrase.

"No, not yet," said Paul. "I think that might be a mistake, if he thinks that there may be a significant religious item hidden somewhere in the building he might try to claim it for the Catholic Church. After all he was a priest at one time! What I want him to do is to help me get inside the church, without anyone else knowing. Then I'm going to go through that place with a fine tooth comb."

The next day, Paul was on tenterhooks waiting for Maria to call and let him know when she would be arriving. He got the call in the early afternoon, Maria would be on a flight that arrived at ten-thirty that night. Yves had very kindly offered Paul his car to go and meet her. He had also arranged with the housekeeper when she arrived that morning, to make up another bedroom for an extra guest.

"You're sure we need to do this," he had asked Paul with a twinkle in his eye. Paul had said, "yes." This was no time to be adding any extra complication to his life.

At the airport that night, Paul paced up and down the terminal. He was far too early for the flight, but had been unable to stay at the house any longer. He checked the arrivals television screen many times to confirm that the flight number he had been given was on time, and that the gate number had not changed. At last, he heard the announcement of the flight arriving, and waited impatiently outside the doors to greet her as she came out.

"Maria," he yelled as he saw her, "over here!"

She saw him, and smiled as he came towards her.

"It's wonderful to see you again," he said. "Let's go and get your bags and get on our way."

"These are my bags," said Maria, handing him a smallish suitcase. "Everything I need is in there, plus this other bag in my hand."

"Ok," said Paul, "let's go. My gosh, it's good to see you again!".

Driving back to Yves' house, Paul filled Maria in on the events of the previous two days. She was very interested in the discovery that Paul had accidentally come across in the Aramiac alphabet, when he had been staying at the hotel.

"You must show me how you reached the conclusions you did," she said. "I know you think we have the solution to the puzzle, but my mind doesn't work like that. I'm suspicious of such an amazing stroke of good luck."

Paul agreed to show her everything as soon as they had settled in. He spoke of Yves for a few minutes, and gave her the background of their friendship.

"You were very lucky to have found him, in the circumstances," said Maria. "I hope he doesn't live to regret seeing you again."

Yves was still up when they arrived, but only long enough to greet Maria and to welcome her to his home. "It's very late for me to be up," he said. "So, I'll just say goodnight, and leave you two to chat. I'm sure you both have a great deal to talk about. Paul can show you to your room when you decide to turn in."

"I'll just freshen up, said Maria, then you can show me the completed phrase and the parts in the books you used to come up with the result."

While she was away, Paul arranged things on the kitchen table and made some fresh coffee. "We could be here for a while," he thought.

When she arrived, he opened the book that had the Aramaic alphabet in it and handed it to Maria. "I don't want to influence you," he said. "You see what you come up with on your own, while I pour some coffee for us."

Maria's eyes flitted back and forth from the design to the book for several minutes. Eventually, she singled out some letters and said: "I think these are the ones that bear a strong resemblance, are they the same ones you used?"

Paul looked at her efforts. "Yes," he said, "exactly. Now, if you place them in the appropriate positions, you can see the results. It's funny when I look at it now, I can't believe I didn't see things more clearly. Of course, we didn't know at that point that we would have to look at the Greek alphabet as well."

Paul then showed Maria the illustrations of the Greek language, indicating the differences between the first pages and those near the end of the chapter, the ones that were said to be from an earlier date. Maria saw, very easily, the way in which the match- up with the design occurred.

"Those books you lent me were an absolute God-send," said Paul. "Without them, I don't see any way in which we could have made such progress. The final part to do with the word Calix was a master stroke," he said, smiling at her. "I'm sure that you have hit the nail on the head. What could be more likely than a Chalice taken from a church or temple that had been sacked by the crusaders. It's exactly the sort of thing they would have made off with - easily carried, probably valuable and with a great deal of significance to any religious order."

"What do you intend to do now?" asked Maria.

"Not a thing until the morning," said Paul. "Now, let me show you to your bedroom, you've had a long day. We'll all be better able to make plans after a good nights sleep."

With that, Paul led Maria up to her room. "I'm so glad you are here with me again," he said. "I've missed you"

"Me too," she replied.

In the morning, the three of them sat at breakfast discussing what the next move should be. There was general consensus that the design in the stonework, in the entryway to the old church in Carcassonne, was a very well disguised clue to some object taken during the time of the crusades. Paul was still marvelling at the way four other languages had been used to hide the meaning of the phrase. If it hadn't been for Maria, he would still be looking for some sort of flowers, or petal shapes in the stonework in and around the building.

Maria was deep in discussion with Yves about the way the church had been built. She remembered that Paul had told her Yves was a structural engineer, and that he had been involved in construction of many large buildings in Toulouse. She assumed that whatever was hidden in the church, would likely be behind some stone, either in the floor or in the walls.

"Is there any way that one could tell where some part of the masonry was different from the rest?" she asked. If Yves had wanted to hide an item, in the walls for instance, was there some structural technique that could be used to make it easy to remove certain stones to retrieve a hidden item, yet make it difficult to detect its location.

Yves explained that there was a technique which allowed certain stones in a structure to be more easily removed than others. It needed something called a double keystone. Basically, this required a pair of interlocking stones to be placed above and around a single keystone. Usually, the interlocking stones had other shallower stones placed in front of them, so that the single stone would be hidden from view. The result of doing this allowed a single keystone to be set in between the interlocking stones, without having to bear any weight from above, or from the sides. At the same time, it would appear that removal of the interlocking keystones would be almost impossible, without weakening the whole structure. It required a very high level of masonry skill to do that, Yves had explained.

While this conversation was taking place, Paul had gone to the telephone to call Father Jacques again. This time he made contact. First, he asked if Father Jacques had noticed anyone following him since the meeting in Gaillac.

The reply caused Paul to feel very concerned. Father Jacques had been followed on more than one occasion, by the same man who had been on the train to Gaillac. There was no longer any attempt made to disguise the fact, the man just watched wherever Father Jacques went.

"It's rather like being followed by a reluctant dog," said Father Jacques.

"Do you think you could avoid being pursued?" asked Paul.

"If I wanted to, I'm sure I could, I haven't needed to so far. I've just been doing my normal work here at the shelter."

"If Maria and I return to Carcassonne, where would be a good place to meet you?" asked Paul.

"I've been thinking about that since I knew you would likely be coming back. I think the best place would be the orphanage, up in the old town. There's not much chance of anyone suspecting you would go there. I'll give you the address," he said. "It's number sixteen, Allee du Bois. You'll enter the old town by the south gate, that's the one that is not used much by the tourists, as it is farthest from the main attractions. But it has the advantage of being very close to the church of the Knights Templar, and I assume that at some point, you will be going there." Paul was about to ask how Father Jacques had gained entry to the abandoned church but decided at the last minute not to. "I must be able to find my own way in," he thought. "Better to keep my plans to myself at the moment".

"When might you be visiting us again?" asked Father Jacques.

"Sometime in the next few days," said Paul. "I'll call you and let you know the night before we intend to arrive. We will be in the old town very early on the following morning," he added. "Goodbye until then." Paul put down the receiver and thought about the fact that he had been reluctant to tell Father

Jacques about the discovery he had made. "I wonder why that is?" he mused.

Paul returned to join the other two, and repeated what Father Jacques had said about being followed. "It makes me worried about you," he said looking at Maria.

Yves spoke up. "When are you two going to leave for Carcassonne?" he asked, "and how are you going to get there?"

"We'll leave very early tomorrow morning," said Paul. "Today we have some shopping to do to prepare us for staying inside the old church - maybe for a couple of days. We will have to be self-sufficient once we are inside.

We will have to rent a car again, so I'll do that from a rental company in the city centre, rather than at the airport. I don't trust that airport."

"I would be happy to lend you my car," said Yves. "I don't use it much, and it would be good for it to go for a run. If I need to go anywhere, Jean or his wife will take me. Please let me do this, it will make me feel as though I am part of the adventure. It will also give you further anonymity from the people pursuing you."

"That is very kind of you," said Paul. "But........"

Yves interrupted, and held up his hand. "No buts please, I insist."

There was no more to be said, they had their transport.

"Off you go and get the things you think you will need," said Yves. "Don't buy blankets, you can take some from here. I also have two good thermos flasks for hot drinks that you can borrow. While you are away, I'll see what else I can think of that might be useful to you. I feel very pleased to be able to help."

Paul and Maria sat together, making a list of things they might need for a two-night stay inside the abandoned church. Half an hour later, they were on their way to a shopping centre to pick up the things on the list, and anything else that they could think of as they worked their way from store to store.

The most important thing for them were two powerful flashlights and some extra batteries. They purchased some fruit and some bread, cold meats and cheese; plus a bottle of good wine.

"Might as well have some comforts," said Paul. "I must remember to get a corkscrew from Yves."

When they eventually got back to the house, Yves presented them with a condensed version of his tool box.

"I hope you have need of some of these items," he said. "If you do it will mean that you have found something interesting."

Paul spent the evening packing the car with the items that they would be taking. He had to keep remembering that whatever they took would have to be carried on their backs into the old town, because of the vehicle restrictions. In the end, they emptied Maria's travelling bag and refilled it. Yves gave Paul a rucksack to use, which he stuffed to the limits, leaving only two side pockets for any last minute additions.

Paul and Maria discussed whether or not to call Father Jacques that night before they left, but in the end decided against doing so. Paul was concerned that perhaps the telephone line might be tapped, and in any case he wanted to arrive in Carcassonne without anyone knowing he was there.

As they all said good night to each other, Yves wished them good luck, he would not be getting up at five o'clock to see them off, he said. But he told Maria, to be particularly careful, as he felt she was the most vulnerable.

Paul and Maria were up at the crack of dawn. Paul filled the two flasks with scalding hot coffee and grabbed two mugs, some cutlery, and a corkscrew he found in the kitchen drawer. Then they were on their way. Paul had filled the car with gasoline and checked the oil and water in the car the day before, so there was no need to stop until they reached the town. He knew from previous experience, that it would take about an hour to get there. The traffic was almost non-existent at this early hour, and except for the usual large trucks that preferred to make up any lost time by travelling through the night, they saw very few other vehicles.

During the journey Maria and Paul talked over how they would spend this first day. For a start, Paul wanted to find the orphanage where Father Jacques had suggested they meet. He wanted to become familiar with the streets around the area, especially those between the abandoned church and the orphanage building. He had been thinking about how useful it had been to know his way back to his hotel in London when he was being chased and wondered if something similar might happen this time.

It was easy enough to find the south gate into the old town, as Father Jacques had said it would be. They were able to park Yves' car very close to the entry. Before they walked inside the walls, Paul had a good look at the map that he had purchased the last time he had visited the town with Maria. He found the street where the orphanage was, and the location of the square where he knew the church was. Interestingly, the church was not shown on the map, though other historical buildings were identified. "That's odd," he said to himself.

They left everything in the trunk of the car and walked hand in hand through the gateway into the old town. Within a few minutes, they were on the street where the orphanage was located. They stopped in front of the building. Paul walked up to the front door and knocked, using the brass door knocker.

"What are you doing?" asked Maria.

"Just follow my lead," said Paul. The door was opened by an elderly nun. "Yes?" she said enquiringly.

"I'd like to make a donation to your good work," said Paul.

"Won't you come in," said the nun. She led them along the hall and ushered them into a room. "Please sit down," she said.

"How many children do you look after here?" asked Paul.

"Oh, we don't have children here any more," said the nun, "we haven't for about twenty years. During the last war we had many children living here. Even after the war, we still had little ones to care for. Then when things were beginning to settle down again, we still took in refugees for several years.

This house is now occupied by the last remaining Sisters of my order. When we are gone, the church will probably sell the property to the town."

"How many of you are here?" asked Maria.

"Just three now," she replied, "we are all getting on in years, but we can still take care of one another. The house is really much too large for us, so, we only occupy the main floor."

At that moment, another of the nuns appeared in the doorway. "Would you like some tea?" she asked.

"Yes, please," said Paul.

"This is Sister Agatha," said the first nun, "and my name is Sister Frances."

Turning to Sister Agatha, she said, "run along then and make the tea."

Sister Agatha bowed and left the room. "I'm afraid Sister Agatha is getting a bit forgetful," she said. "She is quite old now. She was the first Sister here, when the orphanage was started during the war. It was a very difficult time for everyone, and she carried most of the responsibility for running the place. Now, it is our turn to take care of her."

Maria had been looking out of the window at the garden. She commented that the Sisters had certainly been busy, as there were beautiful flowers and a large well-tended vegetable plot.

"Yes," agreed Sister Frances. "Like the house, the garden is too big for us to manage nowadays." At this point Sister Agatha re-appeared with a tray of tea cups.

"I heard you talking about the garden," she said. "Aren't we lucky to have that nice man back here again to help us out. He used to come and help us when the children were here. I remember he repaired the chimney for us, but that was a long time ago," she said. "Now, who wants milk with their tea?" she asked, looking at Paul and Maria.

Sister Frances stood up and took Sister Agatha by the arm. "I'll look after the tea," she said, "you should go and lie down for a while." With that, she escorted Sister Agatha out of the room. "I'll be back in a few minutes," she said.

130

Paul looked at Maria, they both had a question on their lips, but said nothing.

"Milk and sugar I believe," said Maria, lifting the teapot and pouring tea into one of the cups.

"Uh, yes, thank you," said Paul.

Sister Frances returned and sat down again. "Now," she said, "do you still want to make a donation, even though we no longer have an orphanage here? Any money we receive, we give to the church we attend to help in its maintenance."

"Yes," said Paul, "I do." He reached for his wallet and handed the Sister some money.

"Where is the church?" he asked, "I'd like to visit it while we are here."

Sister Frances thanked him and put the money in a drawer in the desk. "It's just two streets away, turn right when you leave the house and then take the second on the left, you'll see it right away."

"That was an interesting story that Sister Agatha was telling about the man who is helping you with your garden," said Paul. Sister Frances frowned for a moment.

"I don't know much about him," she said. He came here about a month ago, and he only ever speaks to Sister Agatha. She seems to think that she knew him years ago, but her memory is not very good. Anyway, he certainly helped us with the heavy digging and planting. He comes and goes as he pleases, through a door in the wall at the back of the garden, by the tool shed. Sister Agatha gives him a bowl of soup at lunchtime, if he is here, and they sit and chat for a while. Now, if you will excuse me, I must get back to my work." She stood up, and indicated that the visit was over.

"Thank you again for the donation," she said, as they retraced their steps to the front door. After the goodbyes, Paul and Maria stood in the street looking at one another.

"Are you thinking what I'm thinking?" she asked.

"If it's Captain Dearborn on your mind, I guess I am. I would sure like to talk to Sister Agatha for a few minutes," he added. "Let's walk over to where the Sister's church is," said Paul, "and then go on to the abandoned church. I want to walk around the sides and the back to see if I can find the place where Father Jacques managed to find a way in."

They followed the directions from Sister Frances and soon found the church where the nuns worshipped. It was a very small, ordinary looking structure on the outside, but once inside, they found a very ornate interior, with a beautiful stained glass window above the altar. An elderly woman was sweeping the floor, she looked up as Paul approached her.

"Is this the place where the nuns from the orphanage come to worship?" he asked.

"Yes," she said, "they are here every evening for mass at six o'clock."

"Thank you," said Paul.

The two of them then left to continue on to the little square, where the abandoned church was located. It took less than ten minutes for them to arrive. Paul had a good sense of where they were as they walked along. He had remembered the street names from studying the map of the area closely. As they crossed the square Paul said, "stay close to the front of the church and face the square, that way if you see or hear anyone coming, you can give me a call. I'm going to climb over the fence again and then go down each side of the building to see what I can find."

Everything looked the same as before as Paul clambered over the railing.

"I'll go along the left-hand side first," he said to Maria. "Don't forget to call me if you see anyone."

With that, he disappeared around the edge of the building. As Paul walked along, he could see the slits in the stonework high up in the walls that had provided some light to Dearborn during the day. The window areas were few, and the boards covering them looked untouched. When he reached the rear of the building, there was a high stone wall which ran from the church wall to an adjacent building.

Paul retraced his steps. When he saw Maria, he asked if she had seen anyone.

132

"Just an elderly couple with a small dog," she said.

So, Paul proceeded down the right-hand side of the church. Again he could see that the window coverings looked old and untouched, he carried on and turned the corner to the rear. Here, there were two more boarded-up windows, very high up in the wall. He walked past a portion of the rear of the building that projected outwards and here he found a small boarded-up window about eight feet off the ground. It was somewhat in the shadow close to the stone wall that he had seen from his exploration of the other side.

Paul managed to climb up the wall enough to get a close look at the boarded-up area. He ran his fingers around the edge of the bottom boards to see if he could move them - he could not. Then he ran his fingers up the side nearest the wall, and felt something projecting out just slightly. He looked up to where his hand was but could not see what it was.

"I wish I had brought a flashlight and an extra hand," he thought.

Paul lowered himself back to the ground to consider this problem. He felt sure that this had to be the entryway that Father Jacques had discovered, there was no other part of the building that gave any chance of easy access.

"I'll have one more go at moving the thing that is attached to the boards and then go back to Maria to tell her what I have found," he said to himself.

He examined the wall more carefully this time before climbing up. He picked out the stones that he was going to try to stand on before he started. This time, he managed to get a few inches higher up and this made it easier to move his hand up the side of the boards. Feeling the projection again, he discovered that it was an ordinary latch. He pushed upwards and felt it move. Pushing again, he felt it release and the boards came away from the wall slightly. He moved his hand to the lower boards where he could get more purchase and pulled outward. The boards came away bit by bit. Paul could hear the squeak of the hinges holding them together.

When he had pulled enough to be able to get his hand inside, Paul could now shift his weight slightly and look up to see what was behind the covered area. It was a gap, roughly thirty inches square. He felt around the edges and found the stubs of metal that must have been bars across the opening at one time.

"This is where Captain Dearborn got in and out of the place for sure," he thought.

Paul pushed back the boards and re-attached the latch. Then he lowered himself back to the ground and hurried back to the front of the church. Maria looked up as he came into view, she could see from the look on his face that he had found something!

"Did you see anybody?" he asked as he pulled himself over the railings.

"No," said Maria, "but you have seen something."

"Yes," said Paul. "I think I've found a way inside. Come on, let's get away from here and go back to the car. I could use a cup of that hot coffee we brought from Yves."

Paul glanced quickly at his watch. "I also want to see how long it takes to get from here to the orphanage, if we go at a good pace," he said.

Maria asked Paul to tell her what he had found, but he insisted that she wait until they got back to the car, then he would tell her all about his discovery. As they passed by the orphanage, Paul made a mental note of the time, a few minutes later they were back at the car. Sitting with a cup of hot coffee each, Paul told Maria about the window opening at the back of the church.

When he had finished talking, Maria said: "do you think I could climb up the wall and pull myself inside?"

"I don't know," said Paul, "how much climbing have you done recently? I've seen you at the dig at Gaillac, and you seemed pretty agile there, but this is quite a bit more difficult than you might realise. I guess if I go inside first, and don't break a leg on the way down, maybe I can help you from there. We'll just have to play it as we find it."

"Are we going to try and get inside tonight?" asked Maria.

"Yes, we are," Paul replied.

"While you were away I've been thinking about Captain Dearborn," said Maria. "If it is him who has been helping the nuns at the orphanage, then don't you think we should try and find him?"

"I've been giving that some thought too," said Paul. "We could go back to the orphanage and see if we can find the door at the back of the garden. From the way Sister Frances spoke, I don't think it will be locked. Maybe we will find whoever has been helping them, working in the garden today. If we don't see anyone, then I am going to try to speak to Sister Agatha at the evening mass. I feel sure that she must have known the Captain when he was helping at the orphanage during the war."

"Are you going to call Father Jacques?" asked Maria. "If Captain Dearborn is here in Carcassonne, surely he would have been in touch with him."

"I agree with what you are saying," said Paul. "However, if Dearborn has been here for a few weeks as the Sisters said, why hasn't Father Jacques told us about seeing him again?"

"Hmm," said Maria, "I hadn't thought about that."

"My guess is that he didn't want anyone to know he was here," said Paul, "even Father Jacques. I'm more interested in finding Captain Dearborn than talking to Father Jacques at the moment. Now, let's finish this coffee, and go and find the garden door."

Locking up the car again, Paul decided to take out Dearborn's hat from the trunk and put it on his head. "If it is Dearborn who is working in the garden, and he is there, he will certainly recognise his hat," he reasoned. "If there is someone working in the garden, and he doesn't recognise the hat, then it won't be the Captain."

As he closed the trunk, he could feel the first few drops of rain falling, looking up at the sky he could tell they were in for a wet walk. Turning to Maria he said: "we had better hurry, anyone working in a garden won't be there for long, if this rain gets any worse."

As they approached the orphanage, they could see an alleyway off to the right of the building.

"It must be down there," said Paul.

Once they had walked past the end of the house, they came to a high stone wall.

"This must be where the garden starts," said Maria, "it can't be far now."

A few more steps brought them to a low, narrow door let into the stone wall.

"Well, here goes," said Paul. "Perhaps finally, I am going to meet the man who has caused me so much adventure and intrigue."

The door opened easily. Paul and Maria stepped inside and looked around. They could hear nothing, nor could they see anyone. "I'm going take a look inside the garden shed, you wait here for a minute."

"I'd rather come with you," said Maria. "This rain is getting worse and I am getting soaked right through."

"Alright, come on then." The two of them ran to the shed and got inside out of the miserable weather. It took a moment for their eyes to adjust to the dim interior. The one small window in the shed was covered in cobwebs and did not let in much daylight. Inside, they found the usual assortment of gardening tools. A lawn mower, some pots and a number of bags of fertiliser. However, at the back of the shed was something they had not expected to find....a camp cot with some blankets, a one-burner kerosene stove and an opened can of milk, along with some teabags. On a small shelf, above the cot, were a number of sheets of paper. Paul picked up a couple of them and brought them to the doorway where there was more light.

What he saw, drawn on the paper in his hand, took him right back to his home in Canada.....the same drawings of the design on the front of the abandoned church that he had found in Captain Dearborn's room!

"Take a look at these," he said, handing them to Maria.

She studied them for a minute, then turned to Paul.

136

"It looks like the Captain is living in this shed, or sleeping in here anyway. What are you going to do now?"

"First, let's put the papers back where we found them, then let's get out of this garden," said Paul. Back in the alley, Paul told Maria that they would go back to the car, drive out of Carcassonne and find a hotel room nearby. Then, they would get cleaned up and into some dry clothing, and do some planning. The two of them were thoroughly soaked by the time they got back to the car. Paul had a quick glance at the map and drove off in the direction of the nearest hotel that was shown on the reverse side of the tourist brochure of the area.

CHAPTER .8.

Less than an hour later, they had their hotel room. Maria was the first into the bathtub, while Paul paced up and down, going over all the things that had happened to them since arriving back in Carcassonne. There was a lot to consider. He thought back to his last conversation with Father Jacques. It was he who had suggested that they use the orphanage for a meeting place. Was that because he knew Dearborn was staying there, or just a convenient place to meet? It seemed obvious from what they had found in the garden shed, that the Captain was here in the town, and that he was not advertising his whereabouts to anyone.

Paul then thought about the abandoned church. He didn't think that any other person had been using the window to gain entry recently, the stiffness of the hinges seemed to confirm that. How was he going to meet Dearborn? Did he want to meet Dearborn before he and Maria had spent some time in the church looking for any hidden item? If he talked to Dearborn, did he want to divulge what he had managed to decipher from the design in the stonework?

Eventually, Maria came out of the bathroom. "How do you like my outfit?" she asked. Paul looked up at her from his chair. She was wearing dark grey slacks and a black turtleneck sweater, she had tied her hair back with a silk scarf revealing her long neck once more. Over her sweater she wore a dark woollen jacket. "Wow" said Paul, "you look wonderful, but this is not a fashion show we're going to, you know.

"Everything I'm wearing is quite practical," she said, "but thanks for the compliment. You can have the bathroom now."

Paul took her place. For the next half an hour, he tried to forget about the days' events, and at last returned to the room feeling refreshed and comfortable, with a new set of dry clothes.

"Let's go down to the bar and have a couple of stiff drinks," he suggested.

Sitting together in the hotel bar, they went over what had transpired that day.

"I was wondering," said Maria, "whether Sister Agatha has seen Captain Dearborn since we met her this morning and mentioned our visit to the orphanage."

"I don't think so," said Paul. "We didn't enquire very much about who the chap was that had been working in the garden while she was in the room."

"No, that's true," said Maria, "but the other Sister might have talked to her after we left."

"Hmm," replied Paul. "Well, I still think our plan should be that we go to the church where the Sisters attend evening mass. I would still like to try to talk to Sister Agatha. Then we'll go on to the abandoned church. If this rain keeps up, we should be able to get inside once it's dark, without being seen by anyone passing by. Do you still want to come with me?" he asked.

"Absolutely," said Maria. "I wouldn't miss the next twenty-four hours for anything. I just hope I will be able to climb up the wall!"

Nothing was said for a few minutes, then Maria suggested that they have an early supper in the hotel before returning to the town. "It could be a while before we eat anything hot, once we leave here," she said. Paul agreed, so, they finished their drinks and walked over to the restaurant across from the bar.

After the meal, Maria went up to the room to pack and Paul went to the front desk to pay for the accomodation. It was difficult explaining to the individual behind the desk, that they would not be staying for the night. In the end, Paul kept his room key and told the girl that they would be very late returning that night. Then he went out to the car and returned with the two flasks that Yves had loaned them. He gave them to the waiter in the restaurant to refill with the hottest coffee the waiter could obtain.

Once they were back on the road, Paul checked his watch, five-fifteen, he noted. "That should be just about right for us," he commented to Maria.

The rain was continuing to fall and though it was early in the evening, the daylight was fading fast. At a quarter to six, they parked the car in the same location as they had done earlier in the day.

"We'll leave our bags here for the time being," he said. "It could be some time before we walk over to the abandoned church."

Maria had discovered an umbrella under her seat in the car and with Paul wearing Dearborn's hat the two of them had some protection from the rain as they walked into the old town. It felt quite different than when they had been there during the daylight hours. There was a definite sense of walking into another, older time. The narrow streets and the buildings which seemed to grow together as they reached upward, kept many areas in shadow, adding to the feeling of being in a part of history, long since past.

Arriving at the small church, they entered and sat down close to the rear. This way, they could see everyone who was there. It was a small group of worshippers, not more than a dozen. Paul could see the three nuns sitting close to the front.

"When the time comes for the bread and wine, I'll go up to the altar," said Maria. "I'll be the last one, so I'll be able to look at everyone as I walk back to my seat."

Paul watched as she walked down the aisle. On her way back, he could see that she smiled at the nuns, as she passed by.

"We recognised each other," she said to Paul as she sat down.

When the service was over, Paul and Maria waited at the entrance. The nuns were in conversation with the priest for a few minutes before they eventually came out of the church. Paul greeted Sister Frances, then turned to Sister Agatha.

"Let me give you my arm," he said. Sister Agatha smiled up at him and together they walked along. Maria had asked to be introduced to the third nun and began a conversation with her and Sister Frances, leaving Paul and Sister Agatha to walk along behind them.

"That was a smart thing for Maria to do," thought Paul, "it will give me a chance to talk to Sister Agatha alone." He purposely slowed down slightly to allow the others to get ahead. He knew he would have to talk fast, as the distance from the church to the orphanage was not great.

"You must have had a great deal to do when you were running the orphanage during the war," he ventured.

"Oh yes, it was a wonderful time," she replied. "I felt I was doing some of God's work then."

"The man who has been helping you with your garden, are you sure he is the same one who repaired your chimney back then?" asked Paul.

"Oh yes," said the Sister. "I know it is the same man. Of course, he looks different now, but so do we all, actually you look a bit like him, ' she added.

"Maybe it's the hat," said Paul. Does he wear a hat?"

"I don't think so," said the Sister.

"Have you seen him today?" asked Paul.

"No, not today," she replied, "maybe tomorrow. He comes and goes at different times, but he usually comes to see me if he is around."

By this time, the group had reached the orphanage, Paul and Maria said goodbye to the nuns and walked on as if returning to their car.

"What did you find out?' asked Maria as soon as they were out of earshot. "Well, Sister Agatha is sure that the man helping them in the garden is the same one who rebuilt their chimney for them all those years ago, and apparently he looks a bit like me. Isn't that a surprise! She also told me that she hasn't seen him today."

"There doesn't seem to be any doubt that this man is Captain Dearborn, does there?" offered Maria.

"No," he replied, "it must be him. Let's turn up the next street and work our way back to the scene of our nights lodging. We'll take one last look before it gets dark."

As they made there way along the gloomy streets, there were a few people about making the most of a lull in the rainfall. Eventually, they arrived at the alley that led up to the church. In the distance, they saw the figure of a man crossing the square. He appeared to be heading in the direction of the abandoned building. Paul and Maria hurried to the end of the alley and looked across the square, they could not see anyone.

"Did I imagine that?" said Paul to Maria.

"No, I saw him too. He must have gone into one of the houses or down another alley."

The two of them stood still, looking and listening for any sound but heard nothing. Then they crossed the square and stood in front of the church. Paul was examining the railing to see if there was an easier place for Maria to climb up. When he reached the part where he had managed to clamber over in the morning, it still appeared to be the best spot. Looking down onto the grass at the other side, he could see footprints, very recent footprints from the look of them. The ground was very soft from the heavy rain all day, anyone climbing over could not avoid making a mark in the earth.

Paul called Maria over to where he was standing. "Look at this," he said, pointing to the footprint. "Perhaps this is where the man we saw just now has disappeared."

Maria could easily see what Paul was showing her, she gripped his arm tightly. "Up to now I haven't been scared. But now I am a bit," she added, looking up into Paul's face.

"I'm not too thrilled to see this myself," said Paul. "Especially this evening! Nevertheless, we'll go back to the car and get things ready. It will be quite dark in the next hour and I am still determined to get inside this old building tonight."

With that said, they retraced their steps back out to the car. The rain still held off, making things a bit more pleasant.

"Do you think that the man we saw was Dearborn?" asked Maria.

"It could be," said Paul. "On the other hand, it could also be one of the men from the Order of St George, the ones who have been trying to find me. Maybe they know that I am likely to be here. Someone might have told them."

"Who?" said Maria, "the only person who knew you were coming back here was Father Jacques."

"Yes that's what I was thinking," answered Paul. "Of course, the nuns know that we are here as well," he added.

When they arrived back at the car, Paul opened the trunk and pulled out the rucksack, along with Maria's bag. Next he opened the tool box that Yves had given them. He took out a length of rope, a couple of chisels and a hammer. These he stuffed into the rucksack.

"What are we going to do with the car?" asked Maria, "do you think we can just leave it here for two days?"

"I can't think of anything else, though we might get a parking ticket. I just hope we don't get towed away." Paul lifted the rucksack onto his back, put on the Captain's hat once more, and picked up Maria's bag. "Let's go," he said.

"We look like a couple of tourists looking for a hotel," said Maria.

"Yes," Paul agreed, "except that the place we're going to stay has no hot water, and no toilet."

"Ugh!" replied Maria.

Paul carried the street map in his hand. "It should make us appear to be visiting tourists, if anyone stops us," he said.

There were very few people about as they made their way towards the square. Though it was not raining, the moon was hidden behind a cover of heavy cloud, making the night quite dark. When they reached the square, they stopped for a moment. They could hear the sound of laughter coming from one of the houses across from the church. There was a light on in the front room and the window was partly open. Listening for a minute or two, they realized that the laughter was coming from a television program.

"I hope no one decides to close the window in the next little while," said Maria.

"Just keep quiet as we get over the railing," said Paul.

Crossing the square, the two of them stood in front of the place where Paul had previously climbed over.

"Here goes," he said taking off his rucksack and hanging it on the rail. "When I get over, pass me your bag."

Once on the other side, Paul took the bag from Maria and lifted the rucksack over.

"Now it's your turn," he said. Maria put one foot on a lower part of the railing and pulled herself up. "Give me one of your hands," said Paul, "now put your other foot on the top part of the rail and lean forward onto me." Maria did as he asked.

"Now give me your other hand," said Paul, "and bring your other foot up onto the top of the railing". Once she was there, Paul told her to put her arms on his shoulders. As she did this, he reached around her waist and lifted her down to the ground.

"Well done," he said.

"Well done yourself," said Maria kissing him on the cheek. Paul looked down at her, pulled her even closer and hugged her. "Now for the real test," he said.

Picking up the baggage, they walked down the side of the church to the rear. Paul led the way, with Maria holding onto the back of the rucksack. Turning the corner, they reached the stone wall.

"This is it," said Paul. Maria looked up and could just make out the boarded-up window.

"My God," she said. "I'm not sure I can climb up the wall, let alone pull myself over and in through the opening."

"First things first," said Paul taking the length of rope and a flashlight from the rucksack. "I'm going to climb up, open the latch and pull myself over. Then, I'll turn on the flashlight and see what's on the other side. If it looks like I can get down, I will. Don't worry if I'm gone for a few minutes, Ok?"

"No, not Ok," said Maria, "but I can't think of any other plan, so, go ahead, but be careful. If you fall and hurt yourself in there, you'll really be stuck!"

Paul climbed the wall again to the point he had reached earlier in the day. Feeling along the boarded-up window, he felt the latch again and pushed it up, releasing it. Again, he pulled at the bottom of the boards and felt them come away from the building. He continued pulling as best he could, making the opening as wide as possible. "Now here's the tricky part," he said to himself.

Pushing off the wall, he grabbed the stone sill of the opening with both hands. Getting the best grip he could, pushing with the soles of his shoes on the stone surface of the building, he pulled himself up so that his waist was over the sill. He could feel one of the bits of the old iron bars pressing uncomfortably into his stomach. Reaching into his jacket pocket, he took out the flashlight. Holding it forward into the interior, he turned it on. He looked around and found that he was off to one side of where the altar would presumably have been. To his left, he could see an opening. "That must be one of the rooms Father Jacques had talked about," he thought. He turned the flashlight to look directly below him, there he saw something that made him feel much better. Propped up against the inside wall, was a wooden ladder. He pulled it closer to where he was. He turned off the flashlight and put it back in his pocket.

For the next few minutes, he tried to figure out some way to get onto the ladder. From where she waited, Maria could see the movement of his legs up and down, and side to side.

"What are you doing?" she called up to him.

"Nothing," he grunted back.

Slowly, Paul twisted himself bit by bit, until he was now sitting on the stone window sill with his back to the interior of the church. Reaching above his head, he felt for any projection he could find to pull himself up slightly to allow him to get at least one leg through the opening and onto the top rung of the ladder. He was able to get his fingers into a small slit between two stones. Pushing with one hand and pulling with the other, he got one leg through and onto the ladder. Then, he was able to put some weight on this and pulled his other leg through. He descended the rungs to the floor, where he stood for a few moments to catch his breath and massage his muscles.

"How the heck am I going to get Maria in here?" he wondered. "She will never be strong enough, or tall enough, to do what I just did. What I need is a second ladder, the same as this one."

Turning on the flashlight he proceeded to examine the inside of the building. He looked carefully at the floor around him but could see no footprints in the dust, which covered everything. "Nobody has been in here for a long time," he thought. Walking over to the open doorway he had seen from above, he entered a small room. The interior was much as it must have been during the time that Dearborn had stayed there. To one side, the two old benches that Dearborn had found were still in place. Paul looked behind the door, nothing there.

Leaving the room, he walked across the stone floor to where another, partly open door was located, he pushed hard on it and it slowly moved inward. He remembered that one of the rooms had a large hole in the floor, which had at one time been a well perhaps, and that Dearborn had used it for a toilet. The door would not open fully and was apparently jammed up against something. Paul got down on his knees and holding the light in front of him, peered around the edge of the door. About five feet in front of him, he saw the edge of the hole in the floor. Lying across the top of the hole was the very item he was hoping to find, another ladder!

When the Captain was hiding people during the war he must have used the two ladders to get men and supplies in and out of this place, he realized. When they weren't in use, they would be kept inside, and the access would be hard to detect. "Very clever," he thought.

Pulling the door toward him again, he reached around and moved the ladder away from the entry, then pushed the door once more to open it as far as he could. Picking up the ladder, he walked back to the window opening. He turned off his flashlight and placed the second ladder alongside the first. Climbing back up he looked out of the opening and down at Maria.

"What now?" she said. "I've been trying to climb the wall and I can't get as far as you did without falling back."

"Not to worry," said Paul. "I've got the answer for getting you inside, but first I'll hand you down one end of the rope. Tie the rucksack to it and I'll pull it up." Maria did as she was asked. Paul took it down inside and returned for the small bag. Maria repeated her task and Paul brought that inside as well.

"Now for you," he said.

He pulled the second ladder up alongside him and out through the opening, then lowered it to Maria.

"Place it against the wall and come on up. I'll stay here and help you over the sill", he told her.

"I'm not very good on ladders," said Maria, "especially in the dark."

"Just go slowly," said Paul. "I can see you all the way."

At last, Maria reached the top and with the help of Paul, who had gone down a couple of rungs, she got her leg over onto the inside and gradually made her way down to the floor.

"Phew!" she exclaimed, "I hope I don't have to do that too often."

Paul went back up the ladder, pulled the outside one inside, and set it next to the one he was standing on. He pulled the boards as close as he could, back to their original position.

"I'm going to make us a warning device," he said to Maria. "Hold the flashlight while I attach a piece of wood to one end of the rope, then I'll attach it to the boards at the window, keeping it fairly taut. If anybody tries to get in through the opening, we will hear the wood being moved." When Paul had finished that task, he and Maria started to explore together, the whole of the inside of the structure.

"I'll keep my light on the floor in front of us," he said, "that way we will avoid bumping into anything. You keep your light up around the walls to see if there is something interesting to examine."

For the next hour, they poked and probed into every area. Once they had established there was nothing on the floor to bump into, or fall into, they separated. Maria concentrated on trying to find any anomalies in the walls. She had remembered her conversation with Yves about a double keystone being one way to disguise the significance of a portion of stonework, and its apparent integrity. She began systematically at the rear of the church and was working her way along.

In the meantime, Paul was exploring the entryway. The main door into the church was a marvellous piece of carpentry. It was hung on huge iron hinges and was ornately carved on the inside. He made his way from the entry looking down at the floor to see if he could find the entry to the crypt that Dearborn had told Father Jacques about.
Finding nothing obvious, he called over to Maria.
"Let's stop and have a cup of coffee, then make a decision about where we are going to sleep tonight."

Picking up the rucksack and bag, he walked into the small room that held the two benches. He turned one of the benches around and pulled it away from the other. Then he picked up two of the planks that were laying there and placed them side by side on the benches, to make a table of sorts.

Maria came into the room. "Look what I've found," she said with a chuckle, holding up an old bucket. "A portable toilet!" Putting the bucket down she reached into her bag and took out several candles and a box of matches. "I thought these might come in handy," she said, "and they will save on the batteries." Paul was smiling as he lit the candle. "What a lucky fellow I am to have found such a smart and lovely companion to share this adventure with," he thought.

The two of them chatted together while they drank the coffee.

"It's kind of spooky in here," said Maria. "Just thinking about all the people who have spent time here since this place was built. I don't believe in ghosts, but if ever there was a place where they might be, this is it!"

"I've been thinking about Dearborn," said Paul. "He must have been some tough individual to stay here doing the work he did, knowing that he might be captured at any time. I'm sure I could not have lasted as long as he did. What a relief it must have been to be able to get outside, and go to help the Sisters at the orphanage."

They sat in companionable silence for a while, each with their own thoughts. Eventually, Paul said, "let's try and get some sleep. I'm going to think about the solution to the puzzle, maybe I'll have a flash of brilliance while I'm unconscious."

Using the two benches as beds, they wrapped themselves in the blankets they had brought and tried to get comfortable.

"Goodnight," said Maria. "See you in the morning."

Paul looked at his watch before blowing out the candle, it was a little after eleven-thirty. Through the night, he shifted around and around, however he lay, or sat, he could not get comfortable for long. He knew he had slept some, as he woke up at one point in the night, dreaming of crusaders smashing down his front door at home and demanding that he give them some item. But he could not understand what it was they wanted.

Periodically he looked over to where Maria lay. She seemed to be sleeping whenever he looked in her direction. At last, he could stand it no more. He switched on his flashlight to look at his watch again, this time it was a little after five. He sat up and stared into the darkness.

"What the heck am I doing here?" he thought. "I could be back in Gaillac with Peter and the rest of them enjoying the pleasure of their company, and without a care in the world. Or I could be in Florence with Maria, she would know all the interesting places to visit. in and around that part of Italy. I could be back at home looking after my flowers." He thought about the three options he had considered. Interestingly, the one that seemed to have the most appeal was the one with

Maria in Florence. For a few minutes, he thought about Carla and felt badly that he had not thought of her more often recently. Then, he remembered her words to him on the tape in her car that day, when he had tried to return the hat to Captain Dearborn. He could hear her voice so clearly. "Take every opportunity to live a full and interesting life, and be an active participant," she had said. Then and there, he recognised that Carla was a part of his life that was in the past and that he should not grieve for her anymore, but take pleasure in her memory.

Paul stood up to stretch and massage his arms and legs, as he did so, he heard a low scraping sound coming from outside the room. Picking up his flashlight, he walked quietly out into the main area of the church. He shone the light at the place where he had tied the piece of wood to the rope as a warning system. The wood moved again as he stood there watching.

"We've got a visitor," he said to himself. "Friend or foe, I wonder." Quickly, he ran back into the room where Maria was sleeping.....he shook her as gently as he could. When she opened her eyes, he whispered to her that there was someone outside. "Just stay in the room here, until I find out who it is" he said. Maria nodded her head and sat up.

Paul turned off his flashlight and picked up the hammer, in case he was about to meet one of his pursuers. He climbed very quietly, part-way up the ladder toward the opening. The boards had been pulled away, and in the moonlight he could see a pair of hands, holding onto the stone window sill. He was relieved to see the absence of any rings on the fingers. As he climbed one more rung, he could see out. At the same time, a man's face appeared at the opening.

"Are you the person who was at the orphanage this morn......, I mean, yesterday morning?" asked the man hesitatingly.

"Who are you?" asked Paul

"My name's Dearborn," said the face.

"Well, I'll be damned," said Paul. "I've waited a long time to meet you! Get back down from there and I'll pass you out a ladder." As Paul reached back to grasp the second ladder, he was not surprised to see Maria standing there with an expectant look on her face.

"Is it Captain Dearborn?" she whispered.

"Well, he says he is," replied Paul, "and we have plenty of ways to check him out." Paul pushed the ladder through the opening. The man outside took it, placed it up against the wall and quickly appeared in the opening. Paul shone his flashlight at the face, his mind recalling the picture he had of Dearborn in uniform. There was some resemblance between that picture and this face. "Come on down," he said.

Paul watched closely as the figure descended. At the bottom of the ladder, the man turned to look at Paul and held out his hand.

"Miles Dearborn is my full name," he said.

"My name is Paul," said Paul not wanting to give his surname, "and this is Maria." Dearborn smiled at Maria and made the gesture of doffing his hat. "Pardon me," he said, "I forgot, I'm not wearing a hat."

For a moment, Maria stood looking at the two men, they were very similar in build, and height. If they had been wearing the same clothes, they could easily have been mistaken for one another she decided.

"What made you come here, looking for me?" said Paul.

"Two reasons," said Dearborn. "One, I saw you both coming out of the church with the Sisters last evening. I followed you, and when you started to come here to the abandoned church, I got ahead of you, only just though. I hid in the entryway to this place, while you were examining the railings."

"We thought we saw someone," said Maria, "but when we got to the square, there was no one around."

"That was me," said Dearborn turning back to face Paul. "I overheard you saying to this lady that you were going to try to get inside this place last night."

"The second reason is that a certain Father Jacques visited the orphanage last evening. He was enquiring from the Sisters whether or not they had received a visit from a couple in the last few days. After he left, Sister Agatha came out to the garden shed, to tell me of his visit. When I first came back to the orphanage this time, I asked the Sisters to let me know if they saw Father Jacques, and not to reveal my presence to him. I'm glad that, so far, they have kept their word."

"Come into our makeshift quarters," said Paul. "We have some hot coffee with us, and I have a lot of questions I'd like you to answer. First though, let's pull in the outside ladder and get the boards back in place. I'll leave my warning device connected, in case we get any other visitors."

This done, the three of them went into the small room. Dearborn stood in the doorway for a moment. "This place brings back a lot of memories for me," he said.

While Maria poured a cup of coffee for their visitor, Paul put the hat on his head. Then, he lit two of the candles and sat down opposite the Captain.

Dearborn lifted the cup of coffee with both hands and sat back. He looked over at Paul expectantly, then a picture of complete amazement came over his face. "My Hat!" he exclaimed. "How....where....how on earth did you get my hat!"

"What makes you so sure this is your hat?"

"I bought that hat in a shop in Canada," said Dearborn, with conviction.

"What was the name of the shop?" Paul questioned further.

"It came from a shop called Winterbourne's in the town of Westport," Dearborn continued. "I can also tell you the name of the hatmaker, it's Burdett and Sons, in London England."

"Then, I would say without much doubt, that it is indeed your hat," said Paul, "and I'm very pleased to be able to give it back to you......"Here you are," he said, taking off the hat and passing it to Dearborn.

"However did it come into your possession?" asked the Captain, holding the hat in front of him.

"I found it in a park in my home town of Cambridge, in Canada, about twenty miles from Westport," replied Paul. "But how you came to lose it is a question I have asked myself many times!"

"Well" said Dearborn, "it s a long and complicated story, but the fact that you are here, in this place, means that you already know some of the details. The fact that you have a lady with you also means that you are not part of a group of men called the Order of St. George. They do not allow females to have any knowledge of their activities. You are also not wearing a ring with the red cross of St. George on it. Members of this organisation are obliged to wear such a ring forever, once they are admitted to the Order. Unfortunately, these same people are trying to locate me and do me some mischief.'

"Go on," said Paul, ".......about losing your hat.'

"I had a lady friend in Cambridge," said Dearborn. "On the day I lost my hat, I had been to visit her. She is a seamstress by profession, and I had asked her on a previous visit, to sew something to the inside of the hatband of my hat.....this hat. I had given her a design I was interested in, and knew that she could sew a very faithful copy of it."

"For a couple of months before this, I had been advised by letter, from a person I had known here in Carcassonne, that an Organisation called the Order of St. George, were searching for me. They apparently believed that I had discovered the whereabouts of a religious icon that had been hidden in this church, by members of their Order, during the time of the crusades. Are you following me so far?" asked Dearborn.

"Absolutely", said Paul and Maria, in unison.

"Could I share a little more of that coffee?"

Maria poured Dearborn some more and gave the other cup to Paul, they had only two. 'We'll share this," said Paul turning to look at her. "Please go on with your story."

"I stayed right here in this abandoned church for a while during the war. It was a refuge for me as I was on the run from the German occupation forces. It became a transit point during the war for servicemen using an escape route to get back to the allies, and I was in charge of the operation here. I've also had an abiding interest in archeology most of my life. While I was living here, I managed to get some reading material on the crusades and the time when this church was built. I also learned quite a lot about the various people who have occupied this place at different times. It is true that I believe there may be something hidden here, perhaps by a group of English Knights who occupied this place at one time, when they were returning from the crusades. However, I have never found anything, despite an exhaustive search.

"Now back to the hat shop in Westport. I had become acquainted with the owner of the business. In the course of many conversations with him, we discovered that we had some areas of mutual interest. He had been a prisoner of war and had made a successful escape, as I eventually had. He was also a student of religious history. Now, I am not particularly interested in religions, but their influence on history has been pretty significant, as far as I'm concerned. Anyway, one of the things that seemed of special interest to him, was my time spent in this church, and the amount of historical information I had. The physical exploration which I had been able to do here during the war, also fascinated him. Though I did not know it at the time, this man was a member of the Order of St. George."

"He must have been in touch with their headquarters in London, and had been told to get from me, all the information I possessed on this place, which was once and is still, owned by the Knights Templar. In any event, I was accosted one night on my way home to my lodgings. I was threatened and beaten up when I refused to divulge any details of what I knew about this place. I was told to think over my refusal and advised that my movements would be monitored. Also, I would be visited again......this second visit would include a severe beating by experts, who would make me beg to tell them anything they wanted to know. I can assure you I believed them!"

Paul shuddered to think of what could have happened to him, if he had been caught in his hotel room, in London.

"A couple of weeks later, St. Valentine's Day, as it happens, I left my lodgings with a bouquet of flowers in hand, hoping to give anyone watching, the impression that I was going to see a lady friend. I was also carrying a small case inside which was a concertina. Inside the concertina, I had hidden some information which was part of what these people wanted. I took the concertina to a pawn shop and left it there. I had a plan as to what I would do with the pawn ticket, if ever I needed to. When I had done that, I went on to Cambridge to pick up the hatband from my seamstress acquaintance. I travelled by bus to my destination. On the journey, I did not particularly notice anyone following me, though as events transpired, I now know that I was being followed!"

"After I had delivered the flowers and retrieved the hatband, this same hatband you see here," said Dearborn, holding the hat close to the candles and pointing at the ornate band. "I left her apartment and was walking across the park on my way back to the bus station, when I was set upon by the same two thugs who had beaten me up before. This time I fought back. I managed to disable one of them with a good shot in the groin, with my knee. I freed myself from the other and ran off as fast as I could. It was during this fight that two things occurred. I saw that one of the men was wearing a ring with a small red cross on a white background, on his right hand, and I lost my hat when I was hit on the side of the head."

" I never went back to my lodgings. I got as far as Montreal under my own steam. I used to live there as a boy, my sister still lives in our old house....she managed to give me enough money to get here."

"Why did I come here and put myself in harms way again...you might well ask! Well, some people think that what I know is pretty important. I've spent a lot of time, on and off over the years, trying to figure out if there is something of value hidden in, or under this building. I am getting to the latter part of my life, but while I can still use my brain, I want to keep on with my search."

While Dearborn was relating his story, Paul had noticed that he was fiddling with the inside lining of the hat.

"The item that you are looking for, which was tucked in the inside rim of your hat, is not there anymore," said Paul. "I found it, when I found your hat. Before I get into all the things that have happened in my life since that day, I think we should get cleaned up a bit and have something to eat. So, let's arrange our makeshift table again. Maria and I have brought some supplies with us and I'm sure we have enough to feed you too."

"Thanks for the invitation," said Dearborn. "I am rather hungry, the last meal I had was at noon, yesterday."

They had brought enough water with them to be able to wash their hands and faces.

"Oh, for a lovely long, hot shower," said Maria. "That's my number one desire when we leave this place, I'm sure I must look a mess."

"I think you look just great," said Paul smiling at her.

The three of them sat down around the makeshift table.

"I would like to know how you got involved in this escapade," said Dearborn to Maria. "I certainly didn't expect to find a woman inside this place."

"If it wasn't for Maria, I wouldn't be here at all," Paul told him. "But let's eat something while we continue this conversation". As they ate, they noticed that it was getting lighter in the room.

"It must be quite sunny outside," said Dearborn, between mouthfuls. "I remember when I lived here, this room got the most benefit from the early morning sunshine, it's not much and I'm afraid it won't last. Once the sun gets higher in the sky and moves around, it comes in on the other side of the building, late in the afternoon, through those slits in the walls."

Maria took Paul's cup from him and poured the last of the coffee from the first flask.

Paul turned and spoke to Dearborn. "Before I tell you how we come to be here, I want you to know that we have met someone that you know, or knew, at one time. That person is the same Father Jacques, the one who came to the orphanage yesterday asking about us. I want you to tell me why you did not go to see him when you came back here, after all, he

156

helped you when you were on the run during the war. Maybe even saved your life."

Dearborn said nothing for a minute. "What you say is true," he agreed. "I have kept up a correspondence with Father Jacques over the years since the war. From his letters, I knew of his recognition by the government, here, for his bravery."

"I knew also that he had been expelled from the Catholic Church through his alleged involvement with a woman. He always felt that he was set up by someone in the Catholic hierarchy here in Carcassonne, and that was very hard for him to bear. As you probably know, he became a history teacher and taught at Toulouse. He became an ardent academic on the subject of the church in medieval and pre-medieval times."

"When I lived in this place, I talked to him about my ideas regarding this church, and the possibility that the crusaders, who came to stay here, may have hidden some of their religious plunder. He always gave me the impression that he thought I was crazy. I have to admit that there were times when I thought I was crazy too. Living in here, which I did for nearly two and a half years, is enough to do that to you."

"Anyhow, about two years ago, his letters became very inquisitive on the subject of this place and he began asking for every detail that I could recall. I sent him anything I could remember that I thought would be of interest. It seems that I was not telling him what he wanted to know, as his last two letters were very accusatory, almost frantic in a way. Because of this, I started to wonder if he had decided that I was right, about there being something hidden here and, if only he could find it, he would be able to ingratiate himself to the Catholic Church, by giving it to them.....hoping that he might redeem himself sufficiently to be re-instated to the priesthood. "Once a priest, always a priest," has been said before. So, that is why I have been reluctant to see Father Jacques since returning to Carcassonne."

Maria looked across at Paul, and raised her eyebrows....the gesture seemed to say, "it's just as well we didn't call him before we left Toulouse."

CHAPTER. .9.

"Very interesting," said Paul. "Now, let me fill you in on some of the things you do not know."

"First of all, I tried to return your hat by going to the store where you bought it. As a matter of fact, I was mistaken for you on more than one occasion when I had it on. I also redeemed your concertina with the pawn ticket I found, for which incidentally, you owe me $32.50. Your concertina works properly now because I removed the piece of paper that was hidden inside it. I also visited your landlady Mrs. MacTavish and rescued some of your books and files, before she threw them out. I might add that your landlady was abused by two thugs who tried to find out where you were. One of these men was wearing a ring similar to the one you described earlier. From what you have told us, it seems likely that they were the same men who attacked you in the park."

"My God, said Dearborn, what a rotten thing to do to poor old Mrs. Mactavish. Was she badly hurt ?"

"No, I don't think so, but she was very frightened. I told her to go to the police, but she seemed to think that she would be left alone when they realized that there was nothing in your room.

Miles Dearborn sat shaking his head. "Those filthy swines," he said.

Paul continued to relate his experiences. "I'm a retired translator, like you, one of my hobbies is archeology and I was invited to join a dig here in France by a friend of mine. The dig is in Gaillac, not far from Carcassonne. I examined the file and the books I took from your lodgings, and the photos of you and Father Jacques taken outside of this church. It seemed to me that the design on the coded message I found hidden in the concertina, and those other things, were all connected in some way. I decided to take some time off from the dig to come here and see if I could make any sense of what I had found. I had been to Carcassonne some years before and, as a medieval site, it is a most interesting place to visit."

"On my way over here, I stopped off in London to visit the maker of your hat and had a rather unpleasant experience, including being chased and having my hotel room ransacked. While I was at the hatmaker, I also saw one of those rings, which I now believe is worn by members of this Order of St George, it was on the hand of one of the employees there When I got to the dig sight in Gaillac, I had the great good fortune to meet Maria. She is an expert on ancient languages and was there as part of the international team of archeologists. She and I spent quite a bit of time trying to decipher the puzzle that you left hidden in the concertina. Have you been able to find any more clues as to what that design means?" he asked Dearborn.

"No, I haven't, but I'm still convinced that understanding the design in the stonework is the first thing that has to be accomplished. If you could comprehend the hidden meaning there, you would be well on the way to discovering what, if anything, is hidden here."

At this point, Maria asked Dearborn if he had any knowledge of ancient languages.

"I'm afraid I don't have much," he replied, "though I did study Greek for a time at University, in Montreal."

"So, you were never able to get any more words deciphered than *Calyx and Blood*," said Paul.

"That's right, that's where I have been stuck for some time, years in fact. However, when I got those two words, English words; it made me think about the time when there were a group of crusaders staying here, who came from England. According to what I know, they were here for roughly three years. I also believe it was during this time that the front entry to this building was added; the part that has the design in the stonework and the skull carved in stone, with the inscription under it."

"The one that seems to translate, "This Is A Terrible Place?",
said Paul.

"Yes," said Dearborn. "I spent a lot of time examining that
part of the exterior, it was definitely added on after the
original building was erected. What the inscription refers to is
a mystery to me, other than the fact that some of those
crusaders died while they were here. Perhaps it was meant as
some sort of warning to others."

"Well, the reason that Maria and I are here, is that we think
we have solved the puzzle. We believe that it was disguised in
several different languages, some as old as the one used at the
time when Jesus was said to have lived."

"What!" spluttered Dearborn. "You know the rest of the
words......you have discovered something that makes sense?
Tell me what it is, you must tell me now. I can't believe what
you just said....tell me, tell me!"

"We think the translation is: *"BEHIND THE MIND LIES THE
CALIX OF BLOOD"*. When we discovered this phrase, it
seemed to us that hidden somewhere here, in the walls or the
floor, is an ancient cup or Chalice, if you like, an item that
was taken from a religious site during the crusades."

"What an incredible moment this is for me," said the
Captain, "vindication at last!" He repeated the phrase again
and again. "I am sure that you are right, it must mean that
there is an object, or an icon of some sort hidden here. Please
tell me exactly how you came to this conclusion....what
different languages you used to come to this result. I must
know everything!"

For the next half hour, Paul and Maria went step by step,
explaining how they had arrived at their deductions and the
various languages they had used. By the time they had
finished, Dearborn was impressed, overawed, and amazed.

"I am convinced from all this wonderful explanation, that
you have indeed solved the puzzle. It must have been a very
devious mind that could come up with such a well- crafted
disguise," he said.

"Not only that," said Paul. "but one with a remarkably wide knowledge of languages."

At this point, the Captain stood up. "I want to salute your fantastic effort," he said, shaking hands with Paul and Maria in a most formal way. "Whatever fame or recognition may come from this, I want you to know that it belongs to you."

"Thank you very much.' said Paul, "however, we haven't found anything yet! Not only that, we are all being hotly pursued by an organisation that thinks what is in this place, hidden or not, belongs to them. I, for one, am very concerned about that. As to fame, I don't want any fame....fame will bring me nothing but trouble. If we find anything at all, I'll be quite content to let those who think they have some claim to it, argue amongst themselves."

"Now, I suggest that the three of us continue to explore the walls and floor of this building, while we have the opportunity. You know that there is a crypt under the floor here somewhere, I believe," he said turning to Dearborn.

"Yes, yes I do," he replied. "Please call me Miles from now on, that's my first name. Yes, if you follow me, I'll show you where it is.....I found it just before I left here. I didn't have much of a chance to explore it at that time."

Miles Dearborn and Paul walked toward the front entrance.

"Over here," said Miles, "next to the second pillar."

With Maria holding a flashlight, Paul and Miles used the chisels to lever up a large slate from the floor and set it off to one side. Shining the light down into the opening, they could see a set of stone steps leading away into the darkness.

"You go first," said Paul, handing him the flashlight, "then me and then Maria."

"Not me," said Maria. "You two go and see what you can find, I think I'll stay up here, thank you!" She watched as the two figures descended the steps, then returned to the small room and picked up the other flashlight. She retraced her steps to the opening in the floor. "Everything alright?" she called down.

"Yes, we're fine," she heard Paul respond, then she walked on to the front of the church. "I'm sure from what Miles said, this is the most likely area where something may be hidden," she said to herself.

Starting at the bottom right-hand side of the main entry, she examined the stones one at a time.....looking for any evidence, a mark in the stone, an odd angle, a different type of stone. When she had reached up as far as she could, she crossed to the other side and started to work down until she reached the floor. She could not find anything. Walking back to the opening of the crypt, she could hear the muffled voices of Paul and Miles. She stood at the opening. "When are you coming out?" she called.

"We'll be there in a minute or two," she heard Miles reply.

The first person she saw was Paul, as he came up he was covered in cobwebs and dust.

"Yuk," he said. "When we got down there, Miles showed me around. It's not a very big area, it's been cut right out of the rock on which this whole place stands. There are two sarcophagi down there, both with the lids pulled off to one side, and broken. Each has a skeleton in it. There are two other skeletons lying against one of the walls. Miles thinks that they were probably two men who were entombed as a punishment, or perhaps they were put down there to die after they had hidden whatever is concealed here. There's not much place to hide anything there, the rock face of the walls is very smooth. I think we can cross that off the list of hiding places."

As Paul was saying this, Miles' head appeared in the opening. He stopped and crouched down. "Shine your light down my left side please," he asked. Maria obliged. "Thanks," he said. She could see him reaching in alongside one of the steps. "Aha," she heard him say. Then he stood up and came out of the hole.

"I remembered putting this here just before I left this place," he said holding a roll of cloth in his hand.

"What is it?" asked Paul.

162

Miles unwrapped the cloth, and the smell of oil greeted them. In his hand, he held a service revolver. "It might prove to be useful," he said, "it's loaded."

"My God," said Maria. "I hope we never need such a thing. You two put the slate back before someone forgets and falls down in there. Then let's stop and have a combined think about what the phrase could possibly refer to."

Maria returned to the small room, a few minutes later the two men appeared. Paul sat down on one of the benches and asked Maria to hand him a damp piece of cloth to wipe the dust out of his eyes and nose. "Thank you," he said returning the cloth to her. Maria did the same for Miles.

"If you think this place is spooky up here," said Paul, "you should have been down in the crypt, that was really horrible. I kept imagining what those two other people must have felt like, knowing that they were going to die in that awful blackness."

"Let's get back to the phrase, and forget about dead men in holes in the ground," said Maria. "Behind the mind....seems to me to be giving a clue to a location in some way. "I'm not so sure," said Paul. "It almost appears to me to be metaphoric, something that we have to think over, an idea or a concept perhaps."

He turned to Miles: "do you have any suggestions?" he asked

"I'm still marvelling over the news that you gave me this morning, to me it's like a huge boulder has been lifted off my shoulders. To have my theory proved correct is the finest feeling I've ever had. I can't wait until we are out of here and you can show me the pictures of those other languages, and how you pieced them all together. I can say though, that I feel Maria is right - the words are giving a message about a location. It is quite possible that there are other graves underneath some parts of the floor, perhaps that is where we should be looking."

"That makes sense to me too", said Maria. "Let's start at the rear of the church, divide the area into three and work our way along, until we get to the front. We can use the two chisels and the hammer to tap the stones and see if we get different sounds from any of them."

They put this idea into action, gradually tapping their way along the floor. When Maria reached the door that led to the room with the well in the floor, which happened to be in her area, she asked Paul to come and tap around that part with her.

"I want to have as much light in there as I can," she said. Paul had already visited the room to empty the bucket that they were using for a toilet. He went in first and Maria followed.

"Be very careful," he said, "there is no raised wall around the hole, though there must have been at one time."
Maria shone her flashlight down into the hole. "What a terrible way to die, falling down there," she said.

"When I emptied the bucket earlier," said Paul, "I listened, but could not hear any sound coming back up to me. It must be very deep."

"Let's just tap the floor together and get out of here!" said Maria.

In a few minutes they had covered the floor area without any sign of a likely spot to examine and returned to the main church floor. They could hear Miles tapping away on the other side, he was repeating to himself: "behind the mind; behind the mind."

It took a long time to cover the whole floor area, every ten minutes they had to stop and stretch their muscles, and massage them. Only two places seemed to give off a different sound than the rest. Each time their hopes were dashed. They had managed to lever up the stones with help of the two chisels, but there was nothing below them. Disappointed with the results of their labours, they adjourned to the small room to have some food and think some more.

While they ate, Paul brought up the subject of Father Jacques again. He related to Miles the visit that they had had in Gaillac, when Father Jacques had been followed. "I forgot to tell you that Maria saw the man who was following him when he came to visit me at the dig site."

"Yes," said Maria, "he was also wearing one of those same rings on his hand."

Miles turned to Maria; "do you think you would recognise him if you saw him again?"

"I think so," she replied. Then he turned to Paul.

"Do you think you would recognise the man called Germain, the one who chased after you in London?"

"I'm quite sure I would," said Paul, "when he was measuring my head, he was barely a foot away from me."

"I've been wondering if it's the same man each time," said Miles. "Just because he played the part of the employee at Burdett's, doesn't mean he isn't the person who runs the Order of St. George. In fact, it may be a very good cover for him - something nice and innocuous to hide behind."

"Well, although I agree it's possible, it seems to me to be stretching things a bit," said Paul. "The other thing I didn't mention, is that Father Jacques told me the last time we spoke on the telephone, that he was being followed, almost openly, by the same man who followed him on the train to Gaillac. You know," he added, "that all seems like a hundred years ago to me now, so much has happened since then. Also, Father Jacques knows that we are here in Carcassonne, through his visit to the orphanage, although I would be surprised if he tried to get in here during the day. It would not surprise me though, if we had another visitor during the night. It could be either Father Jacques, or the man who has been following him."

By now it was the late afternoon and, as Miles Dearborn had predicted, the sun was shining in through the slits in the walls on the opposite side of the building.

"It doesn't last long at this time of the year, but this is as light as it will get," he said.

"Then let's all examine that part of the wall where there is the most light. I think we can say that we've done as much as we can about searching the floor, that leaves the walls and the roof," said Maria.

For the next while, they concentrated on a detailed effort. They moved along with the shafts of sunlight but could only reach up to a certain height. Miles was reluctant to join in this exercise.

"I've studied these walls for days at a time when I lived here. There's nothing to find, I'm sure of that," he insisted.

"In that case," said Paul, "why not go and just think about the phrase. It's new to you. We've known about it for some time and had more time to think it over. You know this place better than anyone else, according to Father Jacques, perhaps you'll get an inspired idea."

Miles agreed and left them. They could here him wandering around, talking to himself, occasionally repeating the words: *'behind the mind'*.

"I hope he isn't about to *lose* his mind," Maria whispered to Paul.

With the disappearance of the sun, the interior was cast in a gloom. Paul and Maria continued on, using their flashlights but nothing of any significance was discovered. Eventually, they all returned to the small room. The two of them were somewhat dejected by the lack of any results. However, Miles was still enjoying the euphoria of finally knowing the meaning of the puzzle. "We should forget trying to find anything," he said, "until we figure out what the phrase means. Once we know that, the search will be a simple thing."

Paul and Maria concurred with this thought.

"Alright," said Maria. "Let's think, especially, let's get 'behind the mind'. With that remark, quiet descended, each of them trying to understand the phrase.

At last Maria stood up. "I'm going to make us an early supper," she said. "I can't think while my stomach is growling so noisily. What about you Paul?" she said. Paul didn't answer. She walked over to where he was sitting, she could see he was fast asleep. She shook him gently.

"I'm going to make something to eat, are you hungry?"

"Uh, oh, sorry," he said, "I must have nodded off. I was having such a nice dream too." He smiled up at her. "All about having a leisurely meal outside a cafe in Florence, with a beautiful woman."

"Well, when we get out of here, maybe we can do that together," she replied.

"I'll open that bottle of wine we brought," said Paul, "and we'll toast the success we've had, finally meeting up with Miles and returning his hat."

While they sat eating the meal, Maria asked Miles to describe, in detail, the main entryway to the church, even the most insignificant thing. 'That's the one part of this place that Paul and I haven't spent any time exploring."

"Ok," he said. "The most obvious thing about the entryway is that it was not built at the same time as the original building. Although the quality of the masonry is superb, the stones used did not come from the same quarry as the main church, the colouring is different. Also, the style is slightly different. You must remember that there is probably a difference of about three hundred years in the times of construction. The stone on which the design was cut out is very hard, it must have taken months to complete."

"Where the new entry meets the outside face of the original building, there must have been some stones removed, and new ones put in that were large enough to make a solid connection with the addition. The finest example of this work is the large stone from which the skull has been fashioned. that stone is called the keystone. It's the most important one of all. The doorway into the church is supported by it."

"Did you say 'keystone'?" said Maria.

"Yes," said Miles, "it is a beautiful piece of workmanship."

Maria jumped up. "Keystone, keystone," she repeated. "I think I may have a clue to our puzzle! Let me tell you about a conversation I had with our friend Yves, in Toulouse, just before we came here. Yves is a retired structural engineer, he was describing to me a way of building using a thing he called a 'double keystone'. Have you ever heard of it?"

167

"No," said Miles. "What is it?"

"Well, the way he described it to me, and I wish I had listened much more closely, is something *like* this. It is a way of building which allows a *'keystone'* to give the appearance of being integral to a structure, when in fact, it is not bearing any weight at all. A *'double keystone'* he called it. He also said that it took great masonry skill to accomplish."

Miles looked at Maria in complete astonishment, then he turned to Paul. "Did you know about this?" he asked.

"I remember hearing a bit of the conversation," said Paul, "but I was out of the room for much of it."

"This lady is quite the most amazing person I have ever met!" said Miles.

"Yes, isn't she," agreed Paul.

Miles asked Maria to repeat everything she could remember about the discussion with Yves. When she had finished, he stood up.

"Brilliant..... amazing.....wonderful," he said. "Now we have a place to look."

"Do you mean we should go outside and start dismantling the front entry?" said Paul. "I don't think that's much of an idea."

"No, no," said Miles. "We will examine the location where the back of the keystone would be, inside the building. Bring the chisels and the hammer. I'll get one of the ladders and bring it along."

At the front of the church where the main entry was, Miles put up the ladder at the mid- point of the archway. "Let me have one of the flashlights," he said, then climbed up.

"Can you see anything?" asked Paul.

"Give me time, give me time," said Miles. After a few minutes he came back down. "There's nothing obvious to me," he said. "You go and take a look."

Paul took the light from Miles and climbed the ladder.

"Remember what I told you about the fact that one or two stones that cover up the double keystone may look just like the others but they are actually quite shallow," Maria called after him.

"Yes, I remember," said Paul. After a few minutes, he came back down. "I agree with Miles," he said, reluctantly; "there is nothing obvious. So, what do we do now?"

"We pick the most likely stone and start chiselling away," said Maria. "You didn't expect it would be obvious, or easy, did you?"

Miles and Paul looked at each other, they both shrugged their shoulders.

"Ok, Maria, you go up the ladder," said Paul, "and you tell us which is the one we should work on."

"Very well, I will", she replied. "You two hold the flashlights on the area. I need both hands on the ladder. Before I go up," she said, turning to Miles, "can you tell me how high above the centre of the entry the keystone is, on the outside?"

Miles thought for a minute. "About two feet above, is where it starts," he answered.

"Right," said Maria in a firm voice, and started to climb. When she reached the area, she examined the stonework in front of her. She had to agree that there were no clues that would identify a false front. Eventually, she narrowed it down to the two most likely ones, both were roughly two feet above the inside of the entryway. "This one," she said to Paul. "Can you see the one I'm touching?"

"Ok," said Paul, 'I see it. Come on down."

"Let's do this in shifts," said Miles. "I'll go first, work away at it for ten minutes, then you come and replace me, fair enough?"

"Fine with me," replied Paul.

CHAPTER .10.

Miles took the hammer and one of the chisels, climbed up the ladder and began chipping away at the edges of the stone. At first he made little impression, but at the end of ten minutes he had a distinct crevice between the stone and its immediate neighbour. When he came down, he told Paul to try cutting away at the edge of the adjacent stone, as that would allow them to get some leverage on the one they were trying to remove.

"If Maria is right and this one is shallow, we should be able to wriggle it out of there once we have chiselled all the way around," he said.

Paul understood what Miles was getting at and took the hammer from him. Once he got in position on the ladder, he could see where Miles had been working. He started in at the same place. Before long his arms were aching and he had hit his knuckles several times but he persevered, only returning to the ground when his time was up. Handing the hammer to Miles, he sat down. "That was tough work," he said to Maria. "Would you mind giving my shoulders a massage, they're very sore."

She did what she could for him. "I usually get this done for me by a professional when I'm at home," she said. "Every couple of weeks, I go and get myself completely pampered, from top to bottom. I wish I was going there in the morning," she sighed. "Are you making much progress on the stone?" she asked

"Yes, I think so. We've cleared one side and just started across the top. I sure hope you picked the right one."

"We'll know as soon as you two have cut all the way 'round," said Maria. "If it is a false front, the stone will not be set very deep, just enough to hide the second keystone."

Miles came down the ladder and handed the hammer to Paul. "Your turn I believe," he said. Maria offered to give Miles the same massage treatment that she done for Paul.

"I'd be very grateful", he said, looking down at the bruising on his hands from the occasional miss with the hammer. "This is going to go on for a few more times yet. It will be a question of *mind over matter*!", he chuckled. The two men continued to trade places for the next while.

When Paul returned to the floor after one of his stints the three of them decided to take a break for half an hour to rest.

"It's hard on the legs as well as the arms," commented Miles.

"Amen to that," said Paul.

Returning to the small room, they sat and finished off the last of the coffee which, by now, was barely luke-warm.

"What time is it?' Miles asked Paul, "I don't have a watch."

Paul checked. 'It's a bit before ten o'clock," he replied. "Does anyone know how long it has taken us to get as far as we have on the stone?"

"About two hours," said Maria. "How much more is there to chisel away before you might be able to move it?"

"I think we're more than half way around it, at this point," said Paul. "Another hour and we should be able to tell if we're on the right track."

"My neck is killing me from staring up at the two of you," said Maria. "I'm going to stay here and rest for a while. You both keep going and I'll make up a meal for us from what we have left. It won't be much, we're at the tail end of what we brought."

Miles and Paul got up and made their way back to the ladder. "After you," said Paul, passing him the hammer.

Holding the flashlight on the area, Paul could tell that the batteries were getting weak.

"Hang on up there while I get some new batteries in this thing," he called up. Returning to the room, Paul looked over at Maria sitting on one of the benches. She was fast asleep.

As quietly as he could he felt around in the rucksack and pulled out two new batteries and replaced the old ones in the flashlight. Then he returned to the bottom of the ladder. He was surprised to find Miles standing on the ground. He shone the flashlight on his face. Miles was laughing to himself.

"What's so funny?", asked Paul.

"It came to me while I was standing up there in the dark," said Miles. When Maria was massaging my shoulders, I told her that we would just have to practise *mind over matter*, and ignore the aches and pains of what we are doing."

"So?" said Paul.

"*Mind over matter......behind the mind*;" Miles repeated, "that's what the phrase said. Well, at the other side of this stone, we hope, is the keystone - on the front of which is carved a skull. I think that's what the phrase 'behind the mind' is referring to....'behind the mind' is 'behind the skull'!"

"That," said Paul "is a flash of genius! Why didn't we think of that before? Of course, it makes perfect sense. Behind the mind - at the back of the head, or skull in this instance, is the *mind*."

"Let's go and tell Maria! said Miles.

"No, not now, she's sleeping," said Paul. "Let's get on with the chiselling and call her when we have found that the stone we're working on is the right one - if it *is* the right one."

Miles agreed and climbed back up. Paul shone the light on the area and Miles chiselled away with a vengeance. For the next hour, they traded places as soon as one of them needed a rest.

At last, Paul, who was up the ladder at the time, called down to Miles. "I've just removed the last of the obstacles," he said. "I'll come down for the other chisel and see if I can wedge the two of them in at different points. Then I'll hammer on the side of the chisels and see if anything moves."

172

Once he got the chisels firmly wedged in place, he started to hit them on their sides - first one, then the other. By the sixth or seventh hit he saw the stone move! "This is it!" he called down to Miles. "I've managed to get the stone to move, it must be shallow or I never could have moved it at all!" Putting the hammer in his belt he wiggled and jiggled the stone, using the two chisels. Gradually, it came away from the wall, toward him. He stopped and put the two chisels in his jacket pockets. Then he got his hands around each side of the stone and pulled it out. Very gingerly, he lowered himself down the ladder, carrying the stone. As soon as he could reach it, Miles took the stone out of Paul's hands.

"Well done!" he said, patting Paul on the back. "Well done indeed! Let's go and wake up Maria - she would not want to miss this moment!"

Paul shook Maria gently. "Wake up," he said. "Wake up! Have we got a surprise for you!"

Maria looked up at the two of them. "It was the right stone then," she said. "I can tell by the look on your faces that something good has happened."

"Yes, yes," they both said. "Come and see, come and see!"

When they reached the foot of the ladder, Paul shone the light up to where they had been working.

"See the hole?" he said.

"Yes, I can see it," said Maria. "Now, where is the stone you took out of there?" Paul turned the light down to the floor, onto the stone. Maria bent down and examined it. Though it was quite big, it was also very shallow, Maria could see and feel where the stone had been reduced to its present depth.

"I feel you should be the first one to go up the ladder and look inside the hole," said Miles, "after all, if it wasn't for you, we wouldn't be at this marvellous moment." Maria looked over at Paul, as if to confirm that this was alright with him. He smiled back at her and nodded. Taking a flashlight with her, Maria climbed up the ladder - she shone the light into the gap.

"I think I can see the back of the Keystone," she said, "but you will have to remove the stone next to the hole on the right.

It should be easier to do that, now that you can get in behind it. Then, I think you will be able to see nearly all of the keystone."

She put her hand inside the hole and felt around, there was nothing there but dust.

Miles took his turn up the ladder, after retrieving his chisel and the hammer from Paul. When he started work, he realized that Maria was right, he could get a lot more done now - partly because he could see what he had to remove, and partly because he could get more leverage.

When they traded places and Paul continued the work, Miles told Maria about his brainwave concerning the meaning of the phrase *"behind the mind"*. Now, with the removal of this first stone, both he and she agreed that his explanation seemed right.

"Congratulations," she said. "Now, if you will keep the flashlight trained on the spot where Paul is working, I'll go back and put together the meal that I talked about earlier."

"Sure I will," said Miles, "we'll come and get you as soon as we've removed the second stone."

Back in the small room, Maria did her best to put some food together. It wasn't much, and what was worse, they had nothing hot to drink, nor any wine left. "I can't remember the last time I ate anything and had to drink cold water afterwards," she thought. "Whether we discover anything or not, I hope that we can leave here sometime during the night and get back to a nice warm hotel room somewhere. I hope the car is still where we left it!"

She sat quietly when she was done, waiting for the men to call her. In the distance, she could here the tap, tap of the hammer. Surprisingly, it had not been very noisy as they had chipped away at the stones. When they had first begun the removal of the them, they were all concerned that someone outside would hear the noise - so far, that seemed not to be the case.

Her mind wandered ahead and she thought about her future. Like Paul, she did not want to be in the limelight, if they discovered anything. She was very happy in her work back at the university. There was no doubt that living alone was not always the best way, but there were compensations and, in any event, she had not found anyone who interested her - "anyone, until recently that is," she thought. Her enjoyment of Paul's company was undeniable, he was a most perfect companion - intelligent, thoughtful, kind. She listed off the virtues that he had demonstrated to her since they had met - it turned out to be quite a long list!

While she was musing this way, she heard them calling her. When she arrived at the foot of the ladder, Miles was handing down the second stone to Paul. After Paul had put it down, he handed the flashlight up to Miles.

"Tell us what you can see now," they asked. Miles climbed back up and shone the light into the hole. "Here's what I can make out," he said. "I can see almost all of the back of the big keystone, and I can also see what looks like a smaller one set into it."

"Aha!" said Maria, 'the *double keystone*. I knew it! I just knew it!"

"Also," said Miles, "there are three holes that seem to be cut into the smaller stone, two at the top and one other directly below. I'll come down and one of you can take a look."

"Let me go next, please," Maria said to Paul.

"Sure, go ahead," he replied.

Maria took the flashlight from Miles. "Boy, oh boy," she was saying, "the person who deserves the most credit in all of this, is Yves. If it hadn't been for him, we would never have thought to look for anything hidden in this manner!"

"I hope I get the opportunity to meet this chap," Miles said to Paul.

"We'll arrange it as soon as we can. He will be tremendously pleased to think that he has been instrumental in assisting us to uncover something."

Paul looked up to where Maria was standing.

"It looks just like Yves explained to me," she said. "I've been trying to get my two middle fingers and my thumb into the holes, but my hand is not big enough. Who has the biggest hands?" she called down to them. "If I'm right, there should not be any pressure bearing down on this smaller stone, nor anything holding it there from the sides. One of you should be able to pull it toward you, once you get your fingers in the holes.

Miles and Paul shone the light on their hands. "It looks like you," said Paul to Miles. "It's Miles," he called up, "come down and let him try to pull it out."

When Maria arrived on the floor, her face was just beaming. "It's just like Yves said," she told them, "exactly as he described it!"

Miles took the flashlight and climbed up to the hole once more. With his right hand holding the light, he placed the two middle fingers of his left hand into the upper holes and his left thumb in the lower one. "They fit comfortably enough....I guess she's right about the purpose of the holes," he said to himself. Setting his feet as steadily as he could on the ladder, he tried to pull the stone toward him. It turned out to be easy - there was no weight being borne by the stone at all!

He called down to the others. "It's moving easily, I'll have it out in a moment." Once the stone was out of it's place, Miles set it to one side. "I'm going to shine the light in the hole now," he called to them. "I can see something there!" He reached into the space where the stone had been and grasped an object.

"I've got something!" he yelled. "I'm coming down."

Paul and Maria stared at one another, knowing that the highlight of their interest and study of archeology, was about to be revealed!

"Here it is," said Miles as he reached the floor. In his hands he held a Chalice, it was covered in dust, but plainly visible.

"Let's take it to the small room and wash it off with some water," said Paul. Back in the room, Paul dampened a cloth they had been using to wash their faces. Once the cup was cleaned and dried, it shone beautifully in the light of their candles. It was certainly made of gold. Around the top edge, there was an embossed design. Maria asked to look at it and held it closely.

"In this light and without my reference books, I can't be sure, but I would bet that this design is more than just a design. I think, when translated, it will turn out to say, "drink this, this is my blood".

For a few minutes, all three of them were lost in thought about what they had found. They set the Chalice on the floor and stared at it, in the stillness that surrounded them. Paul looked at his watch - it was almost one-thirty in the morning. He was about to say, "let's pack up and get of here," when he heard a noise. It seemed to be coming from the outside of the building.

"Did you hear that?" he whispered.

"Yes, I heard something," replied Miles, quietly. All three of them listened intently, they could hear a scraping sound.

"We are about to get another visitor," muttered Paul, "and this time it probably won't be a friendly one!"

He and Miles walked out into the main area. Here, they could tell that the sound was coming from the outside, close to the place where they had gained entry.

"It sounds like someone is putting up a ladder," whispered Miles. "Shine your light on the floor where your warning device is." Paul did so, it had not moved.

"It won't be long before it does move," he said.

Miles turned to look at Paul. "Turn off your light, and leave it off, I'm going to do a disappearing act. Whoever's coming in - you haven't seen me, and you haven't found anything. Ok?"

"Yes, uh, Ok," replied Paul.

Miles ran back into the room, he quickly told Maria what he had said to Paul. Then he picked up the Chalice, stuck the service revolver in his belt and slipped away toward the front of the church into the darkness!

Paul stood and listened as his warning device started to move, then he grabbed the ladder that was still there by the window and took it down, laying it on the floor. "Blow out the candles," he said to Maria.

Then, the two of them stood in the doorway of the room, watching the space where they knew the window was. The scraping noise had stopped. Then they heard the sound of the boards being pulled away. Finally a figure appeared in the moonlight. They heard a click, and a very bright light illuminated the inside of the church. As the light shone down onto the floor, they could see a hand on the windowsill, in it was a pistol! At last, a man's voice spoke.

"I know you're in here," it said in a menacing tone, "come out where I can see you." Paul and Maria did not move.

"Don't be foolish," said the voice. "You can't stay in here forever, but I can stay outside and wait 'til you try to leave."
Paul looked at Maria. "He's right, of course," he murmured. Then taking her by the hand, they walked out of the doorway and into the bright light.

"That's more like it," said the voice. "Is that all of you?"

"Yes," said Paul, "just the two of us."

"Put that ladder up against the wall, here," the intruder ordered, "and step back twenty paces. Don't try anything foolish - I'm an expert shot!"

Paul did as he was instructed, then he and Maria moved away from the wall.

As the figure moved to climb down the ladder, they could see that he was wearing a hard hat, and the bright light was coming from there.

"He must be wearing a miners' hat," Paul exclaimed.

When the man reached the floor, he pointed the pistol toward the doorway to the small room. "In there," he ordered. When they were inside, the man told Paul to light the candles that were standing on the planks. Then he switched off his light.

For a moment, Paul and Maria were blinded.
"Sit over there," said the man pointing at one of the benches.

"Who are you, and what do you want with us?" said Paul.

178

"Shut up," replied the man. "I'll ask the questions and you had better have the right answers. First of all, this is private property. You are trespassing, now tell me why you are in this place. The truth !"

Paul looked at the face of the man.

"I know you," he said. You're Germain, the man who chased after me in London a few weeks ago. I'd recognise you anywhere, even with the moustache you now have."

Then Maria spoke. "I know you too," she said. "You are the person who came to Gaillac, to the house where I was staying, asking questions about the broken sword.....the one we found at the archeological dig. You have a ring on your finger with a red cross on it, too."

"So what," he replied. "Answer my question! What are you doing here, and what have you found?'

"As to why we are here," said Paul, "we're amateur archeologists and this is a very interesting place. We came to explore the inside, to see what was here. You can say that we're trespassing and that s true, but it is also true that this place has been abandoned for many years. Our interest in coming here, is our interest in the history of such a building as this."

The man moved closer to them, waving his pistol in a threatening manner.

"You came here to steal," he said. "Now, tell me what you've found!"

"We found a crypt," said Paul, "and we explored it, we found four skeletons - that's all. I'll show you where it is, if you want to see it."

"Alright," said the man, ' show me."

Paul and Maria led the way to the location of the crypt. When they reached the spot, Paul pointed to the slate in the floor. "It's under here," he said.

"Lift it out of the way," said the man.

"You'll have to help me." said Paul, "it's too heavy for one person."

"You," he said to Maria. "You help him."

Paul and Maria got down on their knees and tried to lift up the slate.

"I need the chisel that I brought," said Paul. "I need something to help me get some leverage."

"Stay here," said the man to Maria. "Don't move."

Then he followed Paul back to the room where Paul picked up a chisel and the hammer.

"Take one of your flashlights too," said the man.

Maria had stood still in their absence.

Getting down on the their knees again, Paul jammed the chisel in between the slate and its adjacent stone, and began to lever it up slightly. He managed to wedge the hammer under the gap and then, he and Maria together, were able to push it to one side - enough that the steps were visible.

"Now," said the man, "you two are going down those steps. I'll follow you, so don't try anything stupid." Paul went first, with Maria. "I'm scared," she whispered, holding onto the back of his jacket.

"Shut up!" said Germain, "I won't tell you again."

When the two of them reached the bottom of the steps, Paul looked back up at Germain.

"Walk as far as you can from the steps!" he called down to them. Paul and Maria did as they were told.

"Sit down," he ordered.

They sat down. Maria could see the two skeletons, she shivered and held Paul's' arm tightly. Then they saw the light from Germain move away and heard the slate being pushed back into place. Paul yelled out, "Stop!" He ran across the floor and up the stairs. Just as he got there, the slate was almost back in place. He got his fingers over the edge of the slate and tried to push it back the other way, but he could get no purchase.

"You two are as good as dead," said Germain. With that he gave one last heave, catching Paul's finger ends in the narrowing gap.

"You bastard!" shouted Paul trying to nurse his right-hand fingers. They were squashed and bleeding.

Maria, who was right behind Paul said; "come down where I can be some help." Paul staggered back down into the crypt.

"Sit here," said Maria, pointing to one of the sarcophagi. She eased Paul's jacket off and tore off one of the sleeves of his shirt. With this she wrapped the worst of his hands. The left one was not as severely squashed.

"I must have got that one out of the way first," he commented. The other hurts like hell."

"I know, I know," said Maria. "What a maniac that Germain is, he's left us here to die. Oh God!" she cried. "Do you think we could push off that slate?" she asked.

Paul shook his head. "Not a chance. Our only hope now, is that Dearborn comes to our rescue, and quickly. I don't know how much air there is in here."

Meanwhile, Germain had returned to the room and was searching through their baggage. Maria's bag was open, so, he simply turned it upside down and checked everything that fell out. Then he turned his attention to Paul's rucksack. In order to open the side pockets, he had to put down his pistol so that he could use both hands to undo the straps.

At that moment, Miles Dearborn pushed the barrel of his revolver into Germain's back.

"Stop right there," he ordered. "Stand up and don't turn around." Germain stood up.

"I'm holding a revolver against you, and it's loaded. I won't hesitate to use it, if you give me half a chance. Now, back out of this room slowly. You and I are going on a short journey."

Once they were out in the main area of the church, Dearborn worked his way over toward the room where the well was located. Finally, he had Germain facing the door to the room, which was partly open. He nudged him forward until he was just a yard from the door.

"Now, take off your hat with the light still on and put it down, facing away from the door." Germain did as he was told. "You're going to be locked in this room until I get the police, so make yourself comfortable." Dearborn pushed Germain in the back again.

"Get going!" he ordered forcefully. Germain walked to the doorway and pushed the door open some more.

"In you go!" said Dearborn, giving him a solid push in the back. As soon as Germain entered the room, Dearborn pulled the door shut tight.

In less than a minute, he heard the sound he expected, a muffled scream of horror, followed by complete silence.

"Well, well," he said to himself, "pardon the pun - no surprise there!"

Picking up the hat with the light in it, he placed it on his head, it was not a good fit, coming down over his forehead.

"My, he had a big head!" he said to himself.

Then he moved over to the entrance to the crypt. He tried calling down to Paul and Maria, but could hear no response. The chisel and hammer were lying on the floor next to the slate. He wedged the chisel back into the edge of the slate and began again to try and lever it up.

With just his own strength, it moved only a little.

"You'll have to help from below," he yelled through the crack.

Again, he tried to lever the slate up. This time it moved a little more easily, enough for him to jam the hammer in the gap.

"Can you hear me?" he yelled into the small opening.

"Yes, I can hear you," said Paul's' voice. "I've got my shoulders under the slate and I'm trying to push upwards. Try and help from the end where the steps are lowest, that's the best place for me to push from."

Relieved, Dearborn moved to the end of the slate, and with the help of Paul pushing from below, he managed to get it moved up and over enough for the two of them to wriggle out.

"Oh, how good it is to be out of there," gasped Maria. "I'm never, *ever*, going underground like that again."

Dearborn grabbed Paul's hand to shake it.

"Ouch!" yelled Paul, "don't do that."

"Sorry," said Miles. "I didn't know you were hurt."

"That swine Germain was going to let us die down there," said Paul. "Where is he! What have you done with him?"

"I'm afraid he's gone down to the bottom of the well," said Miles. "Such an inquisitive chap."

"How ever did you manage to do that?" asked Maria "You didn't shoot him did you?"

"No," said Miles, "but I was quite prepared to."

Then he told them what had transpired while they were stuck in the crypt.

"What a terrible way to die," said Maria.

"No worse than dying down there in the crypt," said Paul, better in some ways, quicker anyway. Now, let's get out of this place before we have any more visitors. I've had just about all I can take, and my hands hurt like hell!"

Miles and Maria pushed the slate back over the crypt, with the help of Paul using his feet. Then they returned to the small room and Maria packed up their things, while Paul sat on one of the benches.

"Sorry I can't be much help," he said.

Maria picked up the pistol belonging to Germain.

"Here," she said to Miles. "you take it."

"I'll throw it down the well, best place for it really," he said.

"Where is the Chalice?" asked Paul.

"It's in the same room as the recently departed Germain," Miles replied. "I went in there when our friend was getting through the window. If worse came to worst, I was going to throw it down the well."

By the time Miles returned, Maria had everything ready to leave.

"Here," he said. "Put the Chalice in one of the side pockets of the rucksack, that seems most appropriate, seeing as that's how I caught Germain without his gun."

"What time is it now?" he asked Paul.

Looking at his watch, Paul said, "it's just after half past two. As good a time as any to go. There won't be anyone about at this hour, I shouldn't think."

Miles carried the bags over to the ladder. "I'll go first and take the bags with me, then I'll give Maria a hand over the tricky part. When she is safely on the ground, I'll come back and give you some help," he said to Paul. "You're going to have a bit of trouble with only one good hand, and not that good either."

Miles switched off the miners' lamp, and made his way out of the window and down the ladder conveniently left by Germain. Putting the bags to one side, he then returned to give Maria a hand getting over the window sill and onto the outside ladder. When she finally stood on the ground, she hugged Miles as hard as she could. "Thanks for saving our lives," she said.

In return, Miles replied: "I will never be able to thank you enough for all that you have done for me, so let's leave it at that, Ok?" Then he climbed back up to help Paul. With a few scrapes and a lot more 'ouch's', he managed to get Paul's legs onto the outside ladder. Then Maria steadied him down the last few rungs, to the ground.

"I'm going to push the boards back and put the latch on again," said Miles. "Then I'll take this ladder and hide it in the undergrowth. In a few weeks it will be covered over."

"That's better," he said when he had finished. "No need to advertise that there's been anyone here."

They walked quietly around to the front of the building in single file. Miles climbed over the railing first and Maria handed him the bags. Then he helped her over in much the same way as Paul had done. The two of them assisted Paul up and over, and at last they were standing in the square.

"What now?" Maria asked

"Let's go and see if the car is still in the parking lot," said Paul. "If it is, then we can make a plan. There aren't too many places open at this hour of the night. Once we find the car, we can get back to the hotel we were at the other day, chances are it is open all night."

"I'll come with you and bring the bags as far as your car," offered Miles, "then I have a plan of my own."

184

They set off across the square. Every few steps, Miles looked back at the abandoned church. "Who would have thought it possible," he said, to nobody in particular.

To their great relief, Yves' old car was sitting alone in the parking lot. On the windshield were two parking fine notices. Paul pulled them off with his good hand, and stuffed them in his jacket pocket. He gave the keys to Maria, who opened the trunk and Miles put their bags inside.

"I'll give you this miners' hat too, if you don't mind," he said. "I prefer the one you so kindly returned to me"; pulling it out from the inside of his jacket. "It's a much better fit."

"Are you coming with us?" asked Maria.

"No," replied Miles. "I'm going back to my cot in the garden shed. I've got some serious thinking to do about where I go from here."

"Well then," said Paul, "we re off to the hotel I mentioned, but we'll be back at the orphanage tomorrow - I mean today, at around three in the afternoon. See you then."

Maria unlocked the passenger door and helped Paul get settled. Then, she started the car and drove out of the lot, in the direction of the hotel.

"Do you remember the way?" Paul asked.

"Yes, I think so," said Maria.

"Good," he replied, "because I'm going to sleep!"

When Maria drove into the hotel parking area, she could see the vacancy sign shining over the entrance.

"Thank goodness," she said. She parked the car, and then gently shook Paul to wake him. "We're here. I'll come around and help you out of your seat." With Maria's help, Paul got out of the car. "I'll send for someone to bring the bags inside," she said.

At the front desk, Maria asked for two rooms, adjacent to each other, if possible. The desk clerk looked suspiciously at them.

"*You* will have to pay *in advance*," he said.

Paul and Maria looked at each other. "Why, what's the matter with us?" said Paul.

"Perhaps you would care to look in the mirror behind you," said the clerk. The two of them turned around and looked at the full length mirror in the foyer. Then they burst out laughing. Their clothes were covered with cobwebs and dust, in short, they were a mess.

"I know what," said Paul. "Reach inside my jacket pocket, the one on the left. I think you'll find our room key from the other day in there." Maria did as he asked. "Give it to the man," said Paul. "If we could stay here a few days ago, we ought to be able to stay here now." Maria put the room key on the desk, along with her credit card.

"Obviously, we don't always look like *this*," she said raising her voice. "If you check, you'll find we were here just a few days ago. We need a bath. Right *now*! My friend has been hurt and he needs a physician. Please, give me the room keys and send someone out to get our bags from our car – it's the old Citroen in the parking lot. Here are the car keys, the bags are in the trunk. Please, have them brought to our rooms *right away*. You can keep the credit card until the morning!" Maria's voice had been getting progressively louder.

The desk clerk hesitated a moment, and then relented, handing her new room keys. "I'll bring your bags in myself," he said.

Paul and Maria made their way to the rooms they had been given. She helped him take off his jacket and shoes, and was in the process of removing his torn shirt, when the clerk arrived with the bags.

"Just leave them there by the bed, thank you," said Maria.

"I can't get a doctor for you until the morning," said the clerk. "Unless you want to drive into Carcassonne...there's a hospital there."

"That's fine," said Paul. "In the morning will be fine, thank you." With that the clerk left them.

Paul turned to Maria. "I think I can manage to undress the rest of me. You carry on to your own room, and thanks again for all your help."

Maria kissed him on the forehead. "I'll leave a message with the clerk to have a doctor come to see you in the morning, around nine o'clock," she said. "Good night now." She picked up her bag and left the room.

Paul walked into the bathroom and turned on the shower. After he had struggled out of the rest of his clothes, he stepped under the stream of hot water and stood there, gradually easing the torn shirt sleeve off his injured hand. Eventually, he got out of the shower and dried himself as best he could. Then he wrapped his hand in one of the face cloths and got into bed. Within a minute, he was fast asleep.

In the room next to his, Maria stripped off all her clothes, got into the hottest bath she could stand and gradually relaxed. "What an incredible day" she sighed, "all the way from a horrible dungeon to a *lovely hot bath*."

Half an hour later, she was also in bed, asleep.

CHAPTER .11.

At a few minutes before nine in the morning there was a knock on Paul's door. "Come in," he said, trying to sit up. The door was unlocked with a pass key and the clerk came in. "This is Doctor Maissoneuve," he said, indicating the lady who had followed him.

"I understand you have hurt your hand," said the doctor. "Please, let me look at it." Paul held out his injured hand. The doctor gently removed the face cloth. "Um," she said, "that's quite a mess. I'll clean it up for you and put a proper bandage on it. You won't be able to use it for a few days. It doesn't look like anything is broken, but the only way to be sure is to have it x-rayed."

Paul nodded. Then he showed her his other hand.

"This one is not too bad," said the doctor. "I'll do the same to this hand, but I'll do each finger separately, that way you will be more mobile." With that, the doctor proceeded to take care of Paul's hands. When she had finished, she stood up. "That's about all I can do for now," she said. "I advise you to get an x-ray in the next day or so. I'll leave my bill with the hotel desk. I'm on a retainer here, so they will look after it."

Paul thanked her for her help. After she had left, he got up and managed to make himself somewhat presentable. He felt absolutely ravenous. "I need some breakfast," he said to himself, "I'll knock on Maria's door and see if she is up yet."

Before he left his room, he checked the side pocket of his rucksack - he could feel the Chalice through the material. "That's good," he said. He left the room, making sure that the door was securely locked and walked along to the next door.

He knocked. There was no reply. A chambermaid came out from a room across the hall.

"The lady is not in," she said. "I spoke to her earlier and she said she was going to the restaurant for breakfast."

Arriving at the entrance to the restaurant, Paul could see Maria sitting there, looking out of the window. "May I join you?" he asked.

Maria smiled up at him. "Please do," she said.

"You look great,' said Paul.

"You look much better this morning, than you did when we first came in here," she replied. "How are your hands? I see you've been attended to."

Paul briefly told her what the doctor had said. A waitress brought welcome, hot coffee and took his order. Paul took a sip and sat back to savour it...."Sure beats where we've been for the last two days," he said.

Maria visibly shuddered. "I still can't forget that man Germain. He was definitely going to leave us to die in that terrible hole."

"I've thought about that too," said Paul. "If it hadn't been for Dearborn, we would never have got out of there. That brings me to something I have been thinking about. I want to give the Chalice to him, to do with whatever he wants. How do you feel about that?"

"Perfectly fine with me," replied Maria. Without a doubt, he saved our lives. He can have anything he wants as far as I'm concerned, perhaps he has something in mind. He said he was going to do some serious thinking when we left him last night."

We should also call Yves," she added, "he will want to know what has happened to us. I can't wait to see his face when we tell him about the double keystone hiding place!"

"Let's do that as soon as we've finished here," said Paul.

After they had eaten, he put through a call to Yves. He was thrilled with the news - "I want a blow-by-blow description of everything as soon as you are back here!" he said.

Paul asked if he could keep the car for one more day, if they needed it.

"Go ahead," Yves had said, "that's no problem."

When Paul got off the phone, he and Maria went back to their rooms and prepared to leave. She came into Paul's room with him. "I'll help you pack," she said, "and also, I want to look at the Chalice again - to see it in daylight." Taking it out of the side pocket, she held it up to see if there was any mark on the base - some way to identify where it came from, or who made it. She could see nothing. They both examined the embossed area around the top edge. Neither of them could make out anything from the design.

"I think I've had enough of deciphering designs," Paul said. "I'll leave that up to some other experts."

"It is very beautifully made, and so delicate," said Maria. "Someone or some group will undoubtedly claim it, if it is brought into public view."

When they had finished packing, Maria paid their hotel bill, retrieving her credit card in the process. The hotel staff loaded the car again and they set out for Carcassonne. Maria had wrapped the Chalice and placed it in her purse. "You had better not try to hold this with your hands, the way they are," she said to Paul, "you might drop it."

She drove back to Carcassonne in a leisurely manner - they had plenty of time before they met up with Miles Dearborn.

When they reached the outskirts of the town, Paul said, "I think we should park somewhere else this time. I don't know how many parking tickets you can accumulate before someone comes and tows you away." So, they found a side street some distance from the gate into the old town.

"I'll enjoy the walk," said Paul, as they got out of the car.

Passing through the old archway into the town, Maria reminded Paul that they may well run into Father Jacques at the orphanage.

"What are you going to say to him?" she said. "He knows that we have been here for a few days now."

"I don't know," replied Paul. "I suppose I will just wait and see what he says, and keep quiet until we've spoken to Miles."

When they reached the entrance to the orphanage, Maria knocked on the door. It was opened by none other than Miles.

"Come in, come in," he said. "There's a bit of activity going on here. It seems our late acquaintance, Germain, was here in the early evening yesterday. He must have been following Father Jacques. Apparently, he broke in not long after Father Jacques left. He forced poor old Sister Agatha to tell him what Father Jacques had been talking about, when he was here. He scared her badly, threatened her and then left. It seems she had a stroke or something during the night, so Sister Frances called the doctor. He gave her an injection to calm her. He left just before you arrived. Sister Frances came out to the garden shed, and asked me to come in and help them. I was even feeling badly for that swine Germain, but not any more - no sir!"

"Is there anything we can do to help?" offered Paul.

"No, I don't think so," said Miles. "The Sisters are looking after her, they know how to tend to her needs. I'll just tell Sister Frances you're here and then we can go out into the garden, if you like. It's probably easier to have any conversation out there."

Miles showed them to a door that led out to the back garden, and soon came out to join them.

"Maria and I have talked about the Chalice this morning," said Paul. "We are in agreement that you should have it, and do what you want with it."

"That's funny," said Miles. "I was going to suggest that you two keep it!"

"Oh no!" the two of them said in unison. "Not us."

"We have no right to it," said Paul. "It should really be returned to whomever it once belonged. I suppose the Order of St. George thinks it belongs to them, though I'm not sure they even know what was hidden in the church. It could be said that it belongs to the government here, in France. It could also be said to belong to some religious group. That's already too many for me! You could give it to Father Jacques. Remember what you told us about him, perhaps wanting to be re-ordained or whatever the procedure is."

The three of them went 'round and 'round the conundrum for several minutes, each trying to find the best solution.

"I've just had a brainwave," said Paul. "You remember me telling you about my friend in Toulouse?"

"Yes," replied Miles, "you mean Yves?"

"Yes," said Paul. "His son is a television news producer. Why don't we get in touch with him and see if we can get him to do a news story on the Chalice? At the same time, maybe we could get Father Jacques to be at the television station to explain the significance of the Chalice. After all, he is recognised as an authority on the subject of medieval religious history."

"That sound like a perfect solution," said Miles, "but I don't want any news hound chasing after me."

"We don't either," said Maria, looking at Paul for his agreement.

Paul nodded his head. "Leave that to me," he said. "Maria and I will go from here, straight to Toulouse and see if we can set it up. I'll call you later this evening and tell you if it's a go or not. I have a good feeling about this though, I think it's going to work. Give me the telephone number here and wait for my call."

They went back into the house, and Miles gave them the number. Sister Frances greeted them. "Hello again," she said. "I'm sorry that you find us in such a turmoil. Whatever have you done to your hands?" she asked, looking at Paul.

"Oh, it's a long story," he replied, and not one for retelling at the moment, you have enough to cope with."

"How is Sister Agatha?" asked Maria.

"I'm afraid she is not doing well, I don't think she will recover from this," said the Sister. "We'll make sure she is not in any pain and pray for her."

Miles showed them to the front door.

"If you see Father Jacques," said Paul, "don't say anything about us. Just our regrets that we didn't manage to see him this time."

"Right you are," replied Miles.

Paul and Maria made their way back to the car. "We should find a public telephone," he said. "I want to call Yves again and warn him that we will be returning this evening. I'll also ask him to call his son to see if he can meet us at his home, tonight, if possible."

As they left the gateway for the last time and walked across the parking lot, they could see a parking attendant placing a ticket under the windshield of another unfortunate car owner. Paul walked over to him. "I wonder if you can tell me where the nearest public phone is?" he asked. The attendant gave him directions to one close by. "Thank you," said Paul, thinking to himself about his own unpaid parking tickets.

When Paul got through to Yves, he told them that they would be arriving that evening. He asked Yves to get in touch with his son, Jean, and have him come to the house.

"I can't tell you why, at this point," Paul said, "but please try to get him there."

There was nothing left to do, except get on the road. Maria drove as fast as she could, though the traffic was heavy once they got on the main road to Toulouse. On the way, they talked about the idea that Paul had thought up, they could see no big flaws in it. It just depended on whether or not Jean would go along with the plan.

It started to rain just as they got to the outskirts of the city. Paul was obliged to do the navigating for Maria, as she could not remember the way to Yves' house. As they drove up the road towards the house, Paul recognised the vehicle parked outside.

"That's Jean's car," he said to Maria. "So he is here."

She pulled the car into the driveway, and turned off the ignition. "Before we go inside I want to say something to you," she said. "In a couple of days, I have to leave and get back to my job in Florence. I want you to know that I have

come to care for you a lot. I want to offer you the chance to come to Florence and experience some of my home cooking."
Paul looked over to her. "I have never met anybody quite like you. You have been wonderful company. I would be honoured to take you up on your offer, at the earliest opportunity."

Then he bent over and kissed her on the lips.

"Ouch," he yelled, as his injured hand got caught on the gear shift. They both laughed for a moment.

"Now to sell the idea to Jean," said Paul. "We'll leave everything in the trunk, just take the Chalice with us."

As they stepped up toward the front door, it opened. Jean held out his hand, then seeing Paul's bandages, he said. "No handshaking today I see."

"This is Maria," said Paul, "my favourite companion."

"Come on in," said Jean, "my father is in the livingroom. He's all agog to know what is going on- so am I!" he added.

Everyone settled down. Jean brought out a bottle of wine, and a toast was made to their safe arrival.

"Before I tell you the reason we wanted to meet with you," began Paul, "I want you to guarantee our anonymity, for the sake of all of us, especially for your father. You will also have to extend this same pledge of anonymity to a friend of ours. There are some people who would not hesitate to harm any one of us if they knew we were connected with what I am going to tell you. We think that that there may be some serious and far-flung repercussions as a result of our discovery. Both of us are leaving here in the next day or so, but your father will still be here. He will need his privacy protected. You must promise me this first."

Jean looked at each of them in turn, he was silent for a minute. "Very well, he agreed, you have my word."

With that, Maria took the Chalice from her purse and unwrapped it. She handed it to Jean.

"We discovered this Chalice, hidden in an abandoned church building," said Paul. For the next couple of hours, he related the whole story - right from the time he found the hat and pawn ticket back in Canada. To say that Jean was amazed would be a gross understatement, to his credit, he only interrupted occasionally. Paul terminated the story when he reached the part about meeting Miles in the orphanage earlier in the day.

Jean looked at each of them again. "I can see why you wanted a guarantee of anonymity, I don't know much about this Order of St. George, but from what you've told me they appear to be a very determined and dangerous organisation. You were very lucky indeed to have escaped." Paul nodded his head. "Yes," he said, "I've thanked Miles Dearborn many times since then!"

"Now, here's my plan. You can bring this Chalice to the attention of the public by introducing it as a part of the evening news. I want you to get in touch with Father Jacques, and invite him here to your television news centre as an authority on medieval religious history. It would be best if you do the program live, with no rehearsal. I think I can assure you that you will have a very interesting show. Father Jacques is no shrinking violet. I am sure you will reach the same conclusion when you meet him. Rest assured also, that he is a legitimate, published scholar on the subject of medieval religious history. So, what do you think of my idea?"

"I like it a lot," said Jean. "We are always looking for newsworthy stories - especially if we can get a scoop! How do I reach this Father Jacques?"

"I can give you the name of the shelter where he works in Carcassonne," said Paul. "After that, it's up to you."

"Give me the name and leave it to me," said Jean. "Now that you have told me your story, I can see why you particularly wanted anonymity for my father. I'll call tomorrow and let you know how we are getting along. Please, keep the Chalice here, I don't want it until we are sure that we have Father Jacques' agreement to come on the program."

With that, Jean stood up to leave. "If you give me the keys to the car, I'll unload your bags from the trunk, your hands look as if they're quite painful" he offered.

When everything was deposited in the hall, Jean turned to Paul and Maria. "Until tomorrow," he said. "I'll phone you when I have news." Then he left.

"Speaking of phone calls," said Paul, "I'd better call Miles and let him know what's happened." He got through to the orphanage with no problem. Sister Frances answered the phone. "Could I speak to Miles, if he is there," said Paul, after identifying himself.

"I'll just get him for you," said the Sister.

"Miles here," he heard, a few moments later.

"This is Paul, in Toulouse," said Paul. "I have an update for you. It looks like the television station is going to do the program, the main problem at the moment is whether or not they can persuade Father Jacques to come on the show. We should know tomorrow sometime."

"I have a bit of news for you, too," said Miles. "Father Jacques is here right now. He has come to pay his respects to Sister Agatha, she died at about six o'clock this evening. Sister Frances called him to let him know. I asked that she say nothing to Father Jacques about Germain breaking in and frightening her. She reluctantly agreed, but didn't like it. He and I are sitting together reminiscing about her life. He knew her better than most, especially during the time when she was running the orphanage. He hasn't asked me how long I have been here, but I can tell he would like to know. We haven't talked about the old abandoned church either and somehow I don't think he believes that I might have been inside."

"Good," said Paul, "let's keep it that way. I don't know if we will see each other for some time," he added. "I'm leaving in the next day or so to get back to my home. What are your future plans?"

"I'll stay for the funeral of Sister Agatha, which is three days from now," said Miles. "Then I am going to fly back to Montreal and stay with my sister for a while. She needs some help running the house, and there is a big garden that has been neglected for a long time - that will keep me fit and busy!"

"Well, I'll call the orphanage when I know the program is a go," said Paul. "I'll pass on the news about Sister Agatha, to Maria, we will raise our glasses in celebration of her life. Goodbye for now."

Paul returned to the livingroom, joining Yves and Maria.

"We were just going over the uncovering of the double keystone again........," she said.

"I have a bit of sad news for you," said Paul. "Miles just told me. I'm afraid Sister Agatha died earlier this evening. I said we would raise our glasses and recognise a truly good woman - so let's do that." They gave Yves what details they knew of the Sister's life.

"Sounds like a wonderful person," he said. "Here's to Sister Agatha."

After some silent reflection by all of them, Maria said: "I'm going to take our bags up to the same rooms, if that's alright with you Yves."

"What? Oh, I beg your pardon?" he said "Yes, of course - same rooms as before."

She turned to Paul, "I'm off to bed - I'm exhausted. In the morning, we'll go to the nearest hospital, have your hand looked at and x-rayed. Goodnight now."

Ten minutes later, Paul was on his way up the stairs.

"Goodnight," he called to Yves, "it's been a long day", but Yves had already nodded off.

In the morning, Maria drove Paul to a nearby hospital emergency department, where he had both hands x-rayed. It transpired that nothing was broken, but the tips of three of his fingers were severely smashed. He was told they would repair themselves with time, but unfortunately, they would always be somewhat crooked, and the nails would also grow in the same way. The other hand was coming along nicely, according to the nurse who replaced the dressings.

When they returned to the house, Yves was up and about, enjoying a cup of tea and studying the Chalice. "It's marvellous workmanship," he commented. "Is there some meaning to the design on the raised edge?"

"We don't know," said Maria, "and I agree with Paul, let someone else figure that out!"

Just around noon, they had a call from Jean. He told them that Father Jacques had agreed to lend his expertise to the program, and that he had seemed rather flattered. The program would be aired as a last part of the regular evening news the following day, at around six-thirty. The television station would pay Father Jacques for his time and his railway ticket; and pick him up from the station in a limousine! "I think it was the limousine that clinched it," added Jean.

"Why not come to the television station at lunch time tomorrow, and bring the Chalice with you," he said. "Don't bring my father with you though, it's not his favourite place to go."

Paul called the orphanage immediately, he got Sister Frances on the other end of the line. It appeared that Miles was not in, so, Paul left the message to say that their plan was successful, and that Miles should watch the television evening news from Toulouse, tomorrow, at six o'clock. He wished the Sister well, and said he was sorry not to be at the funeral for Sister Agatha - then rang off.

Over a late lunch, Paul and Maria sat at the kitchen table. "I'm making plans for my return to Canada," he told her. "I'll call the airlines today and see what I can get in the way of flights for tomorrow. Are you also going home tomorrow?" he asked.

"Yes," said Maria. "There is a flight to Milan every evening from here. I'll change there for Florence."

"You go and make your flight arrangements first," Paul suggested. "I could be on the phone for some time, organising my flights."

Maria was able to book her flight without any difficulty. The plane left Toulouse at seven-thirty in the evening on the following day. Paul then got to grips with the airlines, to see what he could arrange.

After a lot of options that were not very satisfactory, he decided to go direct to London Heathrow, on a flight that left an hour after Maria's - then hang around for four hours at the airport before getting a flight to Toronto.

When they told Yves that they would be leaving the following day, he insisted that they go out for dinner that night, to celebrate the successful outcome of their visit to Carcassonne. So that evening, he took them to a restaurant he knew well - one that specialised in Spanish cuisine. After reviewing the menu, they all agreed to have paella, though if they had known how much food there would be, they could have easily have done with one less serving.

Paul had to get periodic help from Maria, because of only having one good hand to work with. The table-talk centred on the amazing activities of the previous few days, with Yves wanting to have certain parts explained again, in more detail. Paul raised his glass to Yves, for his hospitality and for his generosity in lending them his car. Then, Maria toasted Yves for his explanation of the double keystone! She and Paul knew very well, without that knowledge, they would never have found *anything*.

By the time they got back to the house, it was late. "Too late for me," said Yves, "I'm off to bed, I'll see you in the morning."

Paul and Maria sat in the livingroom for a while. "I'd better make up a separate parcel for you to take on the plane," said Paul. "I've still got those books you lent me, they'll never fit inside that little bag of yours. Do you want some of the papers we worked on as well?"

"No, I don't think so," said Maria, "but I do need the books."

Again there was a quiet pause between them.

"I'll have to phone my neighbour sometime tomorrow and let him know when my plane should arrive," said Paul. "He said he would pick me up, if I gave him enough notice."

Maria looked over at Paul, they both knew that they were just talking for the sake of it - both thinking about the next day, when they would part from each other.

"I'm glad you're leaving first," said Paul. "Let's say 'goodnight' and think about the things that are going to happen tomorrow."

In the morning, the two of them packed their bags for the last time. Yves found a cardboard box in his garage, that was just the right size for the extra items Maria could not get into her bag.

Paul remembered to return Yves' corkscrew to the kitchen drawer. He apologized to Yves, "I'm afraid we forgot your rope and one of the chisels in the church."

"Never mind, I was glad to be part of this adventure!" Yves replied.

Paul and Maria left the house together and drove to the television station. When Paul had suggested to Yves that only he and Maria go, Yves had been quite happy not to accompany them. "That building is one of the ugliest in the city," he had said, "an architectural eyesore - I dislike it intensely!" Paul now knew why Jean had said it would be better if they did not bring his father.

They had put the Chalice inside a box, which had once been occupied by an expensive bottle of wine, wrapped it in brown paper and addressed it to Jean Carbonne, c/o the News Department at the station.

They walked into the foyer of the building and approached the information counter.

"We're expected by Jean Carbonne," Paul said to the receptionist.

"I'll page him for you," she said. "Please take a seat."

While they waited, a courier brought in several parcels and some mail. He placed them on the counter, said hello to the girl and, after receiving a signature for the delivery, he left.

Paul watched this activity closely. "Go and ask the receptionist to direct you to the Ladies washroom," he asked Maria. She looked at him with a puzzled expression.

"Just do what I ask please," said Paul. She stood up and walked over to the receptionist, who was on the telephone, Maria waited. Meanwhile, Paul walked to the end of the

200

counter where the parcels had been left by the courier. As soon as he saw the girls attention being taken by Maria, he slipped the package with the Chalice inside, into the pile. Maria disappeared in the direction of the washroom.

A few minutes later, Jean came out of an elevator and greeted Paul.

"I want you to go over to the desk and pick out the package that has your name on it", said Paul. "Tell the girl you've been expecting it and that you'll take it with you now,'

"Is it the Chalice?" asked Jean.

"Yes."

Jean walked over to the receptionist. "I see the courier has been," he said. "I'm expecting a package, so, I'll take a quick look and see if it's here." With that, he walked over to the pile and picked out the correct one. Waving to the girl, he smiled and walked away.

A few minutes later, Maria arrived and the three of them left the building.

"What was all that about?" she asked Paul.

"Just making an anonymous delivery," he replied. Jean pointed to the package under his arm.

"Aha! I see," she said. "Quick thinking!"

Over lunch, Paul told Jean as much as he knew of Father Jacques. However, it turned out that the station had been checking out the ex-priest as well, and had obtained several of the academic papers that Father Jacques had been able to have published. They also knew of his decoration after the war.

"He should make an excellent guest for this evening," said Jean. "It wouldn't surprise me if we get a lot of response at the station, after the broadcast. On a personal note, I would like you to know how glad I am that you decided to get in touch with my father. He has become a different person since you and Maria arrived on the scene. He is taking much more interest in life - it's almost like he has woken up after a long sleep."

"Without the help of your father, I'm sure we wouldn't have accomplished anything," replied Paul.

They walked back to the station parking lot together and said their goodbyes'.

"I hope all goes well this evening, we'll be watching," said Paul, then he and Maria drove back to Yves' house.

"I must phone Peter, in Gaillac," said Paul, as they entered the driveway. "He will certainly want to watch the television program tonight. I want to thank him too, for his invitation to the dig. Maybe I can get him to invite me back again next year!" Paul made the call as soon as they were in the house; unfortunately, Peter could not be reached. "He's out at the site," Paul was told. So, after identifying himself, Paul could only pass on the information and hope that it was relayed.

Yves insisted on going to the airport with them. "You can drive there," he said, "and then I'll bring the car back."

Maria did the driving, as Paul's hand was still too painful to use. On the way there, they talked about the television program, speculating on Father Jacques' reaction to seeing the Chalice.

"He's no dummy," said Paul, "he'll put two and two together. Don't forget, he knows we were in Carcassonne along with Miles Dearborn, during the last few days. It's too much of a coincidence to ignore."

At the airport, their parting from Yves was mercifully brief. "I have to get back to the house and get settled comfortably to watch this thing," said Yves brusquely. So, after hugs all 'round, they stood together in the parking lot and watched him drive away.

Paul and Maria were both leaving with Air France, so, after checking in and getting rid of their luggage, they made their way to the airport lounge. They sat in a good location to be able to watch the television set and ordered some wine. The news was just about to get started. They chatted together keeping an eye on the television screen and listening occasionally to what was being said.

At last, the item they had been waiting for was announced. The camera zoomed in on the interviewer who made a few introductory remarks about the guest for the program. Then, the camera switched to a view of Father Jacques. He was told he would be asked to look at an ancient item that had been sent to the television station anonymously, and was thought perhaps, to have some religious significance.

The Chalice was then brought to Father Jacques by an attendant. It was quite obvious that he had not seen it before this moment. The look of astonishment on his face was perfection. For a moment, he said nothing. He simply held the Chalice in his hands, turning it around and around.

Then he seemed to gather himself. "This is a cup that at one time was used in the observance of a religious service," he said. "Probably a Christian mass. It would probably have held the wine that symbolised the blood of Christ. As to how old it is," he continued, "that is hard for me to say. I would imagine that it is somewhere around eight or nine hundred years old. From the weight of it, there is no doubt that it is gold, white gold," he added; "a metal that was highly prized, and used only to make the most significant jewellery, or other special item."

He turned to the interviewer. "You say this was brought to the station anonymously?" he asked, incredulously. "Yes," said the interviewer. "It was delivered by courier, along with the rest of the mail for the station".

The camera cut away for a commercial break. When the program returned, the interviewer explained that the station was already receiving calls about the Chalice, and in view of the level of interest shown, they would be devoting a special half-hour on this subject, later that evening.

Father Jacques was asked if he could stay and be part of the show. He said he would be glad to. The camera focused in on the Chalice, which was now standing alone, on a small side table - then the picture faded out.

Maria looked at Paul. "We're getting out of here just in time," she said.

Paul nodded his head. "I thought something like this might happen. Father Jacques will be in his element for quite a while."

203

They heard the airport announcer call the flight for Maria so, they left the lounge and walked over to the gate. They stood quietly together until the rest of the passengers disappeared down the tunnel, toward the plane.

"I must go," said Maria. She hugged him and kissed him gently. "Call me when you get home." Then she gave her boarding pass to the agent and waved goodbye.

Paul stood there alone, for a few minutes. One of the airline employees came up to him. "Are you on this flight to Milan?" she asked.

"Uh, no," said Paul. "But I wish I was," he thought!

He wandered around the airport, while waiting for his own flight to be called, looking in the shop windows. Eventually, he stopped outside the duty-free outlet. Looking at his watch, he saw he had just enough time to purchase the bottle of good brandy that he had promised to bring back for his neighbour. Satisfied with his purchase, he made his way to the entry gate and joined the other passengers waiting for his own flight.

Once on the plane and seated comfortably, he watched out of the window while the plane taxied out to the runway. As it thundered down the tarmac, he closed his eyes and began to think about Florence.

THE END

ISBN 155369143-1

9 781553 691433